Shadows 3

Shadows 3

Edited by
CHARLES L. GRANT

DOUBLEDAY & COMPANY, INC.

GARDEN CITY, NEW YORK

1980

All of the characters in this book
are fictional, and any resemblance
to actual persons, living or dead,
is purely coincidental.

First Edition
ISBN: 0-385-15777-0
Library of Congress Catalog Card Number: 80-651
Copyright © 1980 by Charles L. Grant
All Rights Reserved
Printed in the United States of America

Contents

Introduction

Theories, novels, plays, films, sketches, black outs, and poems about writers have a continuing fascination not only for the reading public, but also for the writers themselves. The former somehow gets the idea that it is being let into deep and arcane secrets about the way mortals put words on paper—confirming an already concrete notion that writers are indeed queer ducks at best, raving lunatics on the average—and the latter attempt to find something of themselves in the experiences of other craftsmen, a kinship that enables them to feel somewhat less alone in what is essentially a lonely business.

Yet most of these novels, plays, films, etc. deal with a writer as he confronts a novel. Seldom do you see an actor hunched over his typewriter trying to put form to an idea that will bear fruit in less than 20,000 words. Perhaps this is because the shorter length seems considerably less heroic in its concept; perhaps it's because a short piece of fiction implies a less grandiose scope than one, three, four, ten times the length; and perhaps, too, the implication is that it's much easier to write a short story than a novel, simply because it's . . . shorter.

I admit to fostering the latter belief myself, for the first five or six years of my career in the profession. After all, once you sweat through 5,000 words, 50,000 seems like an impossible figure to attain. Good God—all that description! all that dialogue! all that plotting! Impossible. Anyone willing to invest the time it takes to write a novel must be crazy.

Then I wrote my first book. And my second.

Now, at this writing, I'm up to something in the neighborhood of twenty-five, and I've discovered something on my own that everyone else who's been around for a while knew all along—it is, without a doubt, much harder to write a short story than a novel. Much more.

And when you add to this the horror-fantasy notion, what you have is a minor miracle when it works; a major one when it's as successful as it should be.

The short story demands an economy of words, the luxury of rambling reserved to the manuscripts that run 250 pages and longer. And this economy of words demands, in turn, a tighter focus not only on plot but on characterization, on description, on the total effect being attempted. In other words, the reader has to be able to "see" the setting quicker, characters have to be given birth virtually instantly, and there can be nothing extraneous along the way to cause the reader to stumble, to lose heart, to remind himself that this is, after all, only a fiction—nothing could be worse for the writer of a horror story than to have the reader realize too soon that he's being, essentially, conned into believing something he would not ordinarily give credence to in broad daylight.

It is not so surprising, then, that there are far more horror-fantasy novelists than there are horror-fantasy short-story writers. The short-story writer (or the novelist who can also write good short stories) is a rare creature indeed. He knows—whether the reading public understands it or not—that short fiction can take just as long as a novel to complete, that the sweating over the proper word is just as intense, that the effect created must be just as *real* as if he had tens of thousands of words to work with.

The physical difference is in the number of pages taken in a volume such as this for an individual piece.

The emotional difference—not to mention the artistic—is incalculable.

Yet, somehow, just when it seems as if there are no more new writers who are willing to take the time (and the disproportionately lower rates) to perfect a story, the threatened void is overcome . . . for the time being. This is why you'll see so many newer (though not necessarily younger) writers in these pages—the total number of men and women devoted to the (yes) delicate craft of conjuring horror in forty pages or less is, in the best of times, no more than a couple of dozen. Good writers, that is; those who enjoy delivering the fright, creating the shadows, letting loose the screams and the shivers we sometimes feel is too childish to admit to.

What happens then depends on one's taste.

But there is seldom a doubt that that shadow over there, the one in the middle of the noonday desert, doesn't belong. Especially when there's nothing around to cast it. Nothing, that is, that's apparent.

Enjoy.

There's no shame at all in sharing someone's horror.

It's fun.

Trust me.

Charles L. Grant
Budd Lake, N.J.
1979

Shadows 3

Introduction

Davis Grubb, who lives and works in West Virginia, is not known for being the most prolific writer in the field. Yet the work that he's done over the past several decades has about it the unmistakable mark of a superior craftsman. His classic The Night of the Hunter *is virtually untouched for its unrelieved suspense and terror, and his trademark—that which you see is not what you're seeing—is doubly true of this novelette.*

It is also true that sometimes, if you blink at the wrong moment, what you think is a shadow . . . isn't.

THE BROWN RECLUSE

by Davis Grubb

I possess, as you can see, the narrowest, smallest, most beautiful foot in the whole town of Glory.

I wear a size five and a half quadruple A, and since no Glory shoe store—and few anywhere in West Virginia, for that matter—carries my size, I have my shoes—my shoe, that is—especially crafted for me in Waltham, Massachusetts.

You see, my left leg below the knee is missing and has been from birth. And now that I have that blunt and admittedly unpleasant detail out in the open I feel well enough to continue my tale of Justice, of fog—and of murder.

Naturally, I adore this perfect right extremity of mine. And yet, having to make my way about on that one foot, with the aid of a particularly heavy orthopedic crutch made necessary by a slight curvature of the spine, this—one would suppose—might tend to make my foot heavy and calloused and broad. O, no, my dear, far from it! My five narrow little toes wink up at me every night as I draw from them my expensive French silk stocking. At night I soak my foot for hours in warm olive oil. I massage the soles and arch and ankle with Lanolin and vitamin E cream then. The result is a foot of perfection—one without callous or blemish. Each tiny nail has been lacquered with a special shade of polish blended for me exclusively by a Pittsburgh cosmetologist—the subtle flaming hue of the nasturtiums that grow in my small, old-fashioned garden. Is the association too farfetched?—the identification of myself with a flower? Yet what is a flower but beauty standing on its one leg and being swayed and bent by the chance wind of Destiny? Should I be compared perhaps to a stork? No; with my beautiful foot, I think of myself as a blossom.

But men are cruel.

Everyone does not see me in this light.

Towns like Glory are cruel.

And so I live alone in this perfectly charming old frame house on Water Street—amid a yard overgrown with weeds and wildflowers; with tan bark walks and a spice bush and azalea and crab apple trees for jelly and Impatience growing all around the crumbling, rococo porches.

My father willed me the property. I was an only child. My mother, Ellen, for whom I am named, died at my birth, which was difficult and which, obviously, injured me as well as her. My father was inconsolable after her death and within a year had resigned his job as Professor of Logic and Oriental Philosophy at the local Glory college.

He lived until I was nine.

I did not grieve for him, or my mother particularly, as I grew up under the austere stewardship of my father's two gaunt sisters who came to the big waterfront house to take over my care and rearing. They did little to help me through a particularly distressing adolescence; and then one of the sisters, the younger, ran away with a carnival medicine man from Chillicothe, Ohio, and the other, within a year, fell asleep after two pints of elderberry wine and drowned in my father's great Grecian bathtub.

I was nineteen, alone, and really quite well off, thanks to

several oil wells which suddenly resumed production on land my father had owned downriver in Pleasant County.

And that was thirty years ago.

Forgive me while I shed my shoe. It is a hot August midday and such humidity—added to the strain of getting about—causes my foot to perspire. I must let nothing strain that exquisite member.

Look at me closely now, if you please, and tell me what you find. A rather pretty spinster nearing fifty, with striking titian hair, slender (if slightly bowed) figure, with one leg missing and at the end of the other, a foot without peer in all of Glory —perhaps in all of West Virginia.

Is that all you see?

Of course it is, since how—unless you were a mystic—could you see behind my large and rather wistful eyes a mind of absolute clarity and of extraordinary powers of ratiocination. Everyone says I inherited such brilliant powers of deduction from my father. I should somehow prefer to think they came from my mother's side of the family, though, I must confess, it is from my father that I derive my intense fascination for mystery stories in general, and for the tales of Sherlock Holmes in particular.

I seldom read mysteries anymore, even though the local Glory library has a quite good and up-to-date selection. They are so predictable. If the author plays fair and gives me the clues as he should, I can generally spot the killer by the end of page one hundred. And I sigh and go back to my father's deep, cool library bookshelves and pull down the bound *Strand* installments of the Master's exploits. I know these tales by heart, of course, and yet I find more real mystery and suspense in them than in any of these jejune, modern exercises in deduction.

Somehow, I believe the fogs we have here in Glory, especially down here on Water Street, account for my fascination with this segment of nineteenth-century London tradition.

Slowly the river fogs creep in from our great Ohio River. The crickets and frogs down in the rushes and cattails, persist for a while, after the world has grown pale and flocculent and peculiarly hushed. But after a time, Mystery wins, and even they grow still.

They seem waiting, listening, watching.

For what?

One stares out the deep parlor windows and the pale lemon-damask curtains hanging there seem part of the piled mists beyond the wrinkled window panes.

Mystery is afoot.

And what *is* the world out there?

Is it truly the majestic Ohio out yonder—running deep and silent over its submerged secrets in the cunning and clandestine night? Or is it not, magically, incontrovertibly, suddenly the ancient Thames? And has not our Water Street and the end of Twelfth Street and the bricked, deserted wharf not suddenly become a fragment of London, east of Mansion House, beyond Limehouse and sinister, sleeping Soho—and those bricks gleaming with mists like black blood out there at the place where the wharf descends to the lapping shore—is not this perhaps actually a piece of London's waterfront with some satanic malevolence implicit within every shifting shadow and mist-drenched bough and glistening cobbled gutter?

Sometimes I stand in those mists, father's old blue-and-green Alpaca shawl hugged round my shoulders, and stare down the curling white phantoms in the moonlit street toward the looming black-brick dwelling, ugly beyond description, which stands at the end of Water Street at the place where the land, defoliated by the foul-breathing zinc smelter, provides its endless treasure of arrowheads and other Meso-American artifacts for summertime boys. This ugly edifice is the home of Charlie Gribble, the town banker, pillar of the community, bachelor, eccentric, sixtyish, irascible, unbending, with no single warm human virtue.

I call him the Brown Recluse. Naturally.

As you doubtless know, the Brown Recluse shares the distinction of being—along with the Black Widow—the most venomous spider in our land. It is sneaking and furtive and bites unexpectedly and is extremely lethal.

My appropriation of the name of this loathsome creature and giving it to Charlie Gribble is, as you shall see, quite natural.

Look at him pass along the misted, glistening, brick sidewalk beyond my honeysuckle and red raspberry bushes, homeward bound, his goldheaded walking stick ferrule ringing resoundingly on the stones as he hunches past in some still hour of the night after long hours at his cluttered, roll-top desk in the frosted-glass office at the bank, hours of piece-mealing painfully through reams of bank loans, mortgages, proposed foreclosures, imminent bankruptcies, corporation claims to mineral rights—the process of squeezing every last penny out of paper until the paper moans in pain.

Just see him hunker past through the mists which seem, like white spectral fingers, to clasp, cling, and then tear free of the shape of him—a veritable mortal incarnation of the Brown Recluse Spider in that particularly hideous and indescribably ugly brown Manx tweed cape he wears in every kind of weather. See how he seems to scuttle on eight legs rather than stride, like a man, on two. See how the furry, brown, venomous hulk of his shoulders in their repulsive vestiture resembles the shape of the insidious and lethal namesake. A moment later and he has scuttled off under the fog, like a Thing hiding under a stone. O, how one longs to overturn that sandstone shelter and drive the creature out into the open, into the light, where it can be seen. And crushed.

Next to money—and I am not even sure of this—the creature I have named the Brown Recluse has one obsession. And I am not sure whether or not I should not put this passion of his first. I mean, of course, his obsession with Sherlock Holmes.

I know it is difficult to imagine this miser, this money-grubber of unmitigated meanness, as the fanatic fan of the most romantic figure in perhaps all of English fiction. I used to ponder it over my solitary suppers in the pantry, when the lovely light of sundown came in golden lacy lights through the leaves beyond the kitchen window onto my mother's white linen tablecloth. Why, naturally, the Brown Recluse worshipped Sherlock Holmes. Sherlock Holmes, wiser even than Inspector Lestrade, was the absolute paradigm of proper law and order. And banking would rot without law and order. Moreover, there was in the Master's patient unraveling of the tangled skeins of proof and guilt, something close to Gribble's own patient, nitpicking perusal of a mortgage, a deed, a contract for coal or oil rights. O, how well I have named him the Brown Recluse. How patiently he would sit in the center of his mercantile web, throwing out sticky, fresh strands when necessary to entrap some poor man and then pounce, kill and suck out the last drops of some pitiful little legacy or the picayune and pathetic residue of some insurance check after hospital and funeral deductions were made. O, like Sherlock he was a patient, painstaking—and logical—man.

He was also my first and only lover.

I shan't distress you with the details of that short liaison—I don't like to dwell on it. Suffice it to say that it happened over a period of three months in the summer and early autumn of my twenty-ninth year and by Christmas—perhaps the saddest since my childhood—I had miscarried a child and almost hemorrhaged to death in the Glendale Hospital.

O, my diabolical, furry, brown darling—how well I have named you!

And you will think me perhaps strange when I tell you that the loss of my good name in Glory, the loss of my maidenhead, even the loss of my baby—these were not the facts that pinched most painfully in the end. What hurt me—what really maddened me—was the knowledge that the Brown Recluse's passion for Sherlock, the Master, had begun in this very room —over there, in the cool, dark shelves where my father's morocco-bound volumes of the *Strand* glow dully in the amber light of sundown from the stirring curtains above my ferns.

I must confess that in the last few weeks of our little interlude the Brown Recluse spent less time in my bedroom and more in that secluded, shrinelike corner of my father's library. It seemed to me at the time disquieting. I mean, I really do think of Father's books as a kind of chapel, a sort of dedicated retreat which somehow seemed more inviolable than my own body. He had no right to be down there! It seemed more of a rape than his taking of myself.

The night we parted he swinishly called me a cripple and when he left, by the side porch, scuttling off into the fog, he stole from my father's desk a silver-framed inscribed sepia photo portrait of Sir Arthur Conan Doyle himself.

In the eyes of the law it would have seemed a small thing, if even provable, and besides I was too sick that autumn to fight.

I wonder if I ever would have summoned gumption enough to fight—ever—if the Brown Recluse had not then done what he did.

The following April he—and six other Glory professional men—formed the first West Virginia chapter of the Baker Street Irregulars. Almost overnight he—this Brown Recluse—had become the county's expert, proprietor, and final arbiter of a subject so very dear to my heart—Sherlock Holmes, dear Dr. John Watson, Mrs. Hudson, Moriarity, Mycroft, and all that enchanted world of vanished, foggy, London nights. How dare he! If it hadn't been for his knowing me—if it had not been for that world I foolishly shared with him in that cool, sacred retreat of my father's bookshelves—he would not—. But wait! I have not told you the most outrageous part of all. This obscene person—this Brown Recluse—had formed a social club of other addicts to Holmesiana—and he had persuaded them *not* to admit me as a member!

How's that for cheek? Can you blame me for what followed?

Yet I won that round with the Brown Recluse, at least. Little, five-foot Harry Hornbrook and Ory Gallagher, Glory real estate partners along with Gene Voitle, the county sheriff—they had all three been students of my father at the Glory college. They had loved him. They had respected him. It was in those sunny campus autumns that Father had initiated them to the inner sanctum of the neat little flat at 221B Baker Street. They had not forgotten.

And so they haggled, bullied, and cajoled the Brown Recluse until he had agreed to my membership.

Ory called me that night and told me the news. I was invited to the spring meeting. I was to be accepted into the organization with full rights and membership.

And pleased and victorious as I felt—how could I know that my troubles had only begun?

The fourth member of the Irregulars was Jake Bardall, who made his living as a carpenter and—in the winters—teaching manual training at Glory High School. The Irregulars had secured rooms on the third floor of the Snyder Hotel, and Jake promptly proposed that, with him and his sons doing all the work, they transform the quarters, and in particular the large front room, into an exact historical replica of the digs at 221B. It took Jake and the boys all that summer. The result was surprisingly good. Wives and sisters provided Victorian oil lamps and curtains and overstuffed turn-of-the-century chairs and a davenport from dusty attics. Abner Snyder, the hotel proprietor, raised some fuss over the bullet-hole pattern of the patriotic VR over the fireplace, but in the end, myth was master, and Ory, with an old banker's special .32, fired the initials into the golden oak mantelpiece. Gribble and the others went to work on the fine details—the hypodermic syringe and the coal scuttle and the files of cases.

And the Persian Slipper. For Sherlock Holmes's tobacco.

I don't know where the Persian Slipper came from. I never did know. I know it caught my eye at our first meeting during which we read aloud, examined, and took apart a fine Vincent Starrett—or was it Christopher Morley?—story in the style of the Canon.

It was the oddest, queerest, most beautiful slipper I had ever seen. It was made of some faded, jade-green stuff, like felt, obviously and authentically oriental. It was curled at the tip like some curious pastry, and from one end to the other it was crusted with tinted sequins and bright paste gems. O, it was so lovely! And something about the size of it caused my heart to stir—gently at first and then with a furious and almost unappeasable longing for possession. It was only a few millimeters greater in length than my foot. O, I knew I had to have the thing the moment I laid eyes on it!

My admission to the Irregulars occurred in the third year of their existence. I was not yet onto all the special rights and duties of the group—one of them, at least, downright eccentric.

I remember that night. Over on Roberts' Ridge men were working in the hay harvest, in the moonlight, and the sweet smell of slaughtered clover drifted down upon the misted, river hush. It was a scent like the great cake of Creation rising in God's ovens! O, I stared across the table at which everyone was speculating on the date of the buried coins in the Musgrave Ritual (as if they were discernible!)—I stared across the glimmering lampshine at the mantelpiece. At the Persian Slipper.

Is it full of perique? I asked with a small smile. Or perhaps a nice latakia and shag cut English Burleigh?

Is what full of perique? asked the Brown Recluse in an unappeasably patronizing manner. Is what full of latakia or shag cut English Burleigh?

Why, the slipper, I said. The Persian Slipper. Isn't that where the Master keeps his pipe tobacco?

Jake Bardall intervened kindly.

Ordinarily, yes, Ms. Lathrop. Tonight being Persian Slipper Night we dumped it out. It's in that twist of paper you see beside it on the manteltop.

Slowly, irresistibly, I arose and left the doilied table and the circle of lampshine and went to the mantelpiece. O, it was so beautiful! I had never seen so lovely a slipper! Old? Of course. A little moth-eaten? Naturally. Eaten first by moths, I would guess, drawn to the halo of Aladdin's lamp in some ancient Arab midnight. Was there a sequin or a paste gem missing here or there? Of course—ripped off in some desperate last moment escape by Sinbad the Sailor. O, I knew this was no stage prop, some scuffed and dusty Atlantic City souvenir donated by one of Irregular wives or sisters. This was *the* Persian Slipper. It was the one, the only, the original Persian Slipper from the Master's mysterious and marvelous abode.

Here was proof (as though any were needed!) that Sherlock Holmes had been real, actual, flesh and blood—and always would be. This had been *his* slipper.

The men were watching me curiously as I stood at this place to which, on my giant crutch, I had hobbled. They seemed to grasp the fact—yes, even the Brown Recluse seemed to know—that they were in the presence of deep human emotion. The room was still, save for the grassy whisper of the clock. Through the open window came faintly the sweetness of the slashed clover up somewhere above the fog which set its wisping, spectral fingers across the weathered sill.

Slowly I reached up and took the Persian Slipper in my fingers. My hand trembled with excitement. O, you dear, lovely, old thing. I must somehow—someday possess you.

Everyone there must have surely heard my murmur. Yes, even the Brown Recluse.

Yet no one moved, no one spoke—not even as I tucked the slipper firmly in the space between head and shoulder and hopped and scraped across the oriental carpet to the deep Morris chair where the Master might once have sat deep in a cocaine revery of Irene Adler or the abominable Dartmoor dog. I lowered myself slowly into the leather and rested my thick crutch on the carved arm. Then I reached down and slipped off my costly, but rather practical looking, five and a half quadruple A shoe. I lay it beside my stockinged foot. I wriggled my pretty painted toes in happy anticipation. Dare I do it?

I knew every eye was upon me in that moment. I did not look up.

I took the Persian Slipper out from the hollow between cheek and shoulder where I had held it and lowered it to my beautiful foot. I slipped it on. I did not stand up—O, no, this was not for walking. It was for feeling, for dreaming, for being in another time, another place. I did not look at the men. I did not look into the bilious, yellow eyes of the Brown Recluse who, even there, in the comfort of that little room, hunkered above us all in his hideous brown-tweed cape. I looked at the window—the pretty lace curtains blowing gently on either side of a potted begonia—and beyond the sill, the fog. And I knew—I mean I was quite logically convinced—that so long as the Persian Slipper so clasped my foot that I was in England—in the London of a misted metropolitan night—with street lamps glowing in the fleecy murk like Van Gogh sunflowers amid some drenching dark. And somewhere up the street, in Buckingham or Windsor, Victoria was sleeping more soundly thanks to me and Sherlock Holmes!

I tore my eyes from Fancy then and faced the five silent pairs of eyes.

It feels—O, it feels as though—as though it has always been there. On my foot. O, and did you each see my foot? Yes, you, Mister Gribble, yes, I know *you* have seen it! Did any of you ever see a lovelier foot?

I kicked my leg like a dancer, there in the lampshine. Now, there were fireflies out in the fog, but they were not really fireflies at all—they were the wink of carriage lamps on fleeing hansom cabs or glimmers of dusky, hangdog flames leaked out of dark lanterns carried by bodysnatchers and Resurrectionists from up in the Mews.

Can't you see? I said, that the Persian Slipper is really mine?

And so it may well be, said Harry Hornbrook with a kindly nod into the smoke of his Marsh Wheeling stogie. Next year.

Next year?

Why, yes, said Gene Voitle. If you win it.

Win it? I murmured. How vulgar. I don't believe I understand.

The Brown Recluse rose. He appeared more menacing, more virulent as his huge, brown-caped figure soared up out of his chair. He glowered meanly down at me.

This year, he said. It seems that I am the winner.

Winner? Will one of you be so kind as to explain?

I shall not tax you with the details of the answer which followed—nor the truly obscene ritual that ensued—save to say that in the initial year of its organization, the local chapter had voted to have an annual award—purely honorary—to the

Irregular who solved a crime to have been committed by someone other than the person charged by the authorities in Glory or in the boundaries of the Ohio Valley.

As this was being explained to me (as I sat listening in disgust), the Brown Recluse came scuttling across the room, lifted the adorable slipper from my reluctant hands and replaced it on the mantelpiece after a moment of proprietary weighing of it in his own fingers.

It is not often, said Ory with a courteous nod to the sheriff, that law-enforcement officials in these times arrest the wrong person. But it does happen.

He lighted his cold bulldog brier. His friendly eyes twinkled as he regarded the sheriff.

No offense of course, Gene.

Voitle nodded and rubbed the tip of his bulbous, shiny nose.

No offense, of course, he said. But at least once a year during the last three years the law has been wrong. The Ashworth burglary three years ago, we arrested the wrong persons. The Moorhead holdup—that was another mistake. And this year we nabbed and charged those three Trentor kids for a car theft in Benwood, and again we were wrong.

He glanced appreciatively in the direction of the Brown Recluse.

But thanks to you, Charlie Gribble, Justice finally triumphed.

I don't understand, I said, though I think I was beginning to.

Simply this, Miss Lathrop, said the Brown Recluse suddenly, in that nasal voice of his which seems to penetrate and spoil every cranny of peace in a room. Every year for the past three years—since, indeed, I founded this chapter of the Baker Street Irregulars—I have proven the true author of a crime instead of the one wrongly accused.

How? I managed to gasp. You?

By the simple application of those rules of logic which your late father expounded and taught, he said. And with the methods of the Master—the great Sherlock Holmes—whom I have adored (and studied) since childhood.

I think not, I said icily. I think much more recently than that, Charlie.

Well, you are mistaken. My father had a large library of great books. He had many original Doyle manuscripts—he had the complete file of the *Strand* Holmes—he had every first edition. He even had—.

Yes, I think I know, I said, getting laboriously to my leg. He had an inscribed photograph of Doyle.

The spidery hulk wavered. A snicker of wet apology was heard.

Why, no, he said. He was never so fortunate as that. But to get on with it—I have won the Persian Slipper for two years and if my fellow members are to be believed—I am to win it again tonight.

A murmur of assent went round the group. The fog piled white as Dickens' dreams against the lacy panes and I was in the midst of a vanished England.

For a year, I said, nervously. You possess it for a year.

A year is the limit, said Ory. Unless—well, we've never been faced with *this* one.

What is that? I asked, my curiosity insatiable now.

The solving of one kind of case, said Harry Hornbrook. By one of the Irregulars—would mean that he could keep the Persian Slipper in perpetuity.

And what sort of case might that be?

Something, luckily, we haven't had to deal with in this fine little community, observed Sheriff Voitle.

I ask what it is—this special crime—to bring so special a reward for solving.

Murder.

Did you say murder?

Yes, murder. Any member who solves a murder is, at the next meeting, awarded the Persian Slipper.

To—to keep?

In perpetuity, said Harry then.

I don't mean to discourage you, ma'am, said Ory, but we

got a pretty clever sheriff here. And we have Charlie Gribble.

Yes, I said, in a voice I struggled to steady. I know you have him. The Brown—

It came out despite myself.

—the Brown Recluse.

What did you say, my dear? asked Harry Hornbrook.

I said you must excuse me, I stammered, and scraped and hobbled to the door. I shan't stay for the award. I shall pass this meeting entirely by, I think, gentlemen. I have the most unremitting headache in years.

And I was gone from them—into the fogs of that London night, along the sacred Thames, along my lovely old Ohio.

The next three years passed by in dreary progression. A horse theft the first year and the true thief unveiled got the Brown Recluse the treasured Slipper award. The second year vandals broke into the Bowser Feed Company and stole six hundred pounds of chicken mash. Again the Brown Recluse got the honor. And the slipper. The third year he won it for locating another stolen car.

Stolen cars, horse thieves, chicken feed!

What a farce it was!

And the lovely Persian Slipper showing a little more wear, a little more age, a sequin missing here or there as the relentless years unfolded.

I determined one chilly September night in that last year that this should end. Abruptly. I had worked hard on all the cases in question. To tell the truth, all of the members were as eager to help me win the award as I was—I think they knew it meant something special to me. They seemed to relinquish all personal ambitions to possess it. But each year—though I did my homework faithfully (and, as nearly as possible, following the Master's methods)—the Persian Slipper went to the Brown Recluse.

Damn him!

I knew that cold September night that this spider must be crushed.

Forever.

I resolved that the Brown Recluse should be dead before morning.

I am not one of your modern cynics writing now in the mode so prevalent that dwells with obsessive and feverish particulars on acts of violence. So I shall be terse.

There is a venerable and gigantic elm at the corner, beyond the single street lamp, at Water Street and Twelfth. The tree is thought to be some six or seven hundred years old, and its great roots have thrust tough fingers under the brick sidewalk, giving it a lovely tilt and bulge and ripple. In the fog, with the feathered luminescence of the street lamp behind it, it looks like some enormous Druid priest—presiding over some mossy, sacred ritual.

It was behind this tree that I waited that biting September night. From where I leaned, I could scarcely make out the shape of my house, though I could distinguish the guttering candle flame in the window of the little fruit and vegetable storage room off the pantry.

I was frightened, but I was determined.

It was perhaps ten-thirty. I kept my eyes fixed, piercing as best they could the scarcely penetrable fog which lay on the land toward the center of town. Every light was a golden spider sending out myriad, shimmering strands to form, in each pocket of dark, a golden web. But the spider for which I waited was not golden. I had taken my crutch from the pit of my arm and braced myself securely against the great, ancient tree. Somewhere out on the river voices drifted from boys in skiffs, out gigging frogs. A dog barked, muffled, secret, beyond the mist. I faced up Twelfth Street, the direction from which he would come from the Bank. At the very moment when the town clock struck eleven in the tower of the courthouse somewhere up in the submerged village, I heard those footsteps. Footsteps and the unmistakable chink of the steel ferrule of the golden-headed walking stick as he struck it ahead of him along the rippled brick sidewalk. But, heavens—he was coming *from* the house, not *toward* it. He had gotten home early, it would seem, and now was returning to the bank for some late work—those dreary mercantile schemes which seem to occupy his professional life, at least.

If you ponder a moment, you will realize that I was on the wrong side of the tree for him not to glimpse me before I struck. He was far, far stronger than I—stronger than some men, I should wager—and I knew if he saw me with my heavy crutch raised he would fend away my blow easily and successfully ward it off. I could not permit that to happen.

With an effort so great that it tore at my very breath I scrambled around the half circumference of the huge tree trunk and stationed myself on the other side—and not a moment too soon.

He was almost opposite me now. I must wait until that split moment when he is past, yet not too far past, out of eyeshot, at least, but within striking distance. The moment arrived and I harvested it well.

I have not yet mentioned the strength in my right shoulder and arm with which almost forty-nine years of crutching myself about have endowed me. On that side I am quite powerful.

I shall never forget that moment. The street lamp like a blinding, baleful moon above us both. He—in that split instant with his back to me—that hated back, the dirty glow of the bilious brown-tweed cape below the scraggled hair and not very clean collar and raddled, fat neck. It was at this target that now, with all my mortal power, I aimed and swung the crutch.

The Circle of Willis, the poets call it. And the doctors. That area of cranial excellence and all living movement—the base of the skull above the nape. I felt the metal of the crutch standard strike and I felt something crunch and I heard an almost mindless gasp—a sound that seemed to have been an afterthought to dying. Without another noise the hideous victim slumped heavily to the glistening brick pavement.

And fitting the armpiece of the crutch back under my arm I hobbled slowly, remorselessly, and feeling wholly at peace with myself, toward the light in the pantry window.

I had a slender stemmed glass of Muscadet Bordeaux from

a bottle my father had left in his small liquor cabinet in the library. I sat a long while in the dark of the parlor. My thoughts were as slow and grave as the procession of numerals on a clock face. My mind was entirely in order. Except for one thought—a fancy, at first, and then presently an obsession.

I thought I should now never possess the Persian Slipper. I thought the ghost of the Brown Recluse—the avenging shade named Charlie Gribble—would come back from the dead and announce (after much showy pretense of deduction) his own murderer. And in perpetuity—even if in Death—possess the adorable award. The more I thought of it the more I trembled. Even at this moment, it seemed, the ghost of the man I had murdered was pacing the sterile linoleum of his bedroom, pondering the solution to this latest and most intriguing of crimes—and then pointing his phosphorescent finger of accusations—quite accurately—at me!

Damn him!

I hobbled to the phone and sank onto the Ottoman beside it. I laid down my crutch (quite unstained by its recent fatal contact) and picked up the phone and dialed his number. O, yes I knew it. I would never forget it—a memory of the nights when—full of his child—I had frantically called and called to a phone which was off the hook or not answered at all.

I listened to the distant drone of the ring—somehow seeming a little fainter because of the fog against the windows.

Again it rang.

And again.

And seven times more. And I sat thinking myself quite mad and quite a silly fool to be sending those rings echoing through a house in which there was no one to answer. The eighth ring.

What kind of little play are you acting out inside yourself, dear Ellen Lathrop? I heard a voice murmur—not unkindly—inside my head.

And then the distant receiver was picked up.

O, I could hear the aching silence of that fogbound bedroom in the receiver at my ear.

I could hear a breathing in the phone, too. But whose? In God's name whose? Tell me quickly before I am struck mad forever!

When the voice spoke I fell back in the chair in a half faint. It was he. Yes, it was his voice. Charlie Gribble. The Brown Recluse.

And, to my even greater horror and dismay, he seemed, for the first time in years, quite affable and even talkative.

Ellen, he said. How nice it is to hear you. How are you. For some curious reason I was thinking about you a quarter hour or so ago. I meant to call you.

Are you—are you all right?

Not really, he said then, in fateful, unmistakable words of doom, though unawares of that. I'm concerned. Jim Smitherman, a colleague of mine from Wheeling has been here for supper and we've been working since then on those old Bow Chemical mineral right suits you may have read about in the Glory *Argus*. Well, it was warm this afternoon when we came home from the bank (Why had I not seen them!) and Jim left his coat in my office. Around ten I asked for a file of documents Jim had brought down with him. It wasn't here. Obviously, Jim had left it at the bank. Jim knew exactly where the file was and offered to go back for it. By then this plagued river weather had changed and the fog was up and it was chilly. Damned chilly. I loaned Jim something to wear and he took it and left, and it's been an hour and he's not back yet.

I began to laugh then. O, I caught it in time, but I am sure he distinctly heard my laugh. And then I said some things I can't quite remember and hung up. Somehow I made it to bed and took some Veronal and slept—astonishingly untormented by the dream of having killed the wrong person.

At daybreak the chain reaction of certain incredible and astonishing events began. I settled down in father's cool library —like a forest cover of ancient oaks—with a bottle of Yardley's Smelling Salts and a box of Kleenex for my tears until sunrise.

Soon the fog would burn off—roll away and wisp away like the departing ghosts of some long white night. Morning sun would filter through the high canopy of maples and sycamores and elms and spin gold coins on the glowing green lawn. Sun motes and dandelions would intermingle there. I stared out through the front window, beyond the tiny statue of Michelangelo's "David" which father always kept there on the deep, white sill. Every morning I sat and stared there at a certain inevitable, unvarying matutinal event that would take place. It would happen almost simultaneously with the striking of father's old Dutch clock. I watched. I waited. Yes, here he came—weaving and stumbling along the uneven brick path: even on this fatal, fateful morning here he came—Ort Holliday, the town drunk, making his way home at sunrise with a skinful of cheap corncob wine or some foul, resinous bootleg distillation.

He was rounding Twelfth Street now and making his way unsteadily to the left and up Water Street toward my house, toward—yes, toward the gigantic old elm beneath which lay, on the wet, glittering bricks—

I watched, enthralled, rapt in suspense as he came closer. He stumbled once where the sidewalk tilted up suddenly and then steadied himself against Mart Brown's big willow and came on, past the street lamp now competing dismally with the misty, yet powerful sun. On and on. Stumbled, staggered, and leaned. And on.

I thought foolishly for a moment he was going to stumble on the body or that he would somehow stagger around it, seeing it but fancying it was merely a sample of the delirium that was waiting for him in his little shack down below the zinc smelter where Water Street dwindles out and is lost amid mesamerican memories. Surely, he had seen it by now! Good God, he has passed it. No. No, he hasn't. He has seen it. He rubs his eyes, his swollen, sweating face. He stares again. He stoops unsteadily to have a better look. A cunning look replaces the fear on his face. He smiles tipsily, looks around to see if anyone may be watching at this strange prebreakfast hour when only coal miners and drunks are up and about. He pauses, his right hand poised unsteadily like the bill of a robin about to pounce on a worm. Now he makes his move. Swiftly the dirty hand darts down and under the dirty tweed cape, the inner jacket pocket, the inside pocket. The purse is in his hands now as he greedily snaps it open, plucks out a rather thick wad of bills, and without counting them stuffs them into his own coat pocket from which peeps the stained corner of a dirty bandanna. He rises, smiling, his raddled, smeary face working in slow emotion as he tries to persuade himself that his fortune is real. He seems curious as to how his obliging victim died. He leans again—almost as if suddenly sober, almost as though arranging things not as they are but as they should be.

Yes, yes, he nods to himself. Yes, yes.

His gray lips working wetly.

He stoops then and picks up a loose, mossy brick at the edge of the stacked, ornamental pavement. He sees blood on it—blood which has coiled oily across the walk from the wound somewhere up under the huddled, staring head.

He is standing there, the victim's purse already in his pocket, a brick smeared with gouts of the victim's own blood in his right hand, a memoryless vacant smile on his dissipated face—yes, standing there so when Sheriff Voitle and his deputy, on a last tour before shift change, came round the corner of Twelfth and Water Street in their Plymouth cruiser.

He was, of course, arrested, advised of his rights, arraigned and locked up in the Apple County jail.

I did something that morning and afternoon I have never done in my life. I went to father's little wine cabinet with its little brass key which chirps like a golden bird in the lock when you turn it. I saw that only one bottle of father's wine was left—the Bordeaux. So I selected one I had purchased and put there five years before—a perfectly delectable 1971 Château Calon-Ségur, Saint-Estèphe.

I drank all that morning. I drank past lunch while all around me Glory buzzed and whispered over the murder within its sacrosanct city limits. I drank until—at four that afternoon—I suddenly realized that the phone was ringing and had been ringing for, perhaps, two or three minutes. I did not stagger. I think, perhaps, that it is, moreover, quite impossible to stagger on one leg. I made my way quite steadily to the phone and picked it up.

It was he—the unspeakable—the dark, the dreary, the intended dead—the Brown Recluse.

I suppose you've heard, he said.

About the murder? Yes.

I was pleased and delighted at how carefully and distinctly my voice sounded. I was really quite drunk, you see, and I somehow believe that the adrenalin already in me from the excitement of the night had counteracted the wine. I had never spoken more distinctly.

I don't suppose you saw anything, Ellen, he said then. You're generally up and about at the time the murder took place. Sitting in the ladder-back chair in your father's library. At the window.

How well, I said, you remember all my night habits, Charlie.

Don't be unpleasant, Ellen, he said. Besides I didn't call you about that.

What then?

There's to be a special meeting of the Irregulars tonight at sundown. I think you might like to attend.

I was silent a moment.

What is the occasion? No meeting was scheduled until the fall meeting in October.

The occasion, he said, is the awarding of the Persian Slipper. This time in perpetuity.

To whom? Gene Voitle, I suppose. He solved the crime, I am told.

That's the plan, he said.

Well, what a windfall for Gene, I said. I mean he didn't really have to do any real detection. Not in the manner of the Master. He just happened round the corner and his two eyes saw Ort Holliday standing there, the brick in his hand, the purse in his pocket.

That is why he is not going to be awarded the Persian Slipper.

Oh?

Well, wait, Ellen. Be at the meeting tonight. I don't want to spoil my denouement to this strange series of events. Be at the meeting. At sundown.

I shall be at the hotel at six at the latest, I said.

O, no, said the Brown Recluse. Not at the hotel.

What do you mean?

I mean this session of the Baker Street Irregulars isn't going to be held at 221B.

Where then?

Why, in front of your house, Ellen, as a matter of fact. At the scene of the murder.

Why there? I whispered.

Because it is there, said the Brown Recluse, that I am going to demonstrate that Ort Holliday did not—and could not possibly—have murdered Jim Smitherman.

Oh? How? Who then—?

You always were impatient, Ellen. A probing, curious mind, you have.

You *know* then?

Of course, I know.

I mean, you know who really murdered your friend?

I do, he said. And I shall prove it. At the big elm which grows in front of your house, Ellen. At tonight's emergency meeting of our dedicated little group.

My mouth opened but the words wouldn't work. I suddenly felt a severe headache. From the wine. From the pressure which seemed to be tightening, like a silver band, around my perspiring brow. From I knew not what.

Are you there, Ellen?

Yes. Yes. Yes, I'll be there. At six, I cried out and slammed down the receiver.

So he knew. How could he know? Had he anticipated such a crime and followed Smitherman's progress through the thick white night? Nonsense. Had he set the whole thing up to trap me?—knowing I would mistake the brown cloaked figure and — O, I must pull myself together. These are chimeras, unbelievable and impossible conjectures.

I drank coffee. Mother's old blue-speckled coffee pot

steamed and puffed all the remainder of that afternoon. As I drank the coffee and smoked cigarette after cigarette (I seldom smoke) a curious and aery self-assurance seemed to overcome me.

By five-thirty I was ready for whatever came. I think I was even quite sensibly resigned to this ultimate victory of the Brown Recluse—his winning of the coveted Persian Slipper in perpetuity. O, it stung. It hurt. I shall not deny that. But I tell you I felt in absolute possession of myself as the sun sank lower over the river, over the stained Ohio Hills, and six o'clock approached. Even the realization that my crime would be exposed and that he and not I would come into eternal possession of that yearned for possession—well, my mind seemed to stop at the threshold of that realization and to refuse to accept it. Somehow, this detestable Brown Recluse should not be so smiled on by Goddess Fortune.

The sun was low on the mine tipple across the great river when we began to gather. There was a chill in the air, as there had been the night before. I had bathed and massaged my foot in its special emollient cream for half an hour. I wore my black silk dress, black stocking, black shoe. I wore my grandmother's black onyx pendant on its tiny platinum chain. I wore my mother's good quarter-length beaver jacket— as soft and fresh as the day she put it in the cedar chest the afternoon of her death. I put a dab of mother's favorite perfume (and mine—Christmas Night by Houbigant) behind each ear and on the instep of my pretty, pretty foot. I gave my shoe a little shine. Then I came out—rather regally, I think —and made my way down the tanbark path toward the brick sidewalk, under the enormous and venerable tree, where the rest of the Irregulars were awaiting me.

Gene Voitle, his big gun clinging to his hip, looked vainglorious and a little defiant. He looked as determined as the Brown Recluse to win that precious award. I smiled. I knew that my expression betrayed nothing. And I was thankful for that, because the Brown Recluse never once took his beady, spidery eyes off my face, as the meeting began.

I don't know what this is all about, grumbled the sheriff. I don't know how there could be any more incriminating evidence than to find a man at the scene of a cold-blooded murder with the fatal weapon in his hand.

But the brick did not kill Jim Smitherman, said the Brown Recluse. Ort Holliday merely discovered the body and being the cut of man that he is and being, moreover, blind drunk, stole the dead man's wallet. Corpse robbing is, of course, a felony. But it is not the felony of first-degree murder, gentlemen.

And Ms. Lathrop. May I remind you I am here. And that I am not a gentleman, Charlie.

Forgive me, Ellen, he said with ungracious politeness. I had not forgotten your presence here. Oh, far from it.

The wind stirred the long, lovely willow fronds down by the landing where the river lapped on the old stones of the now deserted wharf. For a moment I dreamed one of the old steamboats—lovely as a white-clad bride—was feeling her way in for a landing. Sun motes danced like spinning gold pieces in the high grass and clinging, thick green moss on the brick pavement. The wind blew—that cold September wind. Soon the fog would be up—soon it would claim all, everything, the town, the world, in its white embrace—like a lover taking all from a lover, owning the clasped white earth. Soon it would be London out here where we stood and footpads and cutpurses would dart amid the moonstruck and radiant woolly world. Down yonder where the dark water lapped would not be the Glory wharf—it would be Shadwell Stair and the stair named Wapping Old. And the white queen sleeps more soundly in her Windsor bed because of the Master. And because of me.

Now, said the Brown Recluse. Let us stop this child's play, gentlemen. And—and dear Ellen. Let us show who really murdered James Arthur Smitherman quite early this morning.

I spoke recklessly then.

Charlie Gribble, I said, in a level voice devoid of all the bitterness I might well have been justified in showing. Charlie, I guess this is the happiest moment of your life.

He pondered this.

Oddly enough, he said, it is one of the most uncomfortable. Even though I shall gladly accept and treasure forever the result of it. No, Ellen, it is quite a sad occasion, really.

In what way, sir?

Because it involves my proving that the real murderer was not Ort Holliday as Gene proposes, he said, but that it was someone much closer to us.

Closer? How?

One of us, he said, almost in a whisper, his little glass eyes fixed on mine, a faint smile whispering round his thin, gray lips. One of the Baker Street Irregulars is the murderer.

Oh, really, now, blurted two or three of the group at once. Come on now, Charlie. That's a little thick to cut. Who? Which one?

I'll get to that, said the Brown Recluse, strutting back and forth across the blood-stained bricks like some barnyard tyrant, crowing as he went. First though we must establish motive.

Well, the motive was plain enough, said the sheriff then. Robbery. The defendant already had the victim's wallet in his pocket when he was apprehended. With the murder weapon in his hand.

Again I say that was not the murder weapon, said the Brown Recluse.

I stared at him. He was not wearing the bilious brown tweed cape. That, I supposed, had gone to Empire Cleaners, with an admonition to return it to him in pristine, unstained state. Now he shivered in a shabby little Aquascutum trench coat, quite a few sizes too small. He strutted some more, picked his gold tooth, and inspected a particle of food on the end of it. He flicked it into the gold-dappled grass beside the bricks.

The blood on that brick was dry, he said. Already several hours old. For reasons known only to Holliday he picked the brick up—already clotted with the considerable flow from the deceased's wounds a few feet away. The blood was dry, I say. Clearly Holliday arrived at the scene of the crime a full two hours after it took place. Now are you asking us to suppose that he committed the crime say around four in the morning and then stood there till six with the bloody brick in his hand and the victim's purse in his coat—waiting until Gene yonder could chance upon him? I say that is sheer nonsense, gentlemen—Ellen.

O, he was so patronizing when he said my name. And yet I felt that wine of assurance warm in my veins. Somehow I should win. You see the key to the murder—to any murder—is the establishment of the strongest motive.

What was the motive, Charlie? asked Ory then. If it wasn't greed.

Oh, it was greed all right, said the Brown Recluse. But it wasn't the greed of a simple-minded drunkard for a purse containing forty—maybe fifty dollars and a few coins. It was a much greater greed.

Everyone waited. No one spoke.

The evidence of how great that greed is, he went on, is provided by the absence here this evening of one of our charter members.

I cocked my brow. What was happening here? My mind ransacked all possibilities. What was the repulsive creature getting at? O, I was more determined than ever that he should not possess my treasure. Yes, it had always been mine, I thought in that instant.

And everyone was looking around to see who was missing. Gene Voitle was there. I was there. Gribble was there. Jake Bardall, the carpenter was there. Ory looked uncomfortable.

He cleared his throat.

Harry Hornbrook, he said. I know he'd be sorry to miss this meeting. I mean, a special meeting like this.

Where is Harry? Where is your real estate partner, Ory?

He went to Wheeling early this morning, Ory said. Took a plane to Pittsburgh. Planed out of there for Washington.

Tell us, Ory, said the Brown Recluse, strutting all the more, his pale, hairy wrists jutting out of the undersized trenchcoat like naked chicken bones. Tell us, he said, like some popinjay of a small-town prosecuting attorney, why Harry said he was going to Washington.

Why to fight Bow Chemical's mineral rights contract—they bought up hundreds of them last year—to take over his coal lands.

Tell me, Sheriff Voitle, said the Brown Recluse then, would you have any idea where the original deeds for those mineral rights might be?

No, Charlie, I don't.

Perhaps I can inform you, said the Brown Recluse, like some shyster in a thirties movie, that until the murder in the early hours in this September morning, those original contracts—the sole arbitrating fulcrum for any claims in this case —these were in Jim Smitherman's briefcase.

Charlie, that's not so. I gave those contracts to Harry to take to Washington. You must know that.

You did not, said the Brown Recluse, and I knew when he was lying. (When a man lies to a woman in love she can forever spot a lie in that person's mouth.) He was rigging this, the fiend. He was setting up Harry Hornbrook—just so he could claim the Persian Slipper.

You know Harry has those mineral right deeds, said Ory, red-faced and perplexed before this array of unreason. He had to have them to show to the government boys. To make his claim.

I remember sending Jim back to the bank for them, said the Brown Recluse. He was returning with them—through the foggy town—when Harry struck. Struck and took the deeds. And flew the coop.

Ory picked his nose and then flickered his fingers nervously.

By God, Charlie, he said, you'd do anything to win that damned old Arabian nights shoe. Even betray a friend.

Respect for law and order, said the Brown Recluse, goes deeper than friendship. The Master would agree, I think.

Nobody said anything. Nobody argued.

But I knew, I think we all knew that Charlie Gribble was not through.

Relentlessly, he went on, building his vicious and preposterous case against the poor real estate partner. I had earlier noticed the bulge in the tawdry, tight little trench coat. Now his spidery fingers dove into this pocket and took out something round and perhaps four inches in diameter wrapped in a white, though blood-stained, handkerchief.

This, he announced pretentiously, is the murder weapon. I found it a few moments ago under those leaves and moss by the tree.

What is it, Charlie? asked the sheriff drawing near and scratching the back of his neck.

It is a glass paperweight, said the Brown Recluse. Affixed to the bottom of it so that it can be read easily is a printed advertisement for a Glory firm. It is a promotional give-away.

Which one, Charlie? the sheriff asked. Which company?

A real estate firm, it so happens, drawled the dreadful little spiderman. One quite prominent locally.

He cleared his throat in the manner of a bad actor.

The firm of Hornbrook and Gallagher, he said then.

Again all was still save for the wind and the rustle of the dear old tree. I was fascinated, as though watching the filming of something prerecorded and all stacked up by whatever Fates there be. I felt a little giddy.

This paperweight was the weapon that killed Jim, said the Brown Recluse then. There is blood on it. And even a few hairs. And—

Oh, how dare you perpetrate this unbelievable folly! I blurted. You with your widely known shares in every chemical plant between Weirton and Nitro. You—a millionaire in chemical plants. Bow, I am sure, among them. You want that land for Bow, damn you, you—you Brown Recluse!

Ellen, control yourself, he stammered in a faint, scared voice. You shan't snatch this moment of glory from me now.

I shall—damn you. And I shall snatch with the fingers of Truth!

But Harry Hornbrook's fingerprints are on this paperweight, dear lady. Can that be controverted?

Ory Gallagher was standing tensed, half crouching.

Every one of those paperweights has Harry's prints on them, for God's sake, Charlie. He distributed them. Mailed them out personally.

But the blood. The blood, my dear fellow, snapped the Brown Recluse, and I swear his voice had assumed a kind of fake Englishness. As the Master would say in this case, Elementary, my dear Gallagher.

Oh, this was unspeakable. Absolutely detestable.

He had trumped the whole thing up, this greed-head, in the hopes of causing Harry to lose his deed claim with the powerful chemical combine. And to win, as a kind of laniape, the lovely Persian Slipper.

I think, I said, that it is time that the woman's voice be heard, gentlemen.

I hobbled forward and stood swaying amid lovely beams of a sun which burned all the more fiercely as it declined behind a stripped-out hill. The wind blew and stirred my curls across my cheek.

My soul made choices in that instant.

In the manner of the Master, I announced with a modest lilt to my voice, I shall now demonstrate the true manner in which this crime was perpetrated.

I stared across the grass where the Brown Recluse stood, and I stared into the space six inches above his head, putting him forever beneath my regard.

In the first place, I said, we all know that he yonder wants those mineral rights for Bow Chemical. He is therefore prejudiced. He is also stupid—for the blood and hair on the paperweight will probably, under examination, prove to be the blood of one of his own Rhode Island red stewing hens. Establishing that, I shall continue.

Harry Hornbrook is a small man, I said. The deceased was a large man. I do not believe that Harry Hornbrook could have reached high enough to get a proper swing to deliver the fatal blow.

I hobbled around the dear old tree and stared at the empty case of a locust. Blessed creature, you have escaped and flown away into the moon. I plucked it loose and watched it fall to the moss at the base of the tree. I smiled.

How could you, Charlie Gribble—how could you, Sheriff Voitle—be so blind as to have missed *this?*

They all gathered round.

This footprint, I said. In the sweet, thick moss which grows here. It is so clear. It is unmistakable.

The sheriff stooped and stared. Presently he nodded.

It is like the print of a child, he whispered. A child—maybe ten, eleven. Such a tiny shoe.

Oh, yes, I breathed. Do observe how small. In fact—I smiled over their heads. The sun still clung—a bright, striving crumb of fire upon the mine tipple across the already fog-wisping river—I think if you measure the print, sheriff, you will find it was made by a size five and a half quadruple A.

That's amazingly narrow, amazingly small, said Jake Bar-dall, who sold shoes on a commission mail-order business.

Oh, thank you—thank you, I said.

The thought seemed to strike everyone at once for at least three of them asked it.

Where is the other print? they chorused.

The wind blew so sweetly. O, I felt as if I could dance—dance—if only something soft and green, jade green, with se-quins and paste gems were only clasping my dear little foot.

There was none, I said. The murder was committed by a one-legged person—quite strong in the shoulder and arm of the good side, as most such lame people are—and this one-legged person, to judge from the impression of the shoe in the moss, was probably a woman. Surely, no man would wear so small—so delicate—so petite a shoe.

Drawn by the sundown scents of frying steak in river-front pantries, a small brown dog came trotting past along the bricks and disappeared across Twelfth.

The murder weapon was metal, of considerable more weight than the piece of glass that the Brown—that Charlie Gribble has offered as exhibit A. No, this weapon—I leaned against the great, comforting tree and waved my crutch at them—this weapon, I said, was metal and tubular and of great weight. In fact, I went on, I believe this crutch of mine will, upon examination, prove to exactly fit the wound.

The dog barked at the screen door. Steaks and homefries and wilted-lettuce and gravy haunted the river wind.

No one spoke. I broke the silence.

Gentlemen, I said, I have given you your murderer. I have not confessed—I have irrefutably demonstrated. In the method of the canon—the technique of the Master.

I paused like a happy child about to leap a crying, country brook.

May I have the Persian Slipper? I whispered almost coquettishly. In perpetuity now.

The screen door slammed. But the supper sweetness dreamed sweetly on the wind and I could smell my azalea, too.

Yes, snapped the Brown Recluse. It's up in the hotel. At what used to be 221B. On the mantel.

Will you get it for me?

No, damn you. Get it for yourself.

My progress from the big elm and up the town that sundown evening is legend now. A dozen feet behind me purred Ory's Plymouth cruiser. Lord, did they think I'd make a run for it? It took me one hour and fifteen minutes. Word spread fast. Kids and old people, too, came out on porches and stared over iced-tea glasses at a middle-aged cripple slowly hobbling up brick sidewalks toward her freedom. Oh, the poor fools. Didn't they know I had won—won, at last?

The hardest part was making it up three flights of those hotel steps. And the long hallway with a door open and a poor young colored maid making up a room. I got there at last. I took the Persian Slipper down from its resting place on the mantel, under the patriotic VR. I sank into the Morris chair and, after a long spell, while all of them stood in the hall watching and craning their necks to see, I slipped my expensive hand-lasted shoe off my lovely foot. I wriggled my toes in the almost dark. I put on the Persian Slipper.

A strange thing has happened in the year since that night. I am sitting alone in my little room in a khaki, state uniform. The walls of the room are brown. Everything visible is some shade of brown. There is even a brownish cast to the beams of sunlight that manage to poke through my small window. Perhaps I am brown now, too—I have no mirror here. Only one spot of color blazes like a jewel in that dustbin of a place. Jade-green felt that curls into a cornucopia at the end, like a sweet, subtle pastry; bright sequins of lavender and mauve and cosmos blue, a glitter as of rubies and amethysts from the little gems of paste.

And I am free! No longer am I a flower pinned to earth on one leg—a stork incapable of delivering real babies. I am free. And that's because the Persian Slipper is touched with enchantment and makes it be London out there when the fog comes up. When the fog comes up and makes it be Soho and Limehouse in all that fleecy Dickens world of night. Because you see with my marvelous Persian Slipper I can browse and wander through that strip of Thames just east of Mansion House. And every night—when the fog is up—you'll find me there. If you look.

O, do come looking—do find me in that fog some night!

We can sit till morning and tell each other tales of Sherlock Holmes so wondrous that even he will not believe!

Or, if you prefer, we'll go to haunt a spider.

Poor Charlie Gribble. No one believes him when he tells them he's shrinking.

Introduction

Bruce Francis, with this story, makes his first professional appearance in print. His friend and mentor, William F. Nolan, brought this piece to my attention just before the volume closed for submissions. And it's evident that Mr. Francis not only has a long career ahead of him, but he also knows perfectly what makes a shadow not a shadow.

TO SEE YOU WITH, MY DEAR

by Bruce Francis

She was nearly asleep when she heard the voice.

"Lisa, turn out the light."

The beginnings of a dream eddied down, fading as the soft blanket of sleep slipped away, leaving her feeling cold and exposed. She listened, but heard only the steady rise and fall of David's easy breathing next to her on the bed.

He hadn't spoken, she decided. But she was awake. Just a dream, she reasoned, but still, she listened. A breeze stirred the curtain behind her and touched her ear.

"Lisa?"

She shivered.

"Turn out the light."

She squinted at him through her lashes, hoping that he wasn't watching her. His eyes were closed, and in the dim moonlight from the window, his skin shone pale and cold-looking, thin hands folded on his chest. As she watched, one finger began to tap impatiently, ticking off the seconds in unison with the clock that sat on the nightstand.

Okay, she thought, play the game and get it over with. She glanced at the darkened lamp, then turned back to him and spoke softly, "David, the lamp is off."

He spoke without opening his eyes, "You left the light on in the living room, remember?" He smiled; a triumphant, infuriating smile.

Damn these stupid, childish games! He had always used them; little, inconsequential rivalries, manufactured from whim and circumstance. At the start, the games had been innocent and gently probing and there had been times that she had welcomed them as affectionate reminders, small pleas for her reassurance couched in his pride.

"What would you do if I . . . ?" he would ask.

"Anything you asked," she would reply.

But gradually, he had changed the rules. The small pleas had become demands, her replies grudging recitations. The games had become conflicts, a sport of ugliness. But this time, she thought, it won't get that far.

A headache began to throb, working painfully up the back of her neck as she rose from the bed.

"Where are you going?" asked David. She could tell by the sound of his voice, mocking surprise, that he was still wearing that damned smile.

"To the living room."

"Going to turn out the light?" He beamed happily.

"Yes . . . all right?"

He nodded. "That's a good girl," he chuckled.

She stopped and stared at him with a hard, determined scowl. He scowled back. Finally, a smile tugged at the corners of her mouth. He had her. "Damn you," she laughed as she tumbled into the bed. And, as she pulled the covers over her head, she damned her own predictability. Your score, David, she thought. Your score and your move.

"You've forgotten again, Lisa."

"I haven't forgotten."

"You *are* going to turn it off, aren't you." It wasn't a question.

"Forget it." Easy, she thought, go easy. Give him a little time to get tired of this, then you can get up and turn off the light. She waited.

He sighed, and when he spoke his voice was even and maddeningly paternal. "If you don't do what you've been told, you're not going to get to sleep tonight. And, if you do fall asleep, you'll be sorry. That could be bad, hmm? It will, I promise."

She sawed off a phony, vaudeville snore and pulled herself into a tight ball under the covers. She pressed her face deep into the pillow, hoping that she would soon hear the rustling of the sheets as he rolled over and went to sleep. Instead, she heard a tapping behind her, moving along the headboard. Another one of the props from the very limited repertoire of David Gleason, she thought, picturing his thin fingers, curled like spider legs, creeping slowly toward her, then touching, wrapping themselves in her hair, twisting. . . . Quite suddenly, she did not want it to touch her. The tapping stopped. There was a quiet zip-zip as the hand moved across the crisp fabric of the sheets. Then, just below her face, the delicate pressure of the fingers marching themselves up the pillow. She felt a finger brush her eyelash and she could smell the sweat on his hand. She flinched, wanting to move, but afraid it would bring the fingers rushing at her. Then it was gone. Above her in the darkness something moved on the air. She sensed it, flexing, tensed, dangling above her, waiting for her to open her eyes or to speak, waiting only slightly longer if she did neither until it dropped. She listened to the pulse racing in her ears and tried to hold her breath, but it only made her breath come faster as she waited. In an instant, she was off the bed, struggling with what could have been a tangle of bedclothes or David's hands, clutching at her, pulling her back to the bed. As she fought, she felt the straps of her nightgown pull taut, then rip, momentum thrusting her forward. Her breasts bobbed naked and fingers flew at them, snapping, pinching. A swath of fabric caught her ankle and, with a small wounded cry, she fell into the corner, her shoulder colliding painfully with the wall.

David was perched on the edge of the bed, grinning at her, rocking slowly back and forth.

"Stop it, David . . . *please*." She cried softly, her voice broken by sobs.

He moved to the floor, pulling himself toward her with handfuls of thick carpet, moving on his stomach like an animal with a shattered spine. In the moonlight, his eyes were a darker, colder blue, etched with red. Mean, sore-looking eyes where she imagined she saw a flicker of something dark, throbbing, the charred and blackened remains of his sanity. She saw that one of his fingers was badly cut above the knuckle and bleeding heavily, but he didn't seem to notice. She moaned softly. He moved closer, still grinning. A tic fluttered in her eyelid as his face loomed close, blurred by the tears, and she saw a thin glistening thread trickle over his lips, felt it run smooth and warm across the back of her hand. She bolted and turned to the wall, sobbing. One hand felt the windowsill and the other scrambled across the floor until it touched the nightstand. She pulled herself up. Her fingers touched the clock, the telephone and finally, the lamp. The room swirled with sounds as she fumbled with the switch; a voice calling her; her own ragged breathing.

"Lisa, Lisa?" The voice sounded worried. David's back down there, she thought. She screamed when the light finally went on.

The shaking had passed, but her throat felt dry and her eyes were puffy from crying. He spoke to her in soft whispers as his hands moved over her, comforting, soothing. Sometimes, the hands would leave her when he reached for a cigarette or an ash tray, and when they touched her again she would begin to shiver once more. Then he would press her close to him until the trembling had stopped.

"Do you want to talk?" he asked.

She shrugged.

"I'd like to talk about it, Lisa. I mean, I don't think I'll get to sleep if we don't talk this out."

For an instant she wanted to hurt him. "Well, that would make two of us up all night." She was sorry she'd said it.

"Lisa . . ." he pleaded, gently shaking her shoulder.

"All right, David, let's talk about it." Her voice sounded tired and shrill and it cracked as she spoke. "Why do you do this? Do you know? I don't think you do. Do you hate me so much—?"

"No," he whispered, "no."

She touched his shoulder. "David, David," she said, soothing. "You need help, and I don't think I'm the one who can give it to you. You know I love you, but—" But what, she thought. Leave him? If she hadn't by now, she wondered if she ever could. "Don't you see—"

He wasn't listening. He was staring beyond the edge of the bed, at something near the door on the far wall. She turned and followed his stare, straining her eyes until they ached from the darkness. Then she saw what it was. Beneath the closed door a pale puddle of light seeped into the room. The living room light was still on. Oh God, she thought, don't say it.

"David." She shook him. "David!" Harder, but he just stared, his eyes that cold silent blue. "No," she whispered.

"Lisa . . ." he started.

Then she was crying again. She heard him rush from the room, heard him cursing as he twisted and clawed at the hot bulbs, heard their muffled pop as their glass shattered in the sink, heard the clatter of the old plumbing as he ran cold water over his poor, burned hands. It was over an hour before he came back to bed and another hour until he slept.

In the small room, the sound of his breathing hung closer than the darkness. She heard his words echo, like bits of conversation heard in another room—". . . if you sleep . . . that could be bad . . ." She promised herself that she would not fall asleep. The air in the room was hot and thick and she moved to open the window. A cool breeze moved into the room, making her feel less uncomfortable. She listened to the sound of his breathing until she fell asleep.

There was a sloping meadow, and below her, a small pond that sparkled like a field of crystal. At the far edge, a sandy shore disappeared into a forest of slender, dark trees, smooth and tall, that clattered in the wind, a strange, discordant marimba. The air was hot, but fresh with the smell of the pond and long grass and moist soil. Above a distant red plain, the sun rode the horizon like a fiery warrior, half-buried in the dark land.

She lay back on her quilt and listened to the sound of the wind as it moved the strange trees. The dress she wore was of white lace, the color of smoke in winter and her hands fluttered over it, touching here and there as she pressed her fingertips against the delicate patterns.

The wind changed and, from far off, she heard the sound of blowing leaves and singing voices. She strained for snatches of the song and she heard: (sssss) a sibilant hiss; (aaahh) a long hollow sigh; (leeeee) a high keening wail. Her name. Changed, made foreign shaped by strange tongues, but her name. Leeeaaahhleeesssaahh, they chanted and hearing it, she wept. It was a song of prayer or of mourning, surging, sad. Far off, the singers walked from behind the forest across the face of the sun. There were six: tall, the color of charcoal, they marched in a slow deliberate cadence, their heads lowered. On their shoulders they carried one of the dark trees and lashed to it, a small still form. She could not see what it was. Small dogs followed, dancing between the long, dark legs of the men, their yelps rising in wild counterpoint to the sound of the song. The singing stopped. The men lowered their burden to the ground and one of the small dogs, braver than its companions, rushed toward it. A long knife flashed red in the sun and there was a startled yelp, then silence. There was a smell of blood in the air. The wind rose, sailing her bonnet across the meadow to the edge of the pond. But the pond had changed. The sparkling water had become a stagnant pool, only an occasional bubble of gas breaking the still surface. The air smelled of sulphur and salt. At the pond's far edge something moved and she saw a large dog drinking from the still water, his dark fur patched with sores and jagged pink scars. As she watched, he raised his head from the pond and regarded her with the dead white of blind eyes. The air around her grew cold. Sensing her, it almost seemed that he grinned as he started toward her in a loping run around the edge of the pond. The sky had grown dark and the wind had died, but there was a sound like the wind, a sound of breathing. She tried to rise, to call to the dark men, but her legs would not hold her. She saw that they were gone, the wide plain broken only by their long knives stuck deep in the sand, glinting coldly in the remaining sun.

The dog was running, breathing in hard, short gasps, muzzle flecked with foam. His eyes had changed, grown brighter, as if a curtain had been drawn back from a window to reveal an icy-blue waste. They were eyes she knew and she smiled. As he drew close, she reached to touch him, but he crouched before her, just out of reach. He licked her ankle. It was like ice and sand on her skin. She felt the tongue, cold and rough, move along her thigh and broken nails rake across her breasts. And she felt his eyes. The sound of the breathing roared in her ears. A dream, she thought. It's a dream, and she knew, then she laughed, reaching into the darkness. The light, she thought as her fingers touched, pulled, twisted, unable to turn the switch. She drew back her hand, clutching a matted clump of dark fur. "David," she screamed, "this is a dream!" She felt the cold tongue drag once across her throat, then the press of frayed lips and broken teeth. The sound of breathing stopped.

In the morning he awoke before the alarm sounded, feeling fresh and well rested. Odd, he thought, considering the miserable night before and the way he had frightened Lisa. He smiled and looked at where she lay huddled under the covers. He set the alarm so as not to disturb her, then rose quietly, carrying the phone with him into the living room as far as the cord would reach.

It took him ten minutes of explaining, gentle cajoling and the promise of a ride downtown before Doctor Berman consented to see David before the first appointment. He was smiling as he hung up the phone. That morning, for the first time in months, he sang in the shower and whistled happily as he shaved. He felt a twinge of disappointment that Lisa was not yet awake when he stepped into the bedroom, and there was a gnawing urge to wake her with gentle lovemaking as he'd done other mornings, long ago. Better to let her sleep, he thought. Tonight he would tell her of his talk with the doctor and he imagined how relieved and happy she would be. He pulled his yellow sport jacket from the closet, the one that she liked but that he seldom wore, feeling it too loud and conspicuous. Today, he thought, the way he felt, it was just right. Before leaving, he stepped softly to the quiet form on the bed and kissed her ear, hoping for a split-second that she would wake up long enough to say good-bye. Her skin was cool against his lips. Tucking the covers tight around her, he closed and latched the window, then patted her gently on the shoulder. He was whistling as he walked from the house.

Beneath the covers pressed tight against her face, Lisa's eyes were open, the delicate flecks of gold that had once made their greenness sparkle, now dull and tarnished under a haze of white, like frozen tears.

David had trouble parking and finally had to settle for a space nearly a block away from doc Berman's apartment. The walk would be a good opportunity to get back in touch with the old neighborhood, he decided. He noticed the change as he stepped from the car.

Dented garbage cans lined the curb and yellowed newspapers and foul odors leaked from under their ill-fitting lids. Shutters, door frames, and porch rails, once freshly painted each summer, were blistered and peeling, their true color masked by a dingy film of soot and years of fingerprints. One apartment window yawned dark and vacant while in others, old sun-rotted curtains hung limp and unmoving like battle-weary flags. And everything was so . . . small, he thought, diminished. I'm making a diminishing return, he joked lamely, but it didn't help. He wondered why doc Berman had stayed and decided that it must have been because of the memories. Certainly there were enough here for himself, and he'd moved away just after high school; years before doc's patients began to refuse to come into this part of town, forcing him to get an office in the business district. He hoped that doc hadn't changed as much as the neighborhood. Must have been a surprise for the old guy, he thought, hearing from him after all these years. But doc had been the first . . . no, the only one he'd thought of when he decided to get some help. He would listen, really listen, before sending him off to some shrink. It wasn't the sort of thing you took to a stranger, he reasoned, at least not without some advice. Yes, this was the right thing, the right place to be. Why else would doc have come so automatically to mind after all this time? He thought of Lisa and how she would agree, and he began to feel better.

As he turned down the alley toward the apartment, he noticed a large dog standing amid a group of toppled trash cans, lapping water from a dirty puddle. It was an old dog, thin but muscular, with heavy shoulders and a thick corded neck. On one shoulder a fresh wound glistened raw and wet against a dark coat that looked tough and hard, more scar than fur. He moved closer, trying to see how badly the animal was hurt. Stretching a tentative hand from behind the safety of a trash can he called softly, "Hey fella . . . here—" The dog looked up.

"Jesus Christ," he gasped, staggering back. A knot of fear and revulsion twisted in his stomach. The dog stared, cocking its head from side to side, confused by the reaction it had caused.

"Ugly son-of-a-bitch," David muttered, feeling embarrassed for the shock he'd felt when he had looked into that battered face, the diseased white eyes. Slowly, he backed away, then turned and hurried down the alley, breathing hard and trying to warm the chill that had crept into his flesh.

The smell of the man faded with his echoing footsteps. Shadows retreated, vanishing into light as the morning sun flooded into the alley. And with the shadows, the blindness melted away until the sun sparked against gold in the green, almost human eyes. Far down the alley, the man in the bright sport coat moved quickly away. She moved after him.

Introduction

This is Ray Russell's first short story in several years, coming hard on the heels of his new and very well received novel, PRINCESS PAMELA, *published just this September.*

The problem in dealing with people who carry with them monumental egos is that it is so maddeningly difficult to extract, when necessary, anything but the most blatant retribution. It isn't always the case that the sublime works, and works well. But when it does—especially when the sublime is such that it doesn't appear to be so—then the title of this story is much more apt than first meets the eye.

AVENGING ANGEL

by Ray Russell

When I turned the page of my desk calendar this morning, I saw a cryptic reminder scribbled in my own hand: *O S, 1 yr.* A chill rippled through me, and I was buffeted by two opposite, simultaneous reactions:

Has it really been a whole year since I last saw him?

Has it really been *only* a year?

Time is a carnival mirror, stretching a single moment to tenuous lengths, like taffy; squeezing a lifetime into the flicker of an eye. When Pythagoras was asked to define time, he said it was the soul of this world. I've never understood what he meant by that, but I've always liked the sound of it.

I walked slowly, reluctantly, from my desk to the closet on the other side of my study. I opened the door and peered into the darkness. It was musty from being closed so long, and mingled with the mustiness was the incongruous and almost indiscernible aroma of oregano. With hesitant hand, I reached for the wall switch and—after a few seconds of indecision—snapped on the light.

There it was: still propped against the closet wall—that object, that enigma, that unspeakable monstrosity, that thing.

"And why shouldn't it be?" I asked myself. "I hid it here a year ago, didn't I? After all, it couldn't walk away. It couldn't transform itself into a mist and seep out under the door. I don't believe in that occult rubbish . . . do I?"

I couldn't look at it any longer. It was too repulsive. Too disquieting. Too . . . alive. I turned off the light, shut the closet door, and returned to my desk, but I couldn't work. I pulled open the bottom drawer and lifted out a drinking glass and an almost empty bottle of Chivas Regal. There was just about one good stiff shot left, which I carefully poured. I dropped the dead soldier into the wastebasket.

(Fog like thick gray fungus . . . a furry moon seen dimly . . . the click of boot heels growing louder, nearer, in the dark, in the damp and chilly night . . . that would be the proper setting for what happened a year ago. Instead, it had taken place in blinding daylight, in the inferno of noon, in the shimmer and glitter of the sun, the Southern California sun that can char land, boil seas . . .)

I lifted the glass, murmuring, "Here's looking at you, Orlando," and added an old Irish toast: "May you dwell in Heaven for half an hour before the Devil discovers you're dead." I downed the scotch in one gulp.

"Potipharland," a Biblical scholar of my acquaintance calls this stretch of geography, pedantically informing me that the name of the captain of Pharaoh's guard (the one whose wife had a yen for Joseph) was Potiphar or Phutiphar, which means "belonging to the sun." Potland might also be apt, I told him, considering the smoking preferences of many of the inhabitants.

Marty Meyerson and I pulled into the driveway of the little house in the Hollywood Hills punctually at nine A.M. Even that early, the day was beginning to warm up. There was an ivy-strangled trellis on the left of the house, leading to a patio (so called by realtors) about the size of a postcard. While I walked up to the front door and rang the bell, Marty began to set up his equipment on the patio: tripod, strobe, and that umbrella-shaped reflector photographers use.

The door was opened by a breathtakingly beautiful brunette with patrician features and a willowy body. She belonged on the cover of *Vogue*. She greeted me with a Gleem commercial smile and said, in a voice as bright and brittle as a light bulb, "Hi, I'm Nell. Mr. Silone's secretary. He'll be with you in just a minute." She withdrew inside the house again, and closed the door.

The "minute" stretched to fifteen, but Marty and I passed the time constructively by planning the angles and poses of the pictures he would shoot for *Today's Artist,* the small-circulation magazine that had commissioned me to do the Silone interview.

"That secretary of his," muttered Marty, whose photog's eye had spotted her from the patio, and who knew a good subject when he saw one.

"Lovely," I said.

"Oh, a knockout," he agreed, "but there's something about her. Does she look familiar to you?" I shook my head. Marty said, "Well, I've seen her before, I'm sure of it, damned if I know where, though."

A quarter of an hour after our arrival, Orlando Silone erupted out of the house, bellowing a rhyme: "No baloney! Here's Silone!" He had several such rhymes, I'd been told, some on bumperstickers, others on T-shirts, business cards, letterheads—they served to make clear his preferred pronunciation of his name: not "Sil-loan," to rhyme with "alone," or "Silon-ay," like his namesake, the late Ignazio Silone, famous author of *Bread and Wine,* but, rather: "Hail Silone—he's no phony!" and "Big and bony—that's Silone!" and "Matrimony? Not for Silone!" Some of his rhymes stated simple facts: he was, indeed, very tall, and thin to the point of emaciation. And he *had* successfully avoided marriage for four and a half decades. Whether or not he was a phony, on the other hand, was a matter of opinion. I, for one, did not hold his work in high esteem. He couldn't draw very well, so he fell back on the cop-out of pseudo-Picasso abstractions and distortions (Picasso himself, of course, was a masterly draughtsman who learned the rules before he broke them). Silone stressed the ugly, specializing in vomit-encrusted winos sleeping it off in doorways, bloated prostitutes with grotesque leering masks for faces, and several gratuitously nauseating Crucifixion scenes, in each of which a naked Saviour is shown torn to gory shreds, disembowelled, and obscenely mutilated. Silone equated this ugliness with Truth, "telling it like it is." To be blunt, he had ego but no talent; and this lack had barred him from recognition in the more important art circles and among major critics. But, somehow, he had managed to become a minor cult figure, and had slowly gathered about him a small following of very young and extremely unperceptive devotees whose noisy advocacy had attracted the notice of *Today's Artist*. His fans formed a pathetic but not contemptible little coterie: they were mostly of high school and junior college age; yearning, eager, looking for something, someone, anything, anyone, to worship in an age of toppled idols and blighted faith. So they worshipped Orlando. They called him by his first name ("Like Leonardo, Rembrandt, Michelangelo!" he had said).

"No baloney! Here's Silone!" he shouted, suddenly bursting out the patio door, all six-feet three of him, wearing only a pair of shorts made from lopped-off jeans. Bare-footed, bare-legged, bare-chested, his long red beard and longer, redder hair exploding from his leonine head, he looked me up and down and sarcastically remarked, "So you're the lucky dude who gets to interview Silone."

Then turning in Marty's direction and scowling at the photo equipment, he snarled, "What's all *this* junk?" With a wide sweep of his hand, he knocked over the umbrella-reflector and the camera tripod, sending them clattering to the red bricks of the patio floor. Fortunately, Marty had not yet affixed his camera to the tripod, so there was no serious damage. "I deal in Truth!" growled Silone. "The *naked* Truth! Warts and all! I'm no Botticelli, sonny boy—none of this pretty-pretty stuff for me. You just point the damn camera at me and fire away."

Saying not a word, Marty patiently picked up the apparatus and put it to one side. He removed his camera from its case. "Anything you say, Mr. Silone. But don't you want to put something on?"

"No," retorted Silone in a mocking singsong, "I do *not* want to 'put something on.' This is *me!* This is Silone!" He slapped the rust-colored thicket of hair on his stark-ribbed chest. "I have nothing to hide!"

Marty looked at me, quizzically. I nodded him an OK, and he began shooting. The tape recorder dangling from my shoulder had already been turned on, so I began my questions, but before I could finish even the first one, Silone roared in the direction of the house: "Nell! Where are those drinks? Get your gorgeous butt out here on the double!"

Her answering voice caroled, "Coming!" from inside, and soon appeared with a tray of vodka-tonics. The frosted glasses looked temptingly cool, but for me it was a bit early in the day for strong drink, so I declined. "I don't trust a man who won't drink with me," Silone said darkly. As he took a glass from Nell's hand, she made no attempt to hide the way she affectionately tousled his beard. Silone winked at us, saying, "You've met my sex-retary? Can't keep her hands off me, can you, doll?" Nell giggled and disappeared again into the house.

About an hour into the interview, the mercury rising and my tolerance of Silone dropping, he suddenly frowned and barked, "What the hell time is it?" I glanced at my watch and told him.

"Time to go," he said.

"Go where?"

"The Challenge Gallery. That little art joint off La Cienega. The old broad who owns it twisted my arm and got a promise out of me to sign some pictures for my fans today at ten. You and the shutterbug can come along. You'll pick up plenty of good material for the interview."

"Ten?" I said. "It's a quarter *past* ten already, and it'll take us at least half an hour to get there."

"Close enough. They'll wait."

"Shouldn't you phone the gallery, at least, and let them know we're on the way?"

"What for? I *said* they'll *wait*." He pointed to my weathered Volkswagen in the driveway. "Is that your bucket of bolts?" I admitted that it was. "Well," he sighed, "ordinarily I wouldn't be caught dead in a pile of junk like that, but my Alfa Romeo's in the shop for a tune-up, so I'll make the supreme sacrifice." (Alfa Romeo? Silone made a modest living from his meager fan club, but not enough to afford an Alfa Romeo. Could it be that the champion of Truth was—I hated to think it—lying?)

"Nell!" he boomed. "My traveling gear, and don't be all day about it!" In a moment, Nell trotted out with a blue cotton jump suit, a pair of sandals, and an Aussie outback hat with the brim pinned up on the left side. "They love me down under," he explained, jamming the hat on his head. I refrained from asking "Down under what?" as he climbed into the jump suit and zipped it up. Nell buckled the sandals on his feet.

"Got a notepad on you?" he gruffly asked me. "And a pencil?" I handed him my pad and a felt-tip pen. He snatched them out of my hand and began to sketch something. Meanwhile, out in the driveway, Marty was packing his equipment in the trunk of my car and exchanging a few words with Nell. In less than a minute, Silone had finished his sketch. He ripped out the page, returned the pad to me, but pocketed my pen. The sketch was a hasty doodle that looked vaguely like a battered trash can with the tail of a dead cat hanging out of it. "Wait a minute," said Silone. "It needs some flies." Taking my pen from his pocket, he added a few hovering squiggles over the trash can. "There. That's better." Surprisingly, he didn't sign it.

"What's it for?" I asked.

"You'll see. If you can ever get that rattletrap of yours to start, that is."

We walked out to my car, where Marty was waiting for us. The beauteous Nell beat a quick retreat toward the house, as Silone bawled after her, "Hold down the fort, birdbrain!"

Marty climbed into the back seat, while Orlando and I squeezed into the front. My car's engine turned over instantly, much to Silone's vociferous surprise, and we were off.

Even with all the windows wide open, the car was like an oven. As we rolled down out of the Hollywood Hills, my eyes were dazzled by the sun and my ears were pummeled by a stream of non-stop talk from Silone. He had a voice like a busy signal—the difference being that you couldn't stop it by hanging up. His photo had to appear on the cover of *Today's Artist,* he demanded, as well as his name ("in big letters, and ahead of any other name"). He insisted on rewrite privileges of the interview manuscript. Inasmuch as the bulk of the words in the piece would be his, he expected to be paid for them, and he modestly suggested six thousand dollars, causing Marty to gasp from the back seat; although he may have been yawning. The "six gee's," he airily informed me, would *not* include payment for reproductions of his paintings, at least half a dozen of which must accompany the published interview; that would be negotiated later. I didn't bother to apprise Silone of the fact that interview subjects are *never* paid, or that the entire budget for an issue of *Today's Artist* wasn't much more than the sum he had named, and I didn't voice my educated guess that his total income for half a year, despite his big talk, probably didn't amount to that figure.

But I tried not to judge him too harshly. His distrust of journalists may have been justified by a cleverly executed hatchet job a local columnist had done on him in the recent past. Poor Silone had been thoroughly excoriated both as artist and man in that piece, without his name being specified even once. The columnist had foxily disclosed his identity in a dozen or so ways. For example, the Midwestern state of Silone's birth—well-known to his fans—"Wisconsin, or Land of Lakes, as the Chamber of Commerce calls it," had been mentioned; also the curious physiological fact (often discussed by the logorrheic Silone) that, as a result of botched surgery in his boyhood, he had been "left with but one tonsil, one adenoid." That sort of thing, occurring again and again throughout the blind article, had as much as said "Orlando Silone." No wonder he was a bit paranoid. I could hardly blame him. Still, those interview conditions he had imposed were absurd and unacceptable, so I pulled into the next convenient driveway, to make a turnaround. Silone asked me what the hell I was doing.

"Taking you home," I told him. "The magazine will never go along with those demands, so I guess the interview is off."

"*Off?*"

"Sorry."

"Hold it!" he said quickly. I hit the brakes. "Now let's not be hasty," he added. "I can straighten all this out with your editor later on. One quick phone call will do it." Lots of luck, I said to myself.

Without a word, I turned the car around again and resumed the journey to the art gallery. Three blocks away from it, Silone suddenly snapped, "Pull over here." He pointed to an empty parking space in front of a photocopy shop. "I need some copies of this." He waved the trash can sketch. "Let's see . . . a hundred ought to do it. At a nickel apiece . . ." Snapping his fingers impatiently at me, he said, "Gimme a five-spot. I came away without any cash." I knew I'd never see it again, but I dug into my wallet and handed him five dollars. "Be back in a jiff," he said, hopping out of the car and into the shop.

"Sweet guy," I said to Marty, who hadn't uttered a single word from the back seat during the entire trip.

"A prince," Marty replied. "A real prince. Want to hear something interesting? I was talking to Nell while the great man was drawing that sketch. I suddenly remembered where I'd seen her before. She's a model. I did some shots of her for a fashion catalogue last year. I asked her what on earth she was doing, working as a secretary to No Baloney. She said, 'I'm no more a secretary than you are, Marty, and I'm certainly not a sex-retary, to quote the master. I never set eyes on him before. The model agency got a call from him last week, setting up a gig for this morning. He'd seen my composite in the mug book, and he wanted me. Just two or three hours, no nudes or anything like that, and he'd pay the going hourly rate. The agency ran a quick check on him, found out he's a professional artist of some kind, and figured it was legit. I show up here eight-thirty this morning, and I see there's no camera, no lights, no nothing, so I begin to smell a rat, and right away little Nell is on her toes. I don't make any weirdo scenes, know what I mean? Well, turns out he's a weirdo, all right, but not in the way I was afraid of. He doesn't want to take any pictures of me, or sketch me, and he doesn't want to get palsy, either. He says he just wants me to play a part. Pretend to be his secretary, just for a couple of hours. Kind of like a joke on some friends of his. And I'm supposed to behave like I'm crazy about him—just hold his hand now and then, that sort of thing, nothing more. Well, the whole *shtick* was a little too oddball for me, and not really in my line, so I advised him to hire an actress—I'm a model, strictly. But he talked me into it. "What the hell," he said, "you're already here. Why lose a morning's work?" It would all be just in fun, he said, and he'd pay up just the same as if it were a kosher photo session. To tell you the truth, Marty, I didn't dig the deception part of it, but then I asked myself: Who am I to get on my high horse, deceptionwise? Isn't deception my stock-in-trade? When I pose as a mother in a disposable diaper ad, isn't that let's-pretend time? I've never changed a diaper in my life. And, look, a buck is a buck. So I did it. I'm not proud of it, but I did it.'"

Marty paused for a breath and went on: "Then she told me something else. 'What a fake he is!' she said. 'Have you seen those Modiglianis and Mondrians on his walls? No? Well, you will, before this interview gig of yours is finished. He'll make plenty sure of that. Probably want you to snap him standing in front of them. And they're originals, all right, not reproductions. But they're just like me—hired for the occasion to impress you and your friend. Or borrowed, rather, from a rich buddy. Hon, I've never *seen* a bigger phony. I overheard him on the phone, assuring the guy that he'd have his paintings back tonight. Marty, the minute you fellows drive off to the art gallery with him, my job is over, and I *split*. Will I ever be glad to see the last of that creep!'"

I couldn't respond to Marty's fascinating story because Silone was now bounding out of the store with a thick stack of photocopies under his arm. Climbing into the car, he attempted a mimicry of the late John Wayne: "Let's move out!" I pulled away from the curb.

As we approached the Challenge Gallery, we saw a line of young people standing outside, stretching halfway up the block. They were waiting in the blistering sun for Orlando, *their* Orlando, and no doubt had been waiting since ten o'clock, if not earlier. It was now a quarter to eleven. They were misguided, immature, without taste, but how could one despise those earnest young faces? My heart went out to them. These are his children, I said to myself. Orlando, now in his mid-forties, had never married and was childless. These youngsters, so patiently lined up to see him, were offering him the love a child gives a father. And maybe, I told myself, here is where Orlando will be redeemed. If not in any religious sense of that word, then at least redeemed in my eyes. Here, he may show a side of his nature adults had never seen. By returning the warmth and fervent love of these adoring kids, he may earn himself a lifetime membership in the human race. *Suffer the little children to come unto me,* and all that. Silone was no Jesus, not by a long shot, but to his fans he was *some* kind of cut-rate messiah.

I parked the car. As he got out, his young votaries, seeing him, sent up a delighted cheer and broke ranks, swarming around him, calling his name. "Back, *back!*" he shrieked, flailing his arms. "Get back in line, pinheads!"

They fell back, forming a line again, as Orlando strode toward the gallery door. Marty and I followed him; he with his camera, I with my tape recorder. A couple of the kids, awed and transfixed by the Presence, were rooted to the spot at the entrance, unwittingly blocking our way. "Break it up, you turkeys!" Orlando snarled at them. They skittered away like beetles, and we entered. Thanks for small mercies: the gallery was air-conditioned.

The gallery owner was a large, fiftyish spinster with the fanfare name of Dr. Challenge. I knew something about her background. She'd taught a course in modern art at a local university some years before, and had become a bit of a joke because she'd had the gall to list herself in the campus phone directory as *Challenge, Dr. Vera,* thus enjoying the dubious distinction of being the only Ph. D. at the school to insist upon the "Dr." title. She was later discharged from the faculty when it came to light that she had plagiarized her doctorate dissertation on Mirò. "Oh, *dear* Mr. Silone, at last!" she gushed. "We had almost given you up. Now the signing can—"

"I'm not signing anything," he announced, "until I get a pizza."

Dr. Challenge blinked. "A . . . a pizza?"

He jerked a thumb toward the horde of fans pressing into the gallery. "One of these clowns is gonna hafta go get me a sausage-and-anchovy pizza, before I even lift a pen."

"*I'll* do it, Orlando!" piped a young male voice from the throng.

"Don't forget the wine," Silone warned him. "A bottle of good Chianti, well chilled. And I said *good.* Not some cheap red vinegar."

The kid dashed away, thrilled to be of service.

Silone stood up on a chair. "All right, you freaks, gather round and hear the words of The Great One!" The youngsters crowded into the gallery, filling it with wall-to-wall adulation. He held up a fistful of the Xerox copies. "See these? Know what they are? Copies of an original Orlando, created by the master *just this morning,* expressly for this occasion. The dude with the tape recorder can attest to that—he saw me sketch it, less than an hour ago. Right?" I nodded.

He slipped into a sideshow barker spiel, "Tell ya what I'm gonna dew. I'm gonna permit you walking acne-farms to buy 'em for a mere and only ten bucks per copy." A wail of delight rose from the mob. "But wait, it gets better. For twenty-five bucks, I'll *sign* 'em!" They cheered this news. "You can't believe it, can you?" he went on. "You just cannot believe your good fortune. Well, don't go 'way, 'cause you ain't heard *nothin'* yet. Are—you—ready?" A shout of affirmation rocked the gallery. "Then hear this. For *fifty* bucks, I will not only sign your copy, I will inscribe it with *your name* and dedicate it to *you*, 'who inspired me to create it,' unquote. How do ya like *them* apples?"

They liked them apples just fine, and an even louder cheer resonated from their throats. But I thought: Yes, the champion of Truth *is* lying—and is offering to sell his lies, for fifty dollars each, to children. Stendhal was right: Bad taste leads to crime.

But wait, as Orlando would say, it gets better.

In due course, his lunch arrived. Silone accepted it without thanking his fan, and didn't offer to reimburse the boy. As he munched the pizza and slugged wine straight from the bottle, another fan inched forward through the crowd. She was perhaps fifteen or sixteen, shy, overweight, not particularly pretty, but she had a cascade of radiant long corn-silk hair, and she exuded an essence, a nimbus of purity that magnetized my attention. Under her left arm she held a large rectangle wrapped in brown paper. She *had* to hold it under her left arm because her right arm was missing. There was an angelic quality about her, despite her clipped wing. In a tiny voice, she bashfully whispered, "Mr. Silone?"

"Don't mumble, I can't hear you," he said, mouth full.

"I've brought something for you, Mr. Silone. A present. I painted it myself. It took a long time, because . . ."

Silone chuckled nastily. "I've heard of one-armed paper hangers, but never one-armed painters! You want to buy one of these original photocopies, kid?"

"I don't have any money, Mr. Silone. I just came here to give—"

"Step aside, Fatso, I've got business to transact."

"But won't you at least *look* at it?"

"Okay, okay, let's see the stupid thing."

Because of her handicap, she had difficulty removing the wrapping, so I helped her. When her painting was unveiled, I saw that it was a portrait of Orlando. It was not a work of genius, nor even of professional caliber, but it had been done with some skill, great care, and profound devotion. Her draughtsmanship was superior to anything Silone had ever achieved. Working apparently from photographs, the girl had painstakingly developed a picture that looked exactly like him —and didn't look like him at all. His features had been precisely rendered; technically, nothing was awry; but she had left out Orlando's character. Imbuing the face, instead, with her own misplaced love, she had depicted him as a saint, glowing with kindness and benediction. It was Orlando, and it wasn't Orlando. It was Orlando's shell, emptied of ugliness and filled with beauty. It was Orlando as he might have looked if he hadn't been such a thoroughly rotten human being. "Why, honey," I said, "this is very *good.*"

"Like a Corelli sonata!" Dr. Challenge declared.

But it wasn't our praise that the girl craved. She turned to Silone with a beseeching light in her eyes. Silently, I said: This is your chance, Silone. Maybe your *last* chance to save your maggoty soul. Don't blow it. Say something nice to her.

He said something, all right—not to her, but to me: "Good? Did you call this good? How the hell do *you* know what's good? You want to know what this is? *This is garbage.*" He flung a slice of pizza at the portrait.

Even the assembled worshippers were shocked. Dr. Challenge gasped. A silence settled over the gallery like a suddenly overcast sky. The pizza began to slide down the painting, leaving a trail of cheese and tomato sauce, with occasional bits of anchovy and sausage clinging to the gluey mess.

"You bastard!" I yelled.

The girl was in tears—she was destroyed—it was as if God had spit in her face. I put my arm around her shoulders. "Don't cry, sweetie," I said. "The painting will clean up easily. It'll be good as new, you'll see."

"But it's for *him!* I did it for *him!*" She tried to hide her face in her hand. It was hard to do with only one. Gently, I coaxed her to a secluded corner at the rear of the gallery and gave her my handkerchief.

Silone had meanwhile regained the loyalty of his other fans by starting the sale of the photocopies. They went briskly, some for ten dollars, most for twenty-five and the promise of a signature, a few for fifty and the even more glowing prospect of a personal dedication. "Cash, no checks!" he insisted as he passed out the copies and pocketed the money. In minutes, the sale was over. Then he sold the empty wine bottle for twelve dollars. "Okay, troops, get the hell outa my way. I'm late for another appointment." He started toward the door, pushing the kids aside and calling over his shoulder to me, "Hey, you—tapeworm! Let's make tracks!"

A disappointed murmur was rising from the faithful. "You didn't sign my copy!" . . . "You didn't dedicate it to me!" . . . "I paid you twenty-five dollars, Orlando!" . . . "I paid you fifty!" . . .

"No time now," he said. "In a big rush. Catch me later." He walked out to the curb where my Volkswagen was parked. I followed him into the blazing midday sun. Marty was already standing at the car.

"Here's the agenda, guys," Silone said to us. "You drive me back to my place and drop me off. Then come back again at six, snap some pictures of me inside the house, and take me out to dinner. We can wrap up the interview over a Chateaubriand steak. Right? Right. Let's go."

"*Call a cab!*" I shouted, anger choking me. "I'm not chauffeuring you anywhere!"

"What's with him?" he asked Marty.

"You cheated those poor kids," I said. "You stole their money and didn't even take the time to scrawl your name and a few lying words on their copies. Fifty dollars for a nickel Xerox! They saved up their money all year . . ."

"Aw, put a sock in it, willya? When the Orlando spell is on them thar lantern-jawed morons, I can make 'em do anything I please—and if those gnat-brains are dumb enough to shell out legal tender for a lousy Xerox, they deserve everything they get."

"For Christ's sake, Silone, they're *children!* And as for deserving—I hope you get everything *you* deserve. In spades!" I uttered it like a prayer.

Snickering, he walked away, presumably in search of a cab. The sweat of rage and high-noon heat was rolling off me.

Suddenly, I remembered the girl. I ran back into the cool gallery. Most of the fans had disbanded. I looked around for her. She had vanished. But she had left her painting behind. It was leaning against a rear wall, the face still blemished by coagulating pizza. I asked Dr. Challenge: "That one-armed girl, where did she go?" But the good doctor was still dazed by her whirlwind exposure to Silone, and merely shook her head. I picked up the painting and took it out to the car, where I locked it in the trunk. Then I dropped off Marty and drove home.

The first thing I did was to clean the pizza from the painting. It came off easily, as I'd told the girl it would, but I was in for a heart-freezing surprise. I couldn't believe what I saw. A tumult of images rushed over me. In my memory, I glimpsed that girl again, and felt her angelic aura. I heard Silone say, "They love me down under," and now I wasn't so sure he'd meant Australia. I heard my own unspoken words: This is your chance, Silone. Maybe your *last* chance to save your maggoty soul. Don't blow it.

But he had.

I've read *Dorian Gray* several times over the past year, hoping it might contain a clue, a hint; but the situation in Wilde's novel is quite different from this one, and the book couldn't help me. I never heard from Silone again after that terrible day. To my knowledge, nobody has. I tried to phone him, to tell him I wasn't going ahead with the interview, but I kept getting his recorded voice on an answering gadget: "Orlando's Hideaway. Just leave your name and number and I'll catch you later, baby." Day after day, I heard that recording. After a while, I gave up.

There's been a lot of speculation, of course. He's on the lam from his creditors and/or the IRS, some say—fled the city, the state, the country. He's changed his name, shaved his head, and formed a religious cult somewhere. His fans, tired of being treated like dirt, finally turned on him, as worms are proverbially reputed to do, and murdered him, cremated him, scattered his ashes to the winds or, more in the spirit of his work, flushed them down the toilet. Whatever, nobody seems to know where he is. But I think I do.

I think he's in my closet.

When I cleaned off those pizza stains a year ago today, I saw that the painting had become subtly . . . *different*, somehow. My imagination? No; because Marty's photos of the original portrait, snapped that day in the gallery, are available for objective comparison, and still show it as it was. A chemical reaction to the pizza sauce? I think not.

The amateur painting had been transformed into a masterpiece that captured the character of Silone perfectly—and "captured" is the chillingly right word. It now resembles him to the life. The saintliness is gone, and in its place is the man's true personality—loathsome, cruel, evil. He had been given his chance, but he had thrown it away. And in an awesome act of sanitation, some Force, some Power I can never hope to comprehend, had plucked him from this world and hurled him into Hell. His own special, terribly private Hell. Reserved exclusively for him.

Hell is the shadow of a soul on fire, wrote Omar the tent-maker. In *Dr. Faustus,* Mephisto says, *Where we are is Hell, and where Hell is, there must we ever be.* Hell is underground, some believe; Hell is on earth, others say; Hell is on a different plane of existence, a different continuum, still others argue. Orlando Silone's Hell, I suggest, is a layer of paint a fraction of an inch thick. He's screaming silently, trapped forever in the bright acrylic colors of his own portrait, painted by an innocent supplicant whose heart he had stepped on and mercilessly crushed as if it had been a cockroach. And that supplicant, that ray of purity, had then returned to . . . wherever it was she'd come from. Anyway, that's my theory.

Some day, I'm going to burn that painting. I wonder what will happen when I do?

Introduction

R. Chetwynd-Hayes is known in this country primarily for his stint as editor of the British-based Fontana BOOK OF HORROR *series. His fiction, unfortunately, has until now been confined to the United Kingdom. The story below was included in his collection,* THE NIGHT GHOULS, *and appears in the United States for the first time here.*

THE GHOST WHO LIMPED

by R. Chetwynd-Hayes

Mother said Brian was not to play with matches and of course he did, setting light to the old summerhouse, so that Father had to put the fire out with the garden hose.

Father maintained that Brian should be spanked but Mother would not let him, stating with cool simplicity, that words were more powerful than blows.

"That's all very well," Father grumbled, "but one day . . ."

"He's only seven," Mother pointed out, "and we must reason with him. It's not as though any real damage was done."

Julia went out to look at the summerhouse, and truly the damage was negligible. The doorsteps were slightly scorched, but this added to the old-world, time-beaten appearance of the ancient building.

When she came back to the house, Mother was explaining to Brian the virtues and evils of fire.

"The fire keeps us warm; it cooks our food and is nice to look at."

"Makes pretty pictures," Brian stated, "lots of mountains and valleys."

"Yes," Mother agreed, "and therefore fire is a good friend,

but when you set light to the summerhouse, then it was a bad enemy. You—all of us could have been burned to death."

"Death . . . death," Brian repeated the words with some satisfaction. "What is death?"

Mother frowned, then proceeded to choose her words with care.

"The body . . . your arms and legs become still, and you can't use your body any more. You . . . become like Mr. Miss-One."

Brian grinned with impish delight.

"I'd like to be Mr. Miss-One."

Mother took the small boy into her arms and shook her beautiful head, so that the fair curls danced like corn in sunlight.

"No, my darling. No. You wouldn't like being Mr. Miss-One."

Julia came down late for dinner for she had fallen asleep in her room, and dreamed a strange dream. It seemed that she had been in the drawing room when Mr. Miss-One entered. He had limped across the room and sunk down beside her on the sofa; and for the first time, he seemed to know she was present. He stared straight at her and looked so very, very sad, that when she awoke, tears were rolling down her cheeks.

"You look pale," Mother remarked, "and your eyes are red. I hope you aren't sickening for something."

Julia said: "No," then seated herself opposite Brian, who made a face and poked his tongue out.

"Behave yourself," Father warned, "and, Julia, you're not to tease him."

"I didn't . . ." Julia began to protest but Mother said, "You're not to answer your father back."

She hung her head and fought back the scalding tears. The terrible injustice was a burning pain and she felt shut out—unwanted. Brian was a child, a doll for her parents to pet; she was sixteen, tall, awkward, not particularly pretty, which meant being unloved, isolated, scolded—who knows, perhaps hated.

"Julia, sit up," Mother continued with a sharp voice, "don't slouch. Heavens above, when I was your age, I was as straight as a larch. Really, I can't imagine who you take after."

"Listen to your mother," Father ordered, smiling at Brian, whose mouth was smeared with custard. "She is talking for your own good."

They might have been talking to a stranger or casting words at a statue. Her very presence, every action, provoked a series of stock phrases. She moved in her chair.

"Don't fidget," Mother snapped.

"For heaven's sake, sit still," said Father.

Julia got up and ran from the room.

"Oh, no," Mother exclaimed, "not another fit of the sulks!"

"She'll get over it," Father pronounced.

The garden dozed under the afternoon sun, while bees and bluebottles hummed with contentment in the heat. Julia lay back in a deck chair and basked in a lake of misery, wallowing in the melancholy stream of her self-pity.

"I wish I could die. Death is like a beautiful woman in a gray robe who closes our eyes with gentle fingers, then wipes the slate of memory clean."

She decided this was a noble thought, and really she was quite definitely a genius, which explained why everyone was so unkind.

"I am different," she told herself, and at once felt much more cheerful. "I think on a much higher plane. Mother is so stupid, afraid to smile in case she makes a line on her face, and as for Father . . . he's an echo, a nothing. Brian is a horrible, spoiled little beast. But I'm—I'm a genius."

Having reached this satisfactory conclusion, she was about to rise when Mr. Miss-One entered the garden. He was carrying a hoe and, walking over to one of the flower-beds, he began to turn the soil, or rather gave the appearance of doing so, for Julia knew that not even a single stone would be disturbed. She crept up to him like a puppy approaching its master, uncertain of its reception. She stopped some three feet from him and sank down on the grass, gazing up into his face.

He was so beautiful. There was no other word to describe

that kind, sensitive face. Mother was always a little frightened of Mr. Miss-One, saying that though he appeared harmless, nevertheless, he wasn't natural. Father regarded him in much the same way, as if he were a stray cat that refused to be dislodged.

"We must be mad to live in a house with a bally ghost," he had once protested. "Never know when the damned thing is going to pop up."

This attitude, of course, only confirmed their mundane, unimaginative outlook, and showed up Julia's exceptional powers of perception. Mr. Miss-One was beautiful, kind, and must have been, long ago, a remarkable person. Julia had no evidence to support this theory for Mr. Miss-One never spoke, was apparently oblivious of their presence, and only performed little, non-productive chores, strolling aimlessly through the house or garden. Furthermore, Mr. Miss-One was not young, possibly as old as Julia's father, for his black hair was flecked with gray and there were tired lines around his eyes and mouth. But these signs of age enhanced his beauty, making him a strange, exciting figure, combining the attributes of father and lover. Now he stood upright, leaning upon the hoe, and stared thoughtfully back at the house.

"Mr. Miss-One," Julia whispered, "who are you? I want to know so much. How long ago did you live? When did you die? And why do you haunt the house and garden? Haunt! That's a funny word. It sounds frightening, and you don't frighten me at all."

Mr. Miss-One returned to his work and continued to turn soil that never moved.

"Father says you don't exist, but are only a time image of someone who lived here years and years ago. That's nonsense. I could not fall in love with a shadow or dream about a patch of colored air."

"Julia." Mother was standing in the doorway and her voice held an angry, fearful tone. "Julia, come here at once."

Reluctantly she rose and left Mr. Miss-One to his ghostly gardening, willing herself not to look back. Mother slapped her bare arm, a punishment that had been applied in childhood.

"I've told you once, I've told you a thousand times, you're not to go near that—that thing. It's not healthy. It ought to be exercised or something."

"Exorcised," Julia corrected.

"And don't answer me back. I think sometimes, you're a little mad. Go to your room and don't come down until I say so."

From her bedroom window, Julia watched Mr. Miss-One. He was pushing a ghostly lawnmower over the lawn, limping laboriously in its wake, seemingly oblivious that no grass leaped into the box, that the whirling blades made no sound.

"I expect he was killed in a war," Julia thought as he disappeared behind a rhododendron bush. She waited for him to reappear but the garden remained empty, and when, presently, the setting sun sent long tree shadows across the grass, she knew, for the time being at least, the play was over.

"I thought we might run down to the coast today," Father announced over the breakfast table.

"Good idea." Mother nodded her agreement. "Julia, sit up, child, don't slouch."

"Listen to your mother," Father advised. "Yes, a breath of sea air will do us all good. Brian will enjoy it, won't you old fellow?"

"Yes." Brian nodded vigorously. "Throw stones at seagulls."

Both fond parents laughed softly and Mother admonished gently, "You mustn't throw stones at dickybirds."

"Why?"

"Because . . ." For once Mother seemed lost for an explanation and it was left to Father to express an opinion.

"Because it's not nice."

"We won't go," Julia thought. "We never go. Something will happen to stop us."

But preparations went on after breakfast. Mother packed a hamper and Brian produced a colored bucket and wooden spade from the attic, while Julia was instructed to brighten up and look cheerful for a change.

"Maybe we will go this time," she whispered, putting on her best summer dress with polkadots. "Perhaps nothing will happen to stop us."

The feeling of optimism grew as the entire family walked around the house to the garage, Father carrying the hamper, Mother fanning herself with a silk handkerchief, and Brian kicking the loose gravel. Father opened the garage door, took one step forward, then stopped.

"Damnation hell," he swore. "This really is too much."

Mr. Miss-One was cleaning the car.

A bright yellow duster whisked over the dust that remained undisturbed. White liquid from a green tin was sprayed onto the hood but somehow never reached its surface. Mr. Miss-One rubbed the chromework vigorously, but there was no sign that his labor was to be rewarded. The dull bloom persisted, and at times he appeared to be polishing the empty space on either side of the hood, thereby suggesting to Julia's watchful eye that another and much larger car was the object of his ministrations.

"What the hell do we do?" asked Father.

"Well," Mother backed away. "I, for one, am staying at home. Nothing on earth will get me in that car. Heavens above, he might come with us."

"We shouldn't allow it to dominate our lives," Father protested but without much conviction. "I mean to say, it's only a damn time image. Doesn't really exist, you know."

"Thank you very much, but it's got too much life for me." Mother began to walk back toward the house. "Honestly, if you were any sort of man, you would get rid of it."

"What am I supposed to do?" Father was almost running to keep up with her. "I can't kick it; there's nothing solid for me to get to grips with. I do think, my dear, you're being a little unreasonable."

Mother grunted, fanning herself vigorously, then she turned on Julia.

"It's all your fault. You encourage it."

"I . . ." Julia tried to defend herself, but a sense of guilt paralyzed her tongue.

"You ought to be ashamed." Father glared, wiping his forehead with his top-pocket, never-to-be-used handkerchief. "You've no right to encourage it. Spoiling our day out, upsetting your mother, and depriving your little brother of good sea air."

Mother flopped down into a deck chair, where she continued to wave her handkerchief back and forth.

"Yesterday evening I caught her at it. Talking to it, she was. Lying there on the grass, and talking to it. She's mad. Heavens above knows who she takes after. Certainly my family were sane enough. I don't know what's to become of us."

"We could move," Father suggested.

"And to where?" Mother sat up and put away her handkerchief. "Who would buy a house with a ghost—an active ghost? And where would we get another house that's so secluded and off the beaten track? You know I must have solitude, peace, and quiet."

"Perhaps it will go away," Father said after a short silence. "They do, you know. The atmosphere sort of dispels after a bit."

"Not while that girl encourages it," Mother stated. "Not while she moons around it, like a lovesick puppy."

"Keep away from it," warned Father.

Brian punched her thigh with his small fist.

"Keep away from it."

Days passed without an appearance from Mr. Miss-One. Julia wondered if her Mother's anger had built a wall through which he could not pass, and mourned for him, as though for a loved friend who had recently died. Sometimes, when she escaped from the vigilance of her parents, she went looking for him; roamed the garden, or suddenly opened a door, hoping to see him leaning against the mantelpiece, or lounging in a chair. But he had become a shadow that flees before sunlight. Even Father commented on his nonappearance.

"Six days now, and we haven't seen hair or hide of it. What did I tell you? The atmosphere dispelled."

"Stuff and nonsense," Mother snapped. "Atmosphere in-

deed. Lack of encouragement, more likely. I've been keeping
an eye on someone I could touch with a very small stick."

Three pairs of eyes were turned in Julia's direction and she
blushed. Brian kicked her ankle under the table.

"Keep away from it."

"I am of the opinion," Mother went on, "that he must have
been a bad character. I mean to say, respectable people don't
go haunting places after they're dead. They go to wherever
they're supposed to go, and don't keep traipsing about, making a nuisance of themselves. He probably murdered someone
and can't rest."

"No."

All of Julia's reticence, her lifelong submission to her parents' opinions, disappeared in a flood of righteous anger. A
part of her looked on and listened with profound astonishment to the torrent of words that poured out of her mouth.

"He was not bad. I know it. He was sad, and that's why he
walks . . . I know . . . I know . . . Perhaps once he was
happy here, or maybe it is sadness that chains him to this
house, but he's not evil . . . he's not . . . You're bad, small,
stupid . . . and you've driven him away . . . I'll never forgive
you . . . ever . . ."

Mother was so shocked that for a while she was incapable
of speech. Father stared at the rebel with dilated eyes. Finally
Mother's tongue resumed its natural function.

"I always said the girl was mad, and at last I have proof. I
feel quite faint. Heavens, did you see her eyes? Really, Henry,
are you just going to sit there while she insults us? Do something."

"What? Yes." Father rose as though he were about to
deliver a speech.

"That's no way to talk to your parents, particularly your
mother . . ."

"Oh, for heaven's sake!" Mother pointed with dramatic emphasis toward the door. "Get out . . . go on . . . go to your
room, and I don't care if I never see your face again."

But the earthquake was still erupting, and Julia shouted
back, her brain a red cavern of pain.

"I hate you . . . hate . . . hate . . ."

Mother screamed and fell back in her chair, while Father so far forgot himself as to stamp his foot.

"How dare you speak to your mother like that? Go to your room."

Remorse flooded her being and she craved forgiveness like a soul in torment.

"I didn't mean it. Please . . ."

But Father had eyes and ears only for Mother, who was gasping and writhing in a most alarming fashion. Brian watched the ingrate with joyous excitement.

Julia ran to her room. She flung herself face down on the bed and sobbed soundlessly, her slender shoulders shaking, her long fingers clutching the bedclothes. Presently the storm abated and she became still. Her eyes opened and her sixth sense sent out invisible fingers. All at once—she knew.

She sat up and spun around. Mr. Miss-One was standing in the recess by the side of the fireplace. As usual he was busy, but it took some minutes for her to understand what he was doing. A hand drill! He appeared to be making holes in the wall, although of course the pink-flower-patterned wallpaper remained unmarked. Julia got up and walked cautiously toward him, joy blended with curiosity. He slipped little cylinders of fiber into the wall then drove screws into the invisible holes. Light illuminated the darkness of Julia's ignorance.

"He's fitting a bookshelf. How sweet."

She moved a little nearer so as to observe his actions with more clarity. His face was a study in concentration. The teeth were clenched, the muscles round the mouth taut, and once, when the screwdriver slipped, the lips parted as though mouthing a silent curse. She spoke her thoughts aloud, even as a penitent unburdens his soul to an invisible priest.

"Mother is right. I shouldn't be thinking of you all the time. Look at you, fixing a shelf that probably moldered away years ago. If only I could talk to you, hear your voice, most of all, make you realize I exist."

Mr. Miss-One lifted the Formica-covered shelf and fitted it

into position. It immediately disappeared but he continued to work, seemingly content that all was well.

"You are more real to me than Mother or Father and I feel I ought to tell you all manner of things. But there's no point when you ignore me. Is there no way I can reach you?"

Mr. Miss-One took up a hammer and began to tap the wall. Julia moved one step nearer. She could see a small cut on his chin.

"You cut yourself shaving. How long ago did that happen? Ten . . . twenty . . . thirty years ago? Oh, you must know I am here. Can't you feel something? A coldness—an awareness? Surely there must be something; a certainty that you are not alone; the urge to look back over one shoulder . . . Look at me . . . look . . . turn your head . . . you must . . . must . . ."

The hammer struck Mr. Miss-One's thumb and he swore.

"Blast!"

The solitary word exploded across the room and shattered the silence, making Julia shrink back. She retreated to the opposite wall, pressed her shoulders against its unrelenting surface and watched him. He dropped the hammer which fell to the floor with a resounding crash, sucked the afflicted thumb, then stared in Julia's direction. For a period of five seconds, he was a statue; a frozen effigy of a man; then his mouth popped open, the hand dropped away and his eyes were blue mirrors reflecting astonishment—disbelief—fear.

"You can see me!" Julia's joyous cry rang out, and she took two steps forward to find he had vanished. Man, hammer, plus the assortment of tools, disappeared and Julia was left banging her fist against the recess wall. Her voice rang out in a shriek of despair.

"Why . . . why . . . ?"

Mother, Father, even the carefully tutored Brian, treated her to the silence reserved for the outcast. Some speech was unavoidable, but this was delivered in ice-coated voices with impeccable politeness.

"Will you kindly pass the salt," Mother requested on one occasion, "if it is not too much trouble."

Father appeared to be applying the sanctions with some reluctance but he was forced to obey a higher authority.

"More tea . . . ?" His hand was on the teapot, then he remembered his ordained line of conduct and pushed it toward her. "Help yourself."

Brian was more direct.

"I mustn't talk to you."

This isolationist treatment created comfort when it was designed to produce misery. She was no longer the target for admonishing barbs, corrective slaps, or stinging words. She could fidget, sulk, slouch, or spend hours in her room without a single rebuke, although on occasion Mother was clearly sorely provoked, and once or twice her silence policy almost collapsed.

Free from supervision she was able to continue her pursuit of Mr. Miss-One, but once again he seemed to have gone into hiding. The hum and roar of speeding cars drifted across the sleeping meadows. The roar of an overhead jet could be heard above the wind in the trees. Yet the living had no place in Julia's heart, or for that matter, in any place in the house or garden.

Of late a dream had taken root in her imagination. Now it dominated her waking and sleeping life. The seed had first been sown when she saw Mr. Miss-One cleaning his car.

"Suppose," whispered her imagination, "you were to get into the car and let Mr. Miss-One drive you out into the world. Let him rescue you, carry you off, and never—never come back."

The voice of reason, a nasty, insinuating whisper, interrupted with, "But he is dead. A ghost."

Reason was hoist by its own petard.

"If he is dead—if he is a ghost, then there is only one way in which I can join him."

The twin daggers of shock and horror became blunt as the dream grew. It was the solution to all problems, the key to open the door to Mr. Miss-One. She began to consider ways and means.

Poison! She had no means of obtaining any. Cut her throat? Slash her wrists? She shied from such grim prospects like a horse from a snake. Rope—hanging? That would be easy and should not be too painful. There was a length of plastic clothesline in the garage and a convenient beam. If she jumped from the car roof, the leap would be completed in the space of a single heartbeat. It was all so very simple and Julia wondered why she had not thought of it before.

She began to make plans.

From two to four o'clock in the afternoon would be best, for it was then that the family took their after-lunch nap. Mother undressed and went to bed; Father, weather permitting, stretched himself out on a garden hammock, or if wind or rain confined him to the house, he lay prostrate on the sitting-room sofa. Brian slept anywhere. Like an animal, he shut off his consciousness whenever his elders set the example. Without doubt the time to die was between two and four in the afternoon.

The situation was somewhat complicated by Mother suddenly relaxing her rule of silence and making overtures for peace. She actually smiled and said sweetly, "Good morning, dear," before cracking her breakfast egg. "You're looking quite pretty this morning," she went on to remark, an obvious untruth, that suggested a desire to please. Julia was near despair. How could one die with an easy conscience when the enemy spiked their own guns and flew the white flag? Fortunately, Mother had a relapse with the cutting remark, "Prettiness without grace is like a wreath without flowers," and instantly Julia's resolve became a determination. She would die when the sun was high, take the fatal step in full daylight, and refuse to be diverted by smile or insult.

However, she made one last effort to contact Mr. Miss-One, creeping from room to room and searching the garden, praying that he might appear and acknowledge her existence with a smile. For she could not deny the unpalatable fact that on the one occasion when Mr. Miss-One had seen her in the bedroom, his reaction had been one of fear. At least this established him as an intelligent personality, instead of the mindless time image Father so glibly dismissed, but it was, to say the least, a little disconcerting to know one's appearance inspired fear in a ghost. Of course, once she had assumed the same status, there would be no reason for him to fear her at all. Like would appeal to like. She waited with burning impatience for the hour of two.

At the lunch table, all signs indicated that normality had returned.

"Don't slouch," ordered Mother.

"Sit upright," Father chimed in. "Try to be more like your mother."

Brian displayed signs of budding brilliance.

"You're not pretty, you're not ugly. You're pretty ugly."

The fond parents smiled.

"He takes after me," pronounced Mother. "I could always turn a phrase."

Julia's impatience to be gone grew and destroyed her last lingering doubts.

Father had intended to take his nap in the garden, but just before two o'clock the first cold needles of rain began to fall, so he retreated to the sitting room and was soon prostrate on the sofa. Mother climbed the stairs; the bedroom door slammed, and Julia murmured an inaudible good-bye. Brian lay down on the dining-room hearthrug and appeared to fall asleep, but Julia wondered if this was not a pretense put on for her benefit. Fortunately, the door had a key in the lock, so she turned it before leaving the house.

A rising wind drove a curtain of rain across the lawn. It forced proud trees to bend their heads in submission, and turned Julia's dress into a wet shroud. She ran for the garage, water splashing up her legs, dripping down her nose and chin, but it did not feel cold or even wet and she marveled at the sense of well-being.

The garage doors were open and there was no time to consider why this was so, for there, standing in the gloomy interior, was a large red car. Julia stood within the entrance and stared at this stranger with wide-eyed astonishment. There should have been an ancient black family Austin; instead a sleek, rather vicious-looking red monster occupied the entire floor. A creation of highly polished red enamel, gleaming chromework, black tires and bulging mudguards, it seemed to be a thing of latent power, just waiting for the right finger to touch a switch, to send it hurling along straight roads, across the barriers of time and space into a million tomorrows.

The off-side door was open and Julia, her plans for self-destruction forgotten, slid onto the red, plastic-covered seat and feasted her eyes on the complicated switchboard, the black steering wheel, the gleaming gear levers. Curiosity turned to wonderment, then ripened into pure joy.

"A ghost car!"

It must be, of course. This was the vehicle Mr. Miss-One had been cleaning, only then it was invisible, due undoubtedly to the base thoughts of Mother, Father, and that little beast, Brian. Now she could see it, feel it, and heavens be praised, actually smell it. This must be the result of suffering, loving him with all her being. She giggled, clasped her hands, and waited with joyous anticipation.

Mr. Miss-One entered the garage limping, carrying a small overnight bag. He was plainly prepared for a journey. A terrible fear struck Julia: "Please don't make it all disappear. Let me go with him—wherever he goes. Anywhere at all."

He opened the right-hand door, slung his bag onto the back seat, then climbed in. He closed the door, turned a key on the switchboard, and the engine roared with instant, pulsating life.

"Don't let it all disappear. Let me go with him."

The car slid out of the garage. The garden and house swept by the windows and Julia spared a thought for Mother, Father, and Brian, blissfully asleep, unaware that the despised one was passing out of their lives forever.

"It's happening. I'm going out. At last . . . Oh, merciful God—going out."

The main gates, new, glossy with black paint, were open, and Mr. Miss-One swung the car out onto a country road.

They were away at last, speeding along under an arcade of trees, flashing by meadows, snarling past lovely, red-bricked houses, while windshield wipers made neat half-moons in the driving rain.

Mr. Miss-One suddenly reached over and opened a narrow flap in the switchboard. His hand was a bare inch from Julia's breast, and she wanted to touch it, clasp the strong fingers, but was afraid that this wonderful dream might dispel. He took out a packet of cigarettes, adroitly popped one into his mouth, then replaced the carton and shut the flap. He lit the cigarette with a strange contraption from the switchboard, then inhaled, letting the smoke trickle down through his nose.

By the time they had reached the main bypass, the novelty was wearing off, and Julia permitted herself a measure of confidence. The dream, if such it was, displayed no signs of breaking down. The car was solid. She could feel the seat beneath her, hear the muted roar of the engine, smell the smoke from Mr. Miss-One's cigarette, see the road sliding away under the car wheels.

The bypass was straight, a gray ribbon that stretched out into infinity as their speed built up. Sixty, seventy, eighty miles an hour. Julia watched the needle climb on the speedometer. Then she turned her head and looked at Mr. Miss-One.

Poor ghost, entirely oblivious in his ghost car, he did not know she was there. How was she to declare her presence and break through the wall that still separated them? She began to talk, spilling out her thoughts in a jumble of low spoken words.

"Mr. Miss-One—I'm sorry I don't know your real name, but Brian, the horrible little beast, first called you Mr. Miss-One because of your limp. You sort of miss a step. Please, don't think it's meant unkindly, at least by me. In fact, the limp adds to your appearance; makes you more romantic. I guess that sounds silly, but I am silly—I can't help it. I've been in love with you ever since that day when you first walked across the dining room and Mother went screaming under the table. She did look funny. I remember you took something we couldn't see from the sideboard, then disappeared by the kitchen door. Can't you see, or at least hear me?"

It might have been imagination, but Mr. Miss-One did appear to be a little uneasy. He slid down the window to throw away his half-consumed cigarette. Julia sighed.

"I wonder where we are going? Is this your world? Are the people out there wandering shadows left over from yesteryear, or are we racing, invisible, through today? Please try to see me."

She could see his left wrist. His jacket sleeve had slid up and the wrist was bare. Sun-tanned, muscular, covered with fine hair. It was also covered with goose pimples. She gasped, then gave a little cry.

"Oh, you're cold. My poor darling, you're cold."

She had not meant to touch him—not yet—but there was no controlling the automatic impulse. Her hand flew to his wrist. For a brief moment she touched warm flesh, actually felt the fast beating pulse, then the car swerved, and Mr. Miss-One jerked his head round and stared straight at her.

His face was a mask of pure, blood-chilling terror, and his mouth opened as he screamed. His hands clawed at the steering wheel, as though some part of his brain were trying to right the skid, and the scream erupted into isolated words, like black rocks crashing through a sheet of ice.

"Dead . . . family . . . burned . . . dead . . . fifty . . . years . . . dead . . . dead . . . dead . . ."

The screech of tortured rubber mingled with the screaming words. Outside the gray road was spinning around and around. A black shape came hurtling through the rain. There was a mighty, soul-uprooting crash, then for a brief second— nothing. A heartbeat of total oblivion.

Julia was standing by the roadside watching the car burn. Like a giant red beetle it lay on its back, while beautiful scarlet flames rose from its corpse, like poppies from a long-filled grave. The red enamel bubbled and drooled down the seething metal, as blood tears from the eyes of a dying man, and somewhere in the heart of the shrieking inferno, something moved.

Sound flickered, then ceased. Cars drew up, and the occupants climbed out; mouths opened, faces assumed expressions of horror, shock, or morbid excitement. But they were so many, silent, pathetic ghosts.

Julia turned and walked away.

Home was but a few steps away.

Over the grass verge, through a hedge, under some trees, and there were the gates—broken, rusty, one had lost a hinge and was reeling like a drunken man. Once back in the garden, sound returned. Birds sang, bees hummed, and the sun peeped through a broken cloud bank, making the rain-coated flowers glisten like colored fragments. Julia opened the front door and made her way to the dining room. The family was seated around the table, which was laid for tea.

"At last," exclaimed Mother. "I called until my voice was hoarse. Honestly, I don't know who you think you are."

"It's really too bad," Father echoed. "Your mother was nearly out of her mind. Where have you been?"

Julia did not answer, but sank down, staring blankly at the tablecloth. Brian kicked her ankle.

"You locked me in."

"I ask you," Mother addressed the ceiling, "is that the action of a rational person? Locking your little brother in the dining room? Heavens above knows what might have happened. Well, don't just sit there, we are waiting for an explanation."

"Answer your mother," Father instructed.

Julia took a deep breath.

"We're dead. All of us—dead."

The first shadows of night crept in through the long french window and the silence was coated with the dust of long-dead time. Julia looked up. They were watching her with blank, pale faces.

"Don't you understand? We're dead. We died fifty years ago in a fire. Brian did it. He set light to the bedroom curtains. The whole place went up in fire and smoke."

The ticking of the mantelpiece clock seemed to grow louder; Brian stirred in his chair with a frantic denial.

"I didn't."

"You did." Julia turned on him savagely. "You were told not to play with matches. It was you. You burned us all to death."

"I didn't. I didn't."

He hammered the table with his small, clenched fists, while tears ran down his cheeks, then rose and ran to Father, who put his arms around the shaking body.

"Make her stop. I didn't. I didn't play with matches."

"It's all right," Father whispered. "It's all right. Your sister isn't well."

Mother could not speak, could only stare at Julia with wide open eyes. Occasionally she shook her head as though in disbelief.

"Please," Julia pleaded, "try to understand. We are all dead. Mr. Miss-One was the living. We were—we are—ghosts."

"Go to your room, dear." Father's voice was unexpectedly gentle. "Go to bed, like a good girl. We'll look after you. Don't worry."

"Yes." Mother spoke at last. "Please forgive me. I never knew. I'll never say a cross word again—ever."

Julia rose very slowly, and as she did so, understanding exploded in her brain.

"You think I'm mad."

Mother shuddered and Father shook his head firmly.

"No—no, of course not, dear. Just tired, ill maybe. But not mad. Dear God, not mad."

Julia fled before their naked terror, and as always, took refuge in her room. She lay upon the bed and stared up at the ceiling, gradually allowing the veil to fall from the awful face of truth. She could never be happy again. She knew. Knowledge was brutal, knowledge destroyed the comforting curtain of doubt.

Father, clearly ill at ease, brought her some food on a tray, talked much too quickly of the healing virtues of sleep, plenty of good food, peace of mind, then departed. Julia heard the key turn in the lock.

Presently she sat by the window and watched the sun put the garden to bed. Shadows lengthened, flowers folded their petals, trees hung their heads, and the evening breeze went dancing across the lawn. For a while there was a great, healing peace.

Then a dark shape limped up the drive. At first Julia thought it might be Father, but as it drew nearer, she saw the black, charred face. The hands were shriveled, twisted; patches of white bone gleamed through the gaping, roasted flesh. Eyes still glittered in the naked skull, and they stared up at Julia's window.

Julia tried to scream, but her vocal cords refused to function. The most she could make was a hoarse, croaking sound. But out of the heart of her all-demanding terror, a single rational thought ran across her brain like a ribbon of fire.

"Is this how I appear to him?"

All that remained of Mr. Miss-One limped up the front steps and disappeared from view. Julia knew her prayer had been answered. She would never be parted from him again.

Introduction

Juleen Brantingham makes her second appearance in the SHADOWS *series with this short piece about country matters and manners, and a beautiful young girl. It's a love story, though not the kind, thank goodness, we expect to see Ali McGraw in very soon.*

JANEY'S SMILE

by Juleen Brantingham

Janey Harmon was a pretty little thing, with startled-fawn eyes and a smile that was worth waiting for. Wait for it we did because it seemed Janey was always standing in someone's shadow, usually her Pa's because Reverend Harmon cast the biggest shadow in these parts.

"She knows a woman's place," the Reverend was heard to say once when she was four and a half. It may have been the only time he spoke of her for who speaks of the chair that stands in the corner?

It wouldn't be fair to say the Reverend neglected her exactly. In that house she could never starve for her Pa made sure the larder was never empty. It was true that during the week Janey wore the ugliest of cast-offs from the mission box, but on Sunday the women of Cedar Grove had their way and decked her out in white or pink with bits of ruffle and lace. She'd look pretty as an angel.

The Reverend himself didn't pay much mind to what he wore and no wonder. He had his black suits special made, but the generous yards of material were never quite enough. To see him walk from parsonage to church was to behold the miracle of ambulatory fat. Those who met the Reverend and Janey for the first time could not help but question how a whale could have had any part in the creation of that quick-silver child.

Not many people remembered Janey's Ma for she had died shortly after coming to the Grove. The Reverend, with his sausage fingers and his shortness of breath every time he leaned over, could not be expected to care for little Janey, so she was mothered in turn by every one of the nineteen women in the Grove, even Martha Steinhelfer, old Nate's third wife and not long for this world, poor thing. Maybe Janey brought a bit of joy to her final days. In old Nate's house joy must have been hard to come by.

The day of Martha's funeral Janey must have been about five, if I remember right. The whole town turned out for the services. Martha had been a stranger from down south some-where and the way Nate was we had never got to know her well, but we wanted to see that she had the proper words said over her. Reverend Harmon was a bit leery of Nate and might have been tempted to skimp here and there if Nate was in a hurry to get on about his business. You wouldn't know it to look at his rags and his dirty neck, but Nate Steinhelfer is the richest man in the county.

When the words had been said and Martha's box was being lowered into the ground, I saw Janey standing by Hattie Bryant. Her eyes looked dark, like she was holding her tears inside.

"But where did she go?" Janey whispered to Hattie. "Where did Martha *go?*"

Well, I ducked over there real quick and took Janey's hand, leading her away from Hattie and the others. There was no telling what Hattie would say to that, seeing as how her sister had been Nate's second wife and Hattie still hadn't got over what he did to her. It wouldn't do to have Janey hear the wrong things, being the Reverend's child.

"She went to heaven, darling," I said, thinking I must be lying in my teeth.

I got Janey out of the churchyard as quick as I could. Old Nate was raising Cain. I could hear him yelling. He wanted them to open the box and take Martha's dress and shoes. Said she wouldn't need them where she was going and he might decide to get married again. Well, that didn't surprise any of us. We knew how he was. That's why he had to go down south to find his third wife.

Cedar Grove is a quiet place. Not much changes from year to year. We send our boys off to war when the call comes, but except for that we don't pay much mind to the outside world. We like it that way and those who don't, the young ones mostly, move out. We tend our crops, fish a little, and go to church. On nice evenings we like to set on our porches and talk—mostly about our neighbors for what else mattered?

Of course, Janey Harmon wasn't the only youngster growing up in the Grove at that time. Ralph and Helen Foreman had six or seven, Lucy Renkert's little mistake, Katie, was about the same age, and when Mary Shott left her husband, that city man she married, she sent Mike and Laura back here to live with her folks. There were a few others, enough to keep a teacher busy so we didn't have to send our youngsters out of the Grove for their schooling.

Janey was friendly with everyone. She joined in the games and the mischief and had to be fished out of Shott's Creek where it runs fast under the bridge about as often as anyone. But looking at Janey as she tagged along with the bunch, you got the feeling she was set apart from them just the littlest bit.

The boys, they treated Janey like she was made of glass. Even in her everyday dresses, that stuff from the mission box that looked like it was made from feed sacks, with her bright hair floating loosely around her shoulders, she looked like she should be setting on a shelf under glass and only taken out on special occasions. And the girls—well, the girls just put up with her because they'd been told they had to. Janey's looks was enough to make the girls leery, and we grown-ups probably made it worse because we did things for Janey that we wouldn't have done for our own.

Laura Bennett, Mary Shott's daughter, was the worst. She was always teasing Janey and playing tricks on her. Coming from the city the way she did, Laura thought *she* should be the one to get those special favors. Laura's grandma wouldn't put up with city airs and nonsense so Laura took her spite out on Janey every chance she got.

It might have been the piano lessons that upset Laura the most. That would have been when Janey was about thirteen. Hattie Bryant, who played the piano for services, was getting stranger every year and some of us thought it might be a good idea if the Reverend's daughter learned how so she could take over.

Kind of on the sly, so Hattie wouldn't find out about it, someone checked over at the county seat about piano lessons. Since it was for the church anyway we all chipped in to pay and whoever was going over that way on Saturday took Janey to her lesson.

Well, as soon as Laura heard about it she decided she had to learn the piano, too. There wasn't any reason we couldn't have taken two girls as easy as one but Grandma Shott wouldn't hear of it. She'd got it into her head that Laura's mother, Mary, had been all right in Cedar Grove until she got that job over at the county seat and started thinking she was better than the rest of us. Grandma Shott said she wasn't going to lose *two* girls that way and there wasn't anyone could change her mind.

Laura blamed Janey for this, and she must have made the Reverend's daughter cry for a while. I was about to have a word with Grandma when one day Laura turns right around and starts saying sweet things about "my friend Janey." It took me a while to figure out, till I was passing the church one day and heard the most awful racket. I stuck my head in the door and here was Janey teaching Laura what she'd learned. That went on for a couple months and I almost wished Grandma Shott would find out and put a stop to it. Laura didn't have no more an ear for music than Lucy Renkert's bob-tailed cow.

Janey was turning from a pretty girl into a lovely young woman before our eyes. I guess we all took some pride in her, feeling we'd each had a hand in raising her. If the Reverend felt that way too, he didn't give a sign of it. He didn't seem to care what she did as long as there was food on the table, the house was clean, and his suits were pressed. Janey did all that and more besides. She made calls on the shut-ins, taught Sunday school, swept out the church, and made sure there were flowers every Sunday.

Old Hattie was getting more and more strange and some of us were thinking about the old folks' home over at the county seat. Mostly it's for folks too scat-brained to take care of themselves, and Hattie was that.

I had a run-in with Hattie one night. There was a full moon and I was out walking, just enjoying the night air. When I passed the church yard I could see a shadow moving around and hear a sort of muttering. Thinking it might be youngsters cooking up mischief, I went inside. But it was just old Hattie. She had a spoon and was scooping up dirt from her sister's grave, putting it in a bottle.

"Here, now, what do you think you're doing?" I says, going over and helping her to her feet. "You trying to dig her up, Hattie? Your sister's dead. Won't do no good to dig her up."

Hattie turned on me and I swear that in the moonlight she looked as sane as me. But I guess her words proved she wasn't.

"I know that, you fool!" she says. "My sister's dead and there's a full moon tonight and I've got to get some of this dirt so I can fix the man who did it to her."

"Nate? You think Nate killed her? Now, Hattie, I wouldn't invite the man to a dog fight, but he's no killer."

She glared at me. "He sucked out her soul," she said. "Sucked it right out with his mean ways and his bad temper. After that she didn't have nothing to live for. I'm going to make him pay."

I coaxed her to go along home and I laughed to myself awhile at her funny ideas. Poor Hattie. But she wasn't hurting anyone. It would have been a shame to take her from the Grove and put her in with a bunch of strangers.

And at that, I'm not sure Hattie was far wrong about Nate. I'd seen Martha Steinhelfer shortly after she came to the Grove, and it did seem that as time went by, something sort of leaked out of her. She didn't exactly get sick and die, it was more as if she just ran down. Hattie's sister and Nate's first wife were a bit before my time but the way people talked, it must have been the same with them.

Maybe Nate did kill their souls and maybe he just sold them. Nate would have sold anything he had no use for.

It had to have been a coincidence that a short while after Hattie talked about making Nate pay for what he did, he began to complain of stomach pains. The women of the Grove know their duty to neighbors, even ones like Nate, so they looked in on him, took him broths and jellies that were supposed to be good for digestive upsets. But one after another he made them mad and chased them away. Except Janey. I don't imagine he was any nicer to her than he was to anyone else, it was just that Janey would put up with more.

At sixteen Janey was taking Hattie's place at the piano almost every Sunday and for weddings and funerals. No one mentioned it to Hattie and I don't think her mind was clear enough to wonder how we managed without her.

It was Janey who played for the funeral when they sent Junior Foreman's body home from that place in Asia. It was a sad time for Ralph and Helen, with the Army saying they couldn't open the box to look at him. I think it was a real comfort to them to have her there for at one time they'd had hopes Junior and Janey might be planning a future together.

It was Janey who played, too, when Lucy Renkert's Katie got in trouble with the boy from the telephone company and we had to have a hurry-up wedding. Katie was white-faced and so was the boy, probably because the Reverend was glaring at them like he expected the pit of Hell to open up at their feet. The way he carried on you'd think a seven-month pregnancy could never happen in a God-fearing community.

Janey didn't pay any mind to her Pa's thunder, and after the knot was tied she invited Katie and her husband and all their folks over to the parsonage for cake and punch. Before long Janey had Katie smiling and happy as if she'd planned things this way all along.

Nate's stomach upset didn't improve, and he finally had to dig up some of his money to go see a doctor over at the county seat. Some of those faces on the bills must have blinked to see the light of day. Janey borrowed a car—Nate had never seen the reason for that kind of extravagance—and she took him over.

When they came back late in the afternoon, I was fixing my porch steps and I saw her carry a big box of candy into the parsonage. It was a pink, frilly box, not the sort of thing a girl would buy for herself or even for her father.

I tell you, a God-awful chill went through me—and through the whole of Cedar Grove when I told them about it. Never in his life had Nate laid out a penny for a gift. Bribes, yes, when he was sure there was no other way to get what he wanted.

First thing the next morning some of us started finding excuses to drop by and see the Reverend. I talked to him myself. But none of us did any good. In spite of the fact that he was a man of God, he had always paid more mind to Nate's money than to his character.

"I'd be proud to have Mr. Steinhelfer for a son-in-law," he says. "Janey is a flighty girl and she needs someone older to settle her down."

Janey Harmon was about as flighty as the maple tree that stood by the door of the parsonage, but try telling that to a man who can't see past the edge of his plate.

Helen Foreman said she told him how Nate treated his first three wives and all she got was a sermon about bearing false witness. Even Lucy Renkert put in her two cents, or tried to. She came out of the parsonage like her skirt was on fire and I don't like to think what the Reverend said to her. Thank the Lord, Hattie never heard what was in the wind or we'd have had a spitting wildcat on our hands. She still thought of Janey as her baby, and I think she'd have killed Nate before she let him slip a ring on Janey's finger.

Even talking to Janey didn't cut much ice. She wouldn't admit that Nate had spoken for her—but she wouldn't exactly promise to turn him down, either. We were all just sick, thinking she was going to let her Pa push her into this thing.

It was in the middle of all this that Michael Todd came to Cedar Grove.

I first saw him when Ralph and Helen brought him to church that Sunday morning. Ralph said he'd showed up at the farm, day before. He'd been a friend of Junior's in that place in Asia, and he'd come to talk to them about their boy and how he died. Helen—well, Helen never *had* been sure it was Junior in that box. I can't say she was happy to know the truth, but the way she looked that morning, knowing must have been a lot better than wondering.

The boy had been hurt in the same trouble that killed Junior. Hurt bad. He was missing an arm and a leg and there was something funny about his eyes. He told us he could just stay a short while before going back to the hospital.

Michael was from some place east, but in five days he settled into the Grove like he'd been born there. It was Janey was responsible for that. Those two took one look at each other and Nate might as well have asked Janey to give back his box of candy. Knowing Nate, he probably did.

That Michael, he was a good boy. He traded stories with the grandpas sitting in the shade and asked after the farmers' crops. For all that he had only one leg and one hand he helped where he could and wouldn't take any thanks for it. Of course, he wasn't from the Grove and any other time we might have held that against him because anyone could see he was going to take our Janey away. But losing her to a stranger was better than seeing her marry Nate.

Naturally, Nate didn't take it too good. He started carrying on about his stomach again, I guess hoping Janey would feel sorry for him. But Janey took Michael along when she went to call on Nate and that put an end to *that*. Nate gave up his sickbed and started creeping around the Grove like he was spying on Michael and Janey. I would no more have tangled with him then than I would have with a rabid skunk.

The Reverend didn't take it too good either. He kept mouthing charitable words about "that cripple" but he looked like he'd just bit into a lemon when he'd had his mouth set for chocolate cake.

Anyone could see how the two of them felt about each other. Every time I looked at them I started thinking about

things that had been buried long ago. It was sweet and hurt-
ful all at once. We were going to lose Janey—but Janey, she
looked like she thought she was getting the whole world.

It seemed like everyone in the Grove knew about their
plans as soon as they did. Michael was going back to the hospital and when he was well again he was coming back here to
marry Janey in her Pa's church. I guess Janey would have
gone with him right off, but the Reverend was kicking up a
fuss about her leaving him so sudden.

The night before Michael was to leave we had a supper at
the church. I don't know who invited Hattie. I'd just as soon
have left her out of it. She was getting as strange as a barn
owl and ten times as noisy. She didn't take to Michael at all.

All the women brought covered dishes. Even Michael
brought something he'd whipped up at Helen's place. Called
it Kim Chee or something like that. I had a taste of it and it
was sort of like ripe cole slaw all mixed up with garlic and hot
peppers. Damn near curled my hair. Almost everyone had a
taste, but Michael was the only one could eat the stuff. Guess
he got the taste for it over in Asia.

Maybe it was the Kim Chee—but I didn't like the way old
Hattie was chuckling when Michael started getting those
cramps. Janey and Helen took him over to the parsonage to
lie down and I grabbed Hattie and hustled her outside.

"What did you put in that cabbage stuff?" I asked.

She cackled again. "Why, it wasn't much," she says, all innocent. "Just one of my little potions. I got to help Janey."

"What are you trying to do, kill him?"

"Poor boy has enough troubles," she says. "No, I just fixed
it so he'll forget about Janey as soon as he leaves the Grove."

Well, what can you do with a crazy old woman like that? It
was all right when she was just collecting her weeds and dirt
and talking wild, but when she starts poisoning people then
it's time to put her some place safe.

Michael must have recovered all right because Helen said
he left the next morning. Ralph had offered to drive him, seeing as how he was almost family, but Michael didn't like to

put people out, no more than Janey did, and he said he was meeting someone who was going that way.

I didn't have much time to think about Michael that day, nor Janey either. I had my hands full just taking care of Hattie. I practically had to drag her out of that weed-smelly trailer she called home and she screeched at me every mile to the old folks' home.

As I was driving over the bridge at Shott's Creek, I saw Nate walking by the side of the road. I sort of wished I could throw him in the car and take him to the home, too. Get rid of all our problems at once. But it never would have worked. The people at the home wouldn't have kept him. If you have enough money, you don't have to have all your marbles.

Things settled down for a while after that. The Reverend still preached his sermons and if "honor thy father and thy mother" came up a little more often than usual, none of us remarked on it. I guess you don't notice the roof till the tornado tugs at the shingles, and the Reverend was starting to notice how much Janey had to do with taking care of the church and the parsonage and keeping food on his table.

The women and girls were getting excited, the way they do before a wedding, giving showers, helping Janey with her wedding dress, deciding who was going to bake the cake. There was one who wasn't too pleased. Laura Bennett had been planning her own wedding to one of the Foreman boys, and in all the fuss over Janey, Laura's plans took second place.

But Laura hadn't lost her teeth. From time to time I heard her comment how glad she was her husband-to-be had all his limbs.

Janey didn't seem to hear that. In fact, after the first week Michael was gone, Janey didn't seem to hear much of anything. On the outside she was the same as always. But there was something missing. At first I put it down to love for the boy. But love doesn't take away, it adds. Then the whispers started. That would have been about three months after Michael left the Grove.

I knew Laura had something to do with them so I didn't

pay any mind. But a few weeks later, anyone with half an eye could see Janey had good reason to wish for Michael to hurry back.

The Reverend began to thunder. It got worse when Janey broke down and admitted she hadn't heard from Michael since he left. "The boy is never coming back, never meant to come back," the Reverend said, and we began to wonder if he was right. I told everyone it was the war upsetting Michael's mind and we should give him a little more time, but even I knew something was awful wrong.

The Reverend was getting thick with Nate again and then there was just no stopping it. They set a date and announced it in church. Janey didn't seem to care. It was like she'd already started to die a little inside, the way Martha and the others had. That smile of hers was just a memory.

It was that nightmare all over again. As the wedding date got closer I felt like I was in a box. Sweet Janey, our special girl, was being sold for a hand-me-down wedding ring. I guess I went off my rocker a bit because the morning of the wedding I drove over to the old folks' home and did something I hope people in the Grove never find out about. When old Hattie heard about Nate she was glad to burn some weeds and chant some words she said would remove her spell, but I felt like a damn fool.

I didn't have too much time to worry about it though because when I got back, people were already heading for the church. Ralph and a bunch of the other men were standing by the door, looking solemn and talking among themselves, so I went over to see what was up.

"Found him in Shott's Creek a couple hours ago," Ralph said. "Must have been Nate who did it. He's crazy enough."

"Now, you don't know that for sure," someone else said. "Sheriff said it looked to him like an accident. We know the boy was sick."

"Well, why doesn't someone stop the wedding till we find out?" I wanted to know.

But they'd talked to the Reverend and he couldn't be

moved. Nothing was going to keep him from becoming the father-in-law of the richest man in the county.

No one had the heart to tell Janey. One way or another the boy was gone and how was that going to help her now? I guess we were all hoping she would never have to find out about it.

The bell began to ring and we filed inside. From our faces you might have thought it was more likely a funeral than a wedding. And I guess it was.

Janey and Nate were at the altar and the Reverend had turned away for a moment when we heard the noise from outside the door, coming up the walk, slow and painful, the way it always was for him. Nobody moved or spoke at first. Then the Reverend began to quiver, and Nate, he kind of hunched his shoulders like someone was about to hit him. We looked at them so we wouldn't have to turn around.

But Janey turned. She was smiling in a way that made her face glow, like there was a halo around it. She waited for him to open the door.

I can still remember that smile. I always did say it was worth waiting for.

Introduction

Pure Malzberg/Pronzini—to say any more would have this introduction run longer than the story.

OPENING A VEIN

by Bill Pronzini/Barry N. Malzberg

The last man on Earth was a vampire.

So he rummaged around in the ruins until he came upon a copy of *The Rites of Goetic Theurgy,* and then he conjured up the Devil.

"Listen," the vampire said, wrinkling his nose at the smell of sulphur and brimstone that surrounded Lucifer, "I summoned you here because I'm the last living thing on Earth, as if you didn't know, and I want to make a deal for some blood."

The Devil laughed mockingly. "A deal?" he said. "Vampires have no souls, so what could you possibly bargain with?"

"We could work out something—"

"Even if you *had* a soul," the Devil said fetchingly, "I wouldn't bargain with the likes of you. Now that the Final War has wiped the globe clean, I have all the souls I need to last me through Eternity."

"But you've *got* to help me," the vampire pleaded. "I'm starving here all alone!"

"That's your problem," the Devil said and prepared to depart, then hesitated. "The trouble is that I'm a sentimental fool," he said. "It must be my origins." He lifted his head proudly, considering the abysmal landscape. "One taste," he said. "That's all."

"Of *you?*"

"As you pointed out," the Devil said, "your choice is limited."

The vampire sighed. Not unsophisticated in the ways of temptation he suspected the Devil's ploy was to allow him only enough blood to exacerbate desire, sentencing him to an eternity of even greater torment. On the other hand, his desires were immediate and it was perhaps unwise to take the long view. Considering all of this, the vampire leapt upon the Devil (who received him willingly) and drained a considerable amount of blood from the old tempter, finding it to his surprise to be quite fresh and of no noxiousness whatsoever.

The Devil made no effort to fend him off and the vampire was able to feast, if that is the word, at leisure. At length, sated, he withdrew to find that the Devil was a thin and shriveled figure upon the ground, utterly drained of life or fluids.

I've killed the Devil, the vampire thought. It was a pity, under all the circumstances, that there were no witnesses. In simpler times, he thought, he would at least have gotten a medal.

In the abysmal chaos however there were neither medallions or presenters. There was merely the large meal lingering within him and a vague feeling of regret which the vampire, soon enough, interpreted as boredom. There was not even the hope of further meals, now, and an intolerable eternity of solitude.

Thinking this and other despairing thoughts he looked out upon the formless void. Perhaps there was something he could do about that anyway, he thought.

Energized by the blood of the practical Devil he set about doing it.

He waited a while before creating the swimming and crawling things. No sense in haste. Time and his powers made him easeful.

In due course, the game would come.

Introduction

*When asked if there was another Nolan piece available for
this volume, William F. wrote back to say that he had, liter-
ally, seventeen other projects to work on and had no time for
short fiction. Three days later, "The Partnership" came in the
mail; Bill was at an all-night eatery when the idea struck, he
wrote it longhand on the counter, and spent the rest of the
night typing the final draft. It occurs to him, he says, that it's
about time he got back into the field full-strength. It is about
time.*

*It's also about substance that somehow has more impact
when the town is small and the world threatens to pass it by.*

THE PARTNERSHIP

by William F. Nolan

Me and Ed, we're in business together. Which is what I want
to tell you about eventually because I think you folks will find
it interesting. But this is also about the stranger with the
beard. And he comes first.

You like ghost stories? Bet you do! Everybody does. But
this isn't one of those. Not a ghost in it. Still, it's a little
spooky, I'd guess. I mean, to some it will be. Strange—that's a
good word for it.

Strange.

Anyhow, Ed and me, we got ourselves a real nice partnership going. For one thing, we trust each other, and that's the
basis you build on. No trust, no partnership. Learned that
long ago. My Irish grandaddy, bless him, came over from
County Cork. Bought into a saloon in Kansas City with a partner who "stole him blind." That's how he always put it: "That
man stole me blind!"

Now, with Gramps long gone in Missouri earth, I'm as old as he was when I was a tad. That's how I got my first name. Ralph's the legal one, but I've always been Tad since Gramps called me that. Tad Miller. Simple name for a simple man.

I grew up in St. Louis and we moved to Chicago when I was still a boy—but you don't really want to know all about how I got here to this little town stuck down in god-knows-where country. It's in Illinois, a good piece out from Chicago, and we're on the lake. That's what counts—not how I got here or what brought me.

I'm here. That's enough.

Name of this town's not important, so I won't give it out. If I did, some of you folks might come here one day, looking to say hello, and I wouldn't like that much since I'm not partial to meeting just anybody. No offense.

Ed's the same way. When he's ready to meet a stranger he'll go all out, but in between he's like me. Keeps to home.

Don't get me wrong. When a stranger comes to town, and I see he's lonely, I'll strike up a conversation as quick as the next fellow. I just don't *advertise*, if you know what I mean.

This town's on a spur highway into Chicago, and we get our share of hitchers. Road bums, sometimes. Others—like kids on the run from home, heading for life in the big city. Some on vacation. All kinds, drifting in for coffee and grub at Sally Anne's. They all end up at Sal's. Only eatery left in town, so she gets the business.

Real nice sort, too. You'd like her. Kind eyes. I always notice a person's eyes, first off. Windows on the soul sort of thing. And hers are soft and liquidy, like a deer.

Me and Sally kid each other a lot, but we're both too old to have it mean anything. But she likes me. Most folks do. And that's nice. Person wants to know he's liked, even if he keeps mostly to home.

Well, before I tell you about the bearded stranger I met at Sal's last month you need to know some things about this town.

For instance, it's dying fast. Getting smaller every year. Most of the young ones gone now. Us diehards still hanging

on. Me and Ed, we'll have to split up one of these days because this town's due to just wink out like a star in the sky.
Bound to happen. Be a sad day for me. Ed, too. We're not
that close, understand, but there's a lot between us. Still, like
my mama used to say, nothing lasts forever.

Anyhow, the town's slowed down a hellish lot since I first
moved here from Chicago after Mama and Pop died. Super
freeway gets most of the traffic. Put us in the backwash. The
big change came when Moffitt Paper closed their factory.
Town lost its main source of revenue, and things slowed way
down.

That's when I had to leave Happyland. That's what they
call the amusement park on the lake. All closed down now.
Boarded up. Left to rust and rain.

I ran the Funhouse out at Happyland. For twenty years.
Slept there on summer nights. Knew every turn and twist of
the place, every creaking board and secret passage and blind
tunnel in it. Still do, for that matter. Which is where the
stranger comes in, but I'll get to that.

First, a little more about me and this town if you don't
mind. (I'm in no hurry, are you?)

I got married here. Surprise, eh? Guess, on paper, I don't
come across as the romantic type—even though Sally still kids
me that way. But married I was, and to a good woman who
never liked kids so we didn't have any. When she died I was
left alone. No family, not even cousins. (I didn't know Ed
then.)

Her heart gave out. One day, fine, the next she's gone. Hit
me hard. Made me kind of wacky for a while. But I got over
it. We get over things, or things get over us, take your choice.
Nowdays I'm used to being on my own, and I do fine. Enjoy
my privacy. Enjoy the woods and some fishing in the fall.
Like I said, a simple man. I miss her bad some nights, just like
I do Happyland. But they're both gone—and everything has to
die. Nature's way. Accept it. Flow with the tide.

She's buried out at Lakeside. Strangers think it odd, us having our cemetery right there on the lake, smack next to Happyland. Graveyard and amusement park snug-a-bug together

on the lake. Odd, they say. Or *used* to, when Happyland was still open. "Spooky" is what they called it, having them together that way. But I never saw a ghost in twenty years out there. Oh, once in a while some big rats would wander in and give the ladies a real scare in the dark. (I'd always refund when it happened.) They'd come from the burrows under the cemetery, the rats, that is. Big suckers. And scared of nothing. That's the way of a rat; he scares you, you don't scare him.

Anyhow, my good wife's buried out there, or was. Guess the rats have her by now, though that isn't very nice to think about, is it? They got mighty sharp teeth, can gnaw right through the side of a coffin unless you can afford a steel one. Me, I've never had one extra dime to rub against another! Spend what I earn. To the penny. But I pay my way. No debts for Tad Miller.

Better get on with telling you about the big stranger who passed through here last month . . .

I was at Sally's, kidding with her—and we didn't see him walk in. She was joshing me about a new ring I had on. Big shiny thing, and Sal said it looked like I was wearing a streetlight. I was joshing her back about her new hairdo, saying it looked like a hive of bees could make honey in there. That kind of stuff. Just kidding around, passing the time of day.

Next thing, the stranger is banging the counter with a spoon, and yelling for some service. Sal broke off quick and moved over there to ask him what he'd have.

"Coffee and your special," he growled. "The coffee now. And a small tomato juice."

She told him no tomato juice, just orange. That made him madder than before.

He was big and mean looking. Maybe a lumber man. Had one of those shoulder-hike rigs, which he'd taken off and put on the counter next to him. Man of about forty, I'd guess. Muscled arms and a wide back. Thick dark beard. But honest eyes. I noticed his eyes right off.

He wore one of those space-age wristwatches with all kinds of dials and dates on it and little panels that light up. I'd never seen one like it before, and was plain curious, so I took the empty stool next to him. He gave me a scowl for doing that, because the rest of the counter was empty, and I guess he didn't want company.

"Hello, mister," I said. "My name's Tad Miller."

"So what's that to me?"

Hard-voiced. Not friendly at all.

"Want to apologize for all that jawing I was into when you came in. Customers come *first* in this place."

He grumbled "all right" while stirring his coffee, but he didn't look at me. Ignored me. Hoped I'd go away.

I leaned toward him. "Couldn't help but notice that timepiece you're wearing. Handsome thing. Never saw one quite like it."

He swung around slowly, holding up his left wrist. "Got it in Chi," he said. "You like it, eh?"

"Prettiest damn watch I ever did see!"

He was warming up fast. Like a woman will do when you tell her how cute her kid is. Works every time.

"What are all those little dials and things?" I asked.

He worked back his sleeve so I could get a better look. "Tells you the time in ten parts of the world," he said. "Tells you the month of the year and the day of the week."

"Well, I'll be jinged!"

He twisted a doodad at the side of the watch. "Set this," he said proudly, "and it rings every hour on the hour."

By now Sally was spreading out his lunch special, and she couldn't resist getting into the conversation. "What's a thing like that cost?" she asked him.

Bad manners. I'd never have asked it that way, straight out. And he didn't like it. He scowled at her. "That's my business."

Watch could have been stolen, for all I knew. You just don't ask folks about how they get hold of a thing like that or how much they paid for it. But Sal was never one for laying back.

She huffed into the kitchen, all tight-faced.

He was eating in silence now. Sally's question had put him back into his sour mood. I felt bad about that.

"Look . . ." I said, "don't mind her. She don't see many new folks around here. Sticks her nose in too far, is all."

He grunted, kept eating. Really shoveling it in. It was beef stew. I knew Sally made good beef stew, so he was bound to be enjoying it. I tried him again.

"You just . . . passing through?"

"Yeah. Hitching. Can't hitch on the super so I'm on the spur. Not many cars, I'll tellya. Waited two hours for a ride this morning."

I nodded in sympathy. "Like you say, not many cars. But the fruit trucks go through this time of year. In the afternoons. One of those'll stop for you. Those truckers are good people. Just you give 'em a wave, they'll stop."

"Thanks for the tip," he said. "Usually, with trucks, I don't even try. Regulations about riders and all."

"Just give 'em a wave," I repeated.

There was some silence then. Him finishing Sally's stew, me sitting there sipping at my own lukewarm coffee. (I drink too much of the stuff, so I've learned to nurse a cup. Can't sleep nights if I don't.)

Then I said to him, "You ever go to amusement parks as a kid?"

He nodded. "Sure. Who hasn't? Every kid has."

"I ran the Funhouse in one," I told him. "Down by the lake just this side of town."

His face brightened. A smile creased it. His first of the day, I'd wager.

"Hell, I loved those frigging funhouses! Used to sneak into 'em when my allowance was all spent and I couldn't afford to buy a ticket. They had an air vent inside that blew the girls' skirts up. Used to hide in there and watch." He scrubbed at the side of his dark beard. "Haven't been in one since I was eleven—back in Omaha."

"Never made it to Nebraska, but I hear it's a nice state."

"Used to scare myself half to death in those places. Bumping around in the dark . . . Couldn't see a thing. Scary as hell!"

"Folks like to be scared," I said. "Guess it's part of human nature."

"Trick doors . . . blind tunnels leading nowhere . . . things that popped out at you!" He chuckled. "One had a big gorilla with red eyes . . . I musta jumped ten feet when that ape popped outa the floor at me! Had gorilla nightmares for a month after that. Wouldn't go to bed unless Ma left the light on."

I've noticed one thing in the years with Happyland: people love to talk about funhouses. It's a subject everybody just plain likes to talk about—how scared they got as kids, lost in the dark tunnels, with things jumping at them. Funhouses are just that—*fun*.

"I miss running the place," I told him honestly. "Used to get a real kick out of scaring the folks. I'd work all the trick effects . . . and how they'd yell and scream! Especially the girls. Young girls love to scream!"

He nodded agreement.

Suddenly I turned to him, grinning. "I got me an idea."

"What's that?" he said, pushing away his last empty plate. He put his hand on his stomach and belched.

"Why don't you and me go out there—to Happyland? I can take you through the Funhouse!"

He blinked at me, a little confused. "You mean—right *now?*"

"Sure. The park's closed, has been for years, but I can get in. Be no problem for me to show you through my Funhouse. Be proud to!"

The big man shook his head. "Well . . . I dunno. That stuff's for kids."

"Hell, *we're* kids, aren't we? Just wearing adult bodies. No man ever stops being a boy. Not inside. Not all the way." I grinned at him. "Want to have a go? . . . give it a try?"

"Sounds a little crazy."

"Funhouse is for fun!" I said. "It's not even noon yet. You can take the tour with me, come out of the park and still grab a hitch with one of the truckers."

He slapped the countertop. "Why not? Why the hell not?"

I grinned at him. "Be fun for me, too. Haven't been out to Happyland for a longish while. Be like going home."

I own a Ford pickup. Old, like I am. Got a missing taillight. Clutch is bad. Needs a ring job. Tires are mostly bald. And the paint's gone altogether. But it putters along. Gets me where I have to go.

Happyland's only ten minutes out from town. As I said, right on the lake, at the deep end. Lot of boats used to be on the lake, but it's quiet now. Just black water, and too cold to swim in most of the year. Deep and black and quiet.

I parked next to the gate and we slipped under the rusted chain fence. The park was sad to see, all deserted and boarded up and with old newspapers and empty beer cans and trash everywhere. Vines growing right into the boards. Holes in the ground. I told the stranger to watch where he walked.

"Break an ankle out here at night," I said.

"I'll bet."

We passed the old Penny Arcade. All the machines were gone. It was like a dirty barn inside. No color or movement or sound in there now. Just a rat or two, maybe. Or a spider trapping flies.

Sad.

We walked on in the noon heat—past the Loop and the Whip and the Merry-go-Round, with broken holes in the floor where all the painted horses had galloped.

"No gorillas today," I said as we approached the Funhouse. "Electricity's shut down, and they took all the trick stuff away to Chicago. But at least we can run the tunnels. They're still the same."

"This is crazy," said the bearded man. "I've gotta be nuts, doing a thing like this."

"Be proud of yourself!" I told him. "You're not afraid to let out the boy in you! Every man would like to, but most are chicken about it. You've got guts."

We stood outside, looking at the place. The big laughing fatman at the entrance was gone. I can still hear his booming Ha-Ha-Ha-Ha like it was yesterday. Twenty years of a laugh you don't forget. I knew I never would.

The ticket booth was shaped like the jaws of a shark—but

now most of the teeth were missing and the skin was peeling in big curling blisters along the sides. The broken glass in the booth had two boards nailed over it, like a pair of crossed arms.

"How do we get in?" the stranger asked me.

"There's bound to be a loose board," I told him. "Let's take a look."

"Oke," he nodded with a grin. "Lead on."

I found the loose board, pulling some brush away to clear it. Illinois is a green state; we get a lot of rain here, and things grow fast. The Funhouse was being choked by vines and creepers and high grass. It looked a thousand years old.

Sad.

The sky was clouding over. Late summer storm coming. They just pop up on you. It would be raining soon.

More rain, more growth. At this rate, in another fifty years, Happyland would be covered over—like those jungle temples in Mexico. No one could ever find it.

"Watch that nail near the top," I warned, as the stranger stooped to squeeze through with me. "Tear your shirt easy on a nail like that."

"Thanks."

"Got to watch out for my customers," I said.

Now we were inside. It was absolutely tar-pit black in the Funhouse. A jump from daylight to the dark side of the moon. And hot. Muggy hot inside.

"Can't see an inch in front of me," the stranger said.

"Don't worry, I'll walk you through. I've got a flash. It could use a new battery. Kind of dim, but we should be all right with it."

For emergencies, I always keep a flash in the Ford's glove compartment, with a couple of spare batteries. Never know when a tire might let go on you at night. But I keep forgetting to put in the new batteries when the old ones wear out. I guess nobody's perfect!

"Lot of cobwebs in here," I said, as we moved along. "Hope you don't mind spiders."

"I'm not in love with 'em," said the big man. "Not poisonous, are they?"

"No, no. Not these. Mostly little fellers. I'll clear the way for you."

And I did that, using a rolled newspaper to sweep the tunnel as I moved through it.

"Where are we?" he asked. "I mean—what part of the Funhouse?"

"About midway through from where you start," I said. "But the fun part is ahead. You haven't missed anything."

"This is crazy," he repeated again, half to himself. Then: "Ouch!"

I stopped, flashed the dimming light back at him. He was down on one knee.

"Hurt yourself?"

"I'm okay. Just stumbled. A loose board."

"Lots of those in here," I admitted. "Not dangerous, though. Not the way I'm taking you."

As we moved down the narrow wooden tunnel there was a wet, sliding sound.

"What's that?" he asked.

"The lake," I told him. "This part of the tunnel is built over the shore. That's the sound the lake water makes, hitting the pilings. The wind's up. Storm's coming."

We kept walking—going down one tunnel, turning, entering another, twisting, turning, reversing in the wooden maze. Maze to him, not to me. It was my world.

The rain had started, pattering on the wooden roof, dripping down into the tunnels. And the end-of-summer heat had given way to a sudden chill.

"This is no fun," said the stranger. "It's not what I remembered. I don't like it."

"The fun's up ahead," I promised him.

"You keep saying that. Look, I think we'd better—"

Suddenly my flash went out.

"Hey!" he shouted. "What happened?"

"Battery finally died," I said. "Don't worry. I've got another in the pickup. Wait here and I'll get it."

"Not on your life," the stranger protested. "I'm not staying alone here in the pitch dark in this damned place."

"You *afraid* of the dark?" I asked him.

"No, dammit!"

"Then wait for me. I can't lead you back without a flash. Not through all the twists and turns. But I know the way. I can move fast. Won't be ten minutes."

"Well . . . I—"

"One thing, though. I want to warn you carefully about one thing. *Don't* try to move. Just stay right where you are, so I'll know where to find you. Some of the side tunnels are dangerous. Rotting boards. You could break a leg. The tunnels are tricky. You have to know which ones to stay out of."

"Don't worry, I'll stick right here like a bug on a wall."

"Ten minutes," I said.

And I left him there in the tunnel.

Of course I didn't go back to the pickup for any batteries. Instead, I went to the control room at the end of B Tunnel.

The door was padlocked, but I had the key. Inside, feeling excited about the stranger, I let Ed know I was here. Which was easy. I'd rigged a low-voltage generator in the control room, and when I pulled down a wall switch a red light went on under the tunnels and Ed knew I was back with a stranger.

I'll bet he was excited, too. Hard to tell with Ed. But *I* sure was. My heart was pounding.

Fun in the Funhouse!

I didn't waste any time here. I'd done this many times before, so it was routine now: unlock the door, go inside, throw the switch for Ed, then activate the trap.

Trapdoor.

Right under the bearded stranger's feet. Even if he moved up or down the tunnel for a few yards (some of the nervous ones did that) there was no problem because the whole section of flooring was geared to open and send whoever was inside the tunnel down onto the slide. And the slide ended on the sand at the lakefront.

Where Ed was.

He would come up out of the lake when he saw the light. It would shine on the black water and he would see it from where he lived down there in the deep end and he would come slithering up.

Ed wasn't much to look at. Kind of weird. Spooky looking. (Remember, I said *no* ghosts!) His father was one of those really big rats that live in the burrows under the cemetery—and his mother was something from deep, deep in the lake. Something big and ugly and leathery.

They'd made love—the rat and the lake thing—and Ed was the result. Their son. He doesn't really have a name, but I call him Ed the way Gramps called me Tad. It fits him somehow, makes him more appealing. More . . . human.

Ed and me, we get along fine as partners. I bring him things to eat, and he saves the "goodies" for me. Like wallets, and cash and rings (that big one Sally was joshing me about came from one of Ed's meals) and whatever else the strangers have that I can use.

Ed is smart.

He seems to know that I need these things to keep going now that the factory's shut down and I've lost my job here and all. That's why the partnership works so well. We each get our share. After I take what I want (one time I got a fine pair of leather boots) he drags the body back into the lake.

Then he eats.

Lucky for me, one meal lasts Ed for almost a month. So I don't have to worry if no stranger shows up at Sally's for two, three, even four weeks. One always ambles along sooner or later. Like Mama always said, Everything comes to those that wait. Mama was a very patient woman. But she could be mean. I can testify to that.

It gets bad in winter—for strangers, I mean—when the roads are closed, but that's when Ed sleeps anyhow, so things even out.

By the time I got back to the stranger's tunnel that afternoon it was really coming down. Rain, I mean. Dripping and sliding down the cold wood, and getting under my collar.

Most uncomfortable. Somehow, rain always depresses me. Guess I'm too moody.

The stranger was down there with Ed where I expected him to be. Sometimes there's a little yelling and screaming, but nobody ever hears it, so that's no problem either. One fellow tried to use a knife on Ed, but Ed's skin is very tough and rubbery and doesn't cut easy. The stranger was just wasting his time, trying to use a knife on Ed.

I took a ladder down to the sand where the body was.

Ed was off by the water's edge, kind of breathing hard, when I got there. His jaw was dripping and his slanted black eyes glittered. Ed never blinked. He was watching me the way he always does, with his tail kind of moving, snakelike. He looked kind of twitchy, so I hurried. I don't think Ed likes the rain. Ed makes me nervous when it rains. He's not like himself. I never hang around the Funhouse when he's like that.

The bearded stranger was already dead, of course. Most of his head was gone, but Ed had been careful not to muss up his clothes—so it was no problem getting his wallet, rings, cash, coins . . .

When I climbed the ladder again Ed was already sliding toward the body.

Guess he was hungry.

Three and a half weeks later the stranger at the counter in Sally's was looking at my watch.

"I've never seen one like that," he said.

"Tells you the time in ten parts of the world," I said. "Tells you the month of the year and the day of the week. And it rings every hour on the hour."

The stranger was impressed.

After a while, I grinned, leaned toward him across the counter and said, "You ever go to amusement parks as a kid?"

Introduction

Pat Murphy is certifiably crazy. She lives and works in south-ern California, at Sea World, where she spends most of her time writing about tuna fish, going on shark hunts, and cooing over whales and the like. At home, she writes fantasy and sci-ence fiction, takes karate classes, and is never home when you try to call her.

Another small town, in another country. And a good deal more grim than anyone realizes.

WISH HOUND

by Pat Murphy

Alice hugged Tommy at the bottom of the plane's ramp, but the boy did not set down the case he carried to return his mother's embrace. When she released him, the case shifted in his grasp as if something moved within, and Alice heard a muffled whimper through the cardboard.

Tommy, solid and self-assured even at age seven, watched her with steady blue eyes. "Dad gave me a dog," he said. "It's not a very big one."

Alice opened her mouth to speak, but stopped herself—the words she wanted to say were meant for Paul, her former hus-band, not for Tommy. Paul had taken the boy to his ranch for three weeks immediately following Alice's remarriage. He had promised to keep Tommy while Alice and her new husband, Joseph, traveled in England, a trip that they had been plan-ning for almost a year. But when Paul was called away from the ranch on a business trip that would last several weeks, he had shipped the boy back to Alice.

Goddamn Paul, Alice thought with cold anger. He knows that I live in a city apartment, he knows that we are leaving for England soon—and not content with burdening me with a seven-year-old on my honeymoon, he tries to buy the kid's affections with a puppy. Goddamn him.

Alice waited until they got to the apartment, where Joseph was, before tackling the question of what would be done with the puppy. "We can't keep the puppy here, you understand that, don't you?" Alice held Tommy by the arm and tried to speak gently. The apartment seemed too full. With her and Joseph, it had been a comfortable size.

She had missed the boy when he left for his father's ranch, but at last she had had time for Joseph, a patient lover and now a husband. At last she had been able to sleep late with him on weekend mornings without being awakened by the sound of a knock at the door, to stay out late without worrying about the sitter, to putter about the kitchen, cooking dolmas, wonton soup, baklava, and other foods she had never tried to make before, wearing Joseph's robe because she liked its faint aroma of tobacco and aftershave until Joseph complained that it was starting to smell of her perfume.

Tommy looked at the small black dog that wiggled in his arms, trying to lick his face, and did not reply. The puppy whined, then twisted in his grasp, growled a tiny growl, and strove to attack Alice's hand with sharp new teeth.

"Your father should have known better than to give him to you," she said. "Joseph is allergic to animal hair." The boy shot Joseph a look of intense dislike, and Alice continued hurriedly. "Even if it weren't for that, we couldn't take him to England with us."

"I don't want to go to England," Tommy said. "I want to go back to the ranch. I hate England."

"That's silly. You haven't seen England yet. You might like it." Alice strove to be positive.

"I'll hate it." Tommy stood steadfast in the center of the room, puppy in his arms, his face set in a stubborn expression.

For the next week, Alice tried to give the puppy away—to friends, to relatives, to co-workers at the advertising agency where she was receptionist. No one wanted a puppy of uncertain breeding. And no one wanted to babysit a seven-year-old

for a month. Tommy's aunt was planning on having house
guests. His grandmother would be vacationing in Bermuda.
The old lady who sat for Alice on weekends was leaving town.

"It's all right," Joseph said when she told him that Tommy
would have to accompany them. "Tommy and I have to learn
to get along sooner or later." Joseph was an accepting man; a
history professor, he seemed to have adapted his spirit to the
lessons of history. He was willing to compromise, to allow
events to take their natural time.

Tommy was less accepting when she explained again why
the dog had to go, why he could not keep it. He watched her
with sullen eyes. Finally, on the last day before they were
scheduled to leave, she asked Joseph to take the puppy to the
pound while she fixed a bon-voyage dinner for the three of
them.

The boy did not cry when Alice put the puppy in the carrying case and handed the case to Joseph to take to the pound.
He set his jaw in a way that reminded her of Paul.

After Joseph left with the puppy, Alice stood in the doorway of the living room, where Tommy lay on his stomach, his
head propped up on his hands, watching TV. The TV movie
was an old Sherlock Holmes story—the *Hound of the Baskervilles*. On the screen, Basil Rathbone paced and smoked his
pipe with enormous intensity, discussing the spectral hound
with Watson.

"You want to go out to the park, Tommy?" Alice asked.
"We could go to the playground."

Without looking around, Tommy shook his head in firm denial.

"We could go out and get some ice cream for dessert tonight. You can pick the flavor."

Again, a silent headshake. Alice retreated to the kitchen,
unwilling to force Tommy to share his pain with her. While
she chopped vegetables for dinner, she tried to ignore the
baying of a hound on the TV.

That night, as she lay awake in bed, she told Joseph, "I'd
feel so much better about all this if I thought Tommy understood that there's nothing we can do. He seems to blame you

for dragging him away from his father's ranch and for this business about the dog. I just wish I could make him understand."

Joseph put his arm around her. "You're trying to treat him like a small adult and he's not. Kids aren't human. The way a kid feels about things doesn't necessarily make sense—it just is."

"I'm trying to be a good mother." She snuggled closer to him in bed. "You just don't understand him like I do, Joseph. He and I are alike in a lot of ways. But I just wish he could see that having to get rid of the puppy wasn't your fault. The whole thing was his father's fault."

"Well, it isn't really his fault either, is it?" Joseph asked. "He couldn't help having a business deal come up."

Alice kissed Joseph's cheek. "Don't waste your time trying to be fair to him, Joseph. You don't know him like I do. He always put his business before his family. Always."

A shadow of a frown, visible in the faint moonlight that shone through the window, crossed Joseph's face. "You really dislike him, don't you?"

"Hate is the word." Her voice was low but steady. "I save dislike for strangers. I only really hate people I used to love."

"Makes sense, I suppose." Joseph stroked her hair away from her eyes, then hesitated. "The kid's a lot like Paul, isn't he?"

"He's a lot like me, too." She used his shoulder as a pillow and settled down to sleep. "I'll try not to worry about Tommy. There's nothing to be done about it all anyway. And maybe he'll like England."

Tommy hated England. He hated London—complaining loudly in museums so that guards stared indignantly at the family, chasing pigeons in Trafalgar Square so that the old people who fed them scowled in annoyance. He got lost for three hours in Hyde Park and they finally found him talking to an organ grinder with a dancing poodle. He talked to people with dogs and to dogs themselves, but he did his best to ignore both Joseph and Alice except when he was complaining. He moped when they went to the theater without him, but complained that it was boring when they took him with them.

A guidebook to eastern England that Joseph purchased in a bookstore on Charing Cross (while Alice held the hand of an angry child to keep him from ransacking the shelves) suggested a small coastal resort community as an ideal vacation spot for families on tour. As a desperate move, they took the train from London to the coast, and found a bed-and-breakfast place in the little seaside town.

On the first day in the village, Joseph wanted to visit a small church on the edge of town that the guidebook had described. Under protest, Tommy accompanied them. He sulked on the walk through the village, kicking rocks into the gutter, stepping on and off the curb, dawdling at corners.

"Come on, Tommy, let's move it," Alice said, looking back at him.

"I don't want to see a stupid church," he complained. "I don't want to go at all."

"Come on, Tommy, don't make me angry." Alice turned back to Joseph frowning.

"Just keep walking," Joseph advised softly. "He'll realize that we're leaving him behind and he'll hurry to catch up." Joseph gently placed an arm around her shoulders. "And try to relax."

Alice smiled up at him. Having his arm around her reminded her of the idyllic time they had spent together. "You're so understanding," she murmured. "I'll try to relax. I just . . . I wish Tommy liked you better."

He shrugged. "We get along all right. Sure, it's a little tense, but that's only natural. He's a little jealous, that's all."

Alice looked back when they reached the end of the second block, and Tommy was nowhere in sight. She shook her head in disgust. "Where could he have gone?"

They found him a block and a half back, a long enough distance for Alice to forget her resolve to be calm. Tommy was patting a Yorkshire terrier that he had found sleeping in the shade of a fish and chips stand. "He likes me," Tommy said, looking up at Alice. "But he's not as smart as my dog."

"You don't have a dog, Tommy," Alice snapped. "The puppy's at the pound. Now come on." She took the boy's hand and marched him along the village street toward the church. Joseph followed a step behind on the other side of the angry mother.

At the church, Tommy stopped at the door. "I want to go play over there," he said. "I don't want to go inside."

Alice fought the urge to hustle the boy inside as a punishment, guessing that it would be as much a punishment for her as for him. "Where do you want to play?" she asked sternly.

"Right over there." Tommy pointed over the low stone wall that separated the churchyard from the road. They had left the village behind, and the land sloped away from the road in pastureland, covered with clumps of scrubby grass and wildflowers. Beside the church, a wrought-iron fence overgrown with rose bushes divided an area of land from the rest of the pasture.

Alice nodded. "All right. Don't go any farther than that fence."

She released his hand with a feeling of relief and linked arms with Joseph once again. Inside the church, the air was cold and smelled faintly of damp stone and incense. Alice shivered and Joseph draped his jacket over her shoulders. Gratefully, she pulled it on, and smiled at him. "I've been wearing this as much as you have."

He grinned back. "It's the only thing that makes me indispensable. You'd freeze to death without me."

She took his hand. "Not the only thing."

As the guidebook had promised, the church was tiny, but the stained-glass windows were magnificent, far more elaborate than any they had seen in London's cathedrals. And for a change, no complaining child dragged on Alice's hand.

Joseph peered out through a low window that looked out onto the pastureland and reassured Alice that they could relax. "The kid looks happy enough. He's found himself a dog to play with."

Alice looked out. Tommy stood by the wrought-iron fence and as she watched, he hurled a stick high in the air. A black shadow, almost the size of the boy, bounded from the shade of the rose bushes and leaped after the stick. "Yeah, he looks happy."

So they took their time admiring the windows. Joseph read from the guidebook in the hushed tones that seemed appropriate for the quiet church, and they admired the carved pews, the altar stone, the crucifix from which Christ stared down with a sad expression. Even then, Alice lingered, reluctant to return to the outside world.

When at last they stepped back into the sunshine, Alice saw Tommy standing alone by the wrought-iron fence. "I guess the dog's master came and got it," Joseph remarked as they walked along the flagstones to the fenced-off area.

"Look, don't mention dogs around Tommy, will you?" she asked.

"Hey, take it easy." He put his arm around her, stopping her just before they reached the fence. "I won't mention the dog. You've been having a hard time of it, I know." He kissed her, in the sunshine by the fence where the smell of roses filled the air.

When Alice turned her head to lay it against his chest, she saw Tommy watching them, through the mesh of rose branches. Beneath his shock of hair, his blue eyes burned; his small face was distorted by a look of hatred.

"Tommy!" she said, startled by his expression. And the boy's face changed, assuming the sullen look that had become habitual to him. She hesitated, uncertain of what to say. Joseph had said that jealousy was natural, but she had not thought that the boy could hate the man so much. "How did you get in there?"

Tommy pointed to a gate in the fence a short distance from them.

"Hey, Tom, I bet you've found all kinds of things to show us," Joseph called. His attempt at joviality was met by a frown, but he led Alice to the gate and they entered the smaller yard. Tombstones—weathered so that names and dates were no longer legible—stood at drunken angles within the bounds of the fence. "It's the old graveyard that the guidebook mentioned," Joseph said to Alice. "I'd guess there's a lot to see here."

Alice tried to join in Joseph's attempt to generate enthusiasm without much success. She peered at the headstones and wandered along the edge of the fence, kicking at rocks. In one corner of the fenced yard, she found a small grave, a quarter the size of the others, set apart from the rest by several feet. She pointed it out to Joseph. "Look. I guess it was a child—it's so small."

Joseph glanced inside the book and shook his head. "Nope, it's not a person at all. It's the first grave in the yard, though. Apparently, it's the guardian of the churchyard." He ran his finger down the page. "Says here that they figured that the first one to be buried in a new cemetery had to stand guard over it, so rather than burying a person, they buried ah . . . a dog." He looked at Alice half-apologetically.

"Yeah?" Tommy's face showed signs of interest. "What was the dog supposed to do?"

Joseph looked at Alice and she nodded. "Well, the spirit is called a church grim, and it's supposed to guard the cemetery against wickedness. It says here that the legend of the church grim may be related to the legends of the Wild Hunt—magical hounds that were supposed to roam the moors and chase people who were foolish enough to venture out after dark."

"They chase people like the hound of the Baskervilles did. What do they do if they catch them?" Tommy was still interested.

Joseph shrugged and closed the book. "It doesn't say."

"I'll bet they rip them up." The considering tone in the childish voice made Alice frown. She did not care for the turn the conversation had taken.

"That doesn't sound very nice, Tommy," she admonished him.

"It's okay if it's a wicked person," he argued. "Then it's okay."

Alice let the subject drop and they walked to the heart of the village in the growing twilight. Birds sang in the hedges and wildflowers grew by the side of the road. Tommy seemed happy for a change—he had picked up a stick and was using it to tap out a rhythm on the road as he walked a few paces behind Alice and Joseph. But when Alice looked back, she caught him watching them with a measuring look and she remembered his expression when he saw Joseph kiss her. She linked an arm with Joseph's protectively.

It was not until after they had gone out to dinner, returned to the bed-and-breakfast house, and Alice had put Tommy to bed, that she realized that the jacket she had worn was gone. She tried to remember whether she had worn it on her way back from the church, and she seemed to remember dropping it on a chair by the door in the entry hall of the house, but it was not there. Joseph shrugged when she mentioned it, saying, "If you left it in the churchyard, it'll still be there tomorrow."

"Maybe I dropped it in Tommy's room. I'll check." For some reason, the loss disturbed her.

Tommy's room was empty. His clothes were gone and his pajamas lay in an untidy heap on the floor. The full moon flooded the room with light and suddenly she felt cold. The only place the boy would have gone was back to the graveyard. She remembered the black beast that had leaped from the shadow of the fence and she shivered.

Joseph was already in bed when she returned to the room. She hesitated, then slipped on a sweater. He rolled over in bed to look at her. "Aren't you coming to bed?"

She paused. If he were to know where she was going, he would insist on accompanying her. She realized that it was foolish to worry about the jealousy of a seven-year-old, foolish to hear the wild baying of a hound in the back of her mind. But the jacket was gone and Tommy was gone. And Tommy hated Joseph.

"I'm still a little restless," she said. "I thought I'd go out for a walk before bed."

The crickets that chirped in the hedges lining the road fell silent when she passed. She walked quickly, clutching her sweater tightly around her against the chill night air.

Tommy was like her, she thought as she walked. He had

the capacity to hate. Joseph did not understand that—he thought the child would learn to accept him. But Alice had seen the look in Tommy's eyes.

She reached the churchyard and paused by the stone wall. The scent of roses seemed stronger in the darkness than it had in the day. Over the sound of the crickets, she heard another sound—like the click of toenails on flagstones. A cloud had covered the moon and the church and graveyard lay in darkness.

"Tommy!" Alice called over the wall. "It's time to come home." The crickets were silenced by her voice and she paused, listening to a hush that breathed. She stepped through the gap in the stone wall and followed the flagstones toward the iron fence. The scent of roses became almost overpowering.

A dark shadow separated itself from the darker shade by the fence, and she could dimly see a black beast with red-rimmed eyes, standing in her path. She froze in the darkness. Remembering advice that Paul had given her long ago, she spoke to the animal quietly and firmly. "I don't know what the hell you are—dog or guardian spirit, but you won't get my husband. I'll protect him."

The beast growled—a deep-throated sound that rose and fell, rose and fell. The animal stepped forward and still she stood frozen, confident that the animal would not attack. She had seen Tommy playing with it in the graveyard.

"I am your master's mother, dog. You are making a mistake."

Then another shadow stepped out from the shade of the fence as the moon came out from behind the cloud. Tommy held in his arms Joseph's jacket, which she had worn so often, the jacket that still carried the scent of her perfume. The moonlight shone on Tommy's eager eyes and she knew that it was no mistake.

Introduction

This is the kind of story I was brought up on and still love—where clues and hints are little more than flickerings at the corner of one's eye, where endings aren't what they seem to be, and where people and shadows are not always defined as one or the other.

ANT

by Peter D. Pautz

Autumn in the East is, as nowhere else, better called fall. The heat of August is long forgotten and remembered only as the last burst of life and sun. As leaves twist down upon themselves and fracture beneath the car tires, the everlasting gales of the tenth month hurl all into a frantic jumble of activity that can end only enshrouded in ice. Toil begins its time again, knowing it must pass through death at least once more, knowing again that this is the last.

And the children watch everything fall around them.

Ant among them.

His spirits had been the first to go this time. Usually the bodies were first, falling around him like piles of squaw wood laid carelessly on end in the blustery gusts by the front door. He had learned quickly about the wood: kindling inside where it could be gotten at quickly, corded oak in the woodbin on the porch to season. But now it wasn't the fall of the wood or the leaves or the bodies that dabbed at the corners of his thoughts, irritatingly, incessantly prying with jagged nails at his pain. It was the fall of faith. He knew they wouldn't come to watch the bodies. They never did.

Not even when they promised. Like now.

He wished for once he could see them green, fall.

From where he sat on the low redwood porch, the long front yard fell away to a sweeping and gentle slope. In the months to come he would use it as a beginner's run, swooshing and slicing the crystal powder with all the power and ferocity his ten-year-old frame could muster. Being the best, the fastest. And waiting the hardest for the holidays and their return. Finally, and again.

He couldn't count the trees before him, bordering the slope and the far field where the bodies would lay and stand and lay again. Poplars, elms, cypress, hemlocks. More pines and firs than the whole forest floor could take its bedding from. Their scents blended and wafted up to him, heavy even in the wind. Their colors speckled like a naked ear of Indian corn.

Vaguely, just enough to rob his eyes and nostrils of the world before him, a door opened quietly in the cedar-shingled house at his back. The boards' soft creakings carried the steps of a pair of well-cared-for work boots to his ear, but he fought the urge to look up. He did not want to see the smile, the understanding that he knew would be there. He thought for a moment if he didn't move at all the steps would retreat, but they never did, they never did.

"Use some company, Ant?" Greg Tammaris asked softly.

He shrugged. Would it make a difference what he said? He didn't think so. Greg sat next to him and looked out.

"Sure is pretty. I can never really get over it myself."

Ant sighed to himself and shifted to look at him. He was a tall man, so tall he almost looked like a stack of folding chairs slumped in a corner of a room whenever he sat down. Light brown hair flickered against his recessed cheekbones and his eyes and mouth were guarded half shut against the chilly northeaster. He smiled and Ant returned the grin. Greg looked as he hoped he would someday: fleshed-out, strong, hair—anything other than the frail lifeless ebony it was now.

"So, how you doing?" It was the way Greg began most of their conversations, hesitant, yet straining to be more than friendly.

Ant shrugged again, and slowly rolled his gaze back over the carpet of colors before him. Its nap soon to change from green to white, its borders from yellow-red to stark brown. Soon, but not soon enough.

A low huff passed through Greg's nose, blowing away the hurt and slight disappointment he was probably feeling. "Anthony," he began again, "I know how . . . bad you must feel, but you know that they just couldn't get away to come back here just now. I know you understand—" Ant shut him off. He could do without the soft words and the understanding and the knowing. He didn't feel "bad." He was disappointed, hurt, angry. He wanted to run through the bodies, make them fall around him like sheets from a clothesline at the ripping wind that was himself. "Maybe they can—"

They would fall hard, and still.

Littering the field.

The bodies. The bodies.

Two more Sundays of bodies passed. And he saw them green, and lay upon the field. Lay and rise again. Waiting for the blue, to charge and put him upon the ground. It happened again and again. Green, green most of the time, but more and more blue.

And then came the body that did not rise.

Little men all in white huddled together into a knobbled mushroom, blue characters of place stitched on their backs and jersey fronts. Ant was calling signals.

"Jet 36, on 2," he said sharply, the way he called all his plays. A moan came from Donnie Ryerson on his right. But that was just too bad; this was business. Stretching forth his hands, he received all theirs and led their cry of "Break!" and the Grizzlies shot to their positions. As they settled into stance, Ant scanned right and left like Greg and Coach Tyler had taught him, but now, as more often than not, he searched the long stretched-out line of parents and friends on the sidelines—the bleachers a mocking gray bird cage of fallen bars behind them—instead of studying his own backfield. They could just pop in, he thought. They popped out often enough.

Forcing his attention back to his men, he stomped up behind his center and cupped his hands beneath the boy's rump.

"Green 'em down, Anthony," someone on the left line yelled. He was glad it had worked out that way. If the guys had had to yell "Blue 'em down," he knew the older boys would have made fun of him something fierce. It was something he had heard the roughnecks in the higher grades say to each other, snarling it across the walks outside the school. (Or, once he had heard them saying it quietly, in a small group, talking about someone's girl friend named Judy.)

They had been falling around him all through the first half and his team was six points ahead. But in the third quarter, the blues had found him and he'd been sacked four times, and it was getting worse. The last three plays had all been blue. He knew it couldn't go on much longer that way, and he promised himself that if this one was blue too he wouldn't pass off the next play. He would take it himself. Whatever it was.

Hunkering down behind his center once more, he eyed the defensive line.

Blue.

He could feel it. He could just feel it.

"Damn," he mumbled, then realizing he had said it too loud began the count off quickly. "Set. Hup-One! Hup-Two!"

Everything went off smoothly. The ball hit his hands and was planted there, tight and secure. He backstepped three quick paces and spun. Donnie was there. Slamming the ball into his stomach, Ant curled in the opposite direction hoping to draw at least one of two chargers his way and off of his halfback.

It felt good. A beautiful play.

Two blitzers skimmed over his back—he could feel them brush harshly against his ribs—fighting clumsily to turn and pursue the real ball-carrier. Ant was on his knees between them waiting for the light curses he knew would follow. "Christ! Shit!" Field words. But they didn't come, and the legs didn't move from in front of him.

Twisting, he came up on one knee and saw Donnie not five feet from him, bent double, holding his middle instead of the football. A flicker of gourd-brown caught his eye and disappeared quickly into a dive of bodies, all scurrying for possession. Both teams converged on the pile of midget madmen, thrusting hands and arms and legs into the mess, like greedy monkeys after a piece of fruit.

A whistle blew and the referees arrived, pulling apart the players. One reached into the midst of the scattering bodies and plucked the ball from some vicarious handhold. Stepping away, he carefully placed his foot at the far left hashmark and pointed a flattened hand toward the other team's goal. It was still the Grizzlies' ball.

Ant sighed heavily in relief. He knew he would carry most of the blame if they lost the game. Even if his teammates didn't blame him, he would make sure to heap it all on himself. After all, he was the quarterback, it was his team. But those thoughts left him immediately as he stood. The sky seemed different. Rain? he thought. It didn't look cloudy, just darker somehow. Like looking through a piece of smoked glass at an eclipse: purply, blue and—

"Anthony," the coach yelled from the sidelines, "move it! Come on. Huddle."

He staggered a little, not from dizziness. He didn't know from what. I'm afraid, he told himself, and felt a shiver at the thought. Then, slowly he shook it off. Afraid of what? A stupid football game? A little rain?

It was ridiculous. "Huddle," he cried, and felt the comforting circle of bodies press around him. But still something told him to be careful. He didn't understand the sensation and promptly overruled it. Again he called, "Jet 36, on 2," and broke the huddle before he remembered that he had wanted the ball this time, wanted it for himself. Not for Donnie. Donnie was his friend. But the sky . . .

It was too late. He was already yelling for the ball, feeling it slap into his hands, into Donnie's stomach. But before he could spin away, drawing tacklers, he saw them fly through the air. Arcing, slashing.

Cleats.

When Ant woke in his own room the bloody numbers on his
night stand told him it was after midnight. Quickly he turned
his head away, closing his eyes. Greg was in the living room,
talking softly, his hill-toned voice easing through the closed
door. Ant relaxed. He was very glad to know his friend—he
never knew what else to call him, (certainly not Dad; no
never Dad)—was close by, up and about should he be needed.
Like this afternoon.

Now that he was awake his eyes no longer carved out the
grisly scene behind the lids. Instead, consciousness brought
back complete memory and sensation: Donnie's screams as he
was flipped onto his back; long flashing scythe-sweeps, silver,
then red, then white in the air; warm and sticky smatterings
on his face and the backs of his hands, liquid and half liquid;
the smell of rust pulsing away in his nostrils. Human rust.

And, somehow, the taste of it.

Ant cried. It burst sharp and hoarse from his mouth. Like
the rain of blood and gristle from Donnie's jaw and throat.
(The rain he should have feared.) Other memories faded
through annihilation and were gone: Rising; Greg bent over a
shattered little man in white; cries for a doctor, for help;
hands working under a tiny chin, but not knowing what to do.
And finally he recalled his own screams, the doctor over him
with a needle. Remembered and forgot. Everything.

Except Donnie. And the sky.

In the moment oblivion took to guard his mind, the door
slammed open and he ceased in mid-wail. She stood there,
and behind her—

The room shriveled so that she was on his bed without
seeming to have moved. Her arms clamped around him clumsily, straitjacketing him beneath the covers. She rolled him attempting to comfort, flapping his limp form up and down
lengthwise as if square sheeting an air mattress. Crooned to
him. And he did not move. Reaction caught in his throat and
in his heart. He did not know how to respond.

Mothered.

The next he knew the night was gone. Ant was alone in his

room. The stark, bright sunlight shining outside the straight columns of heavy curtains surrounding the window told him it was well into morning. So subtle it took him several moments to notice it, a sweet and flowery scent pervaded the bedroom. As his mind took hold of the fragrance and accepted its reality, he bolted from the bed, without glancing again at his clock, and raced to the closed door that led into the large living room.

He threw the heavy oaken door open, letting it bang sharply against the wall. "Mom!" he cried. A small scraping sound came from beyond the ell of the room, from the kitchen. Before she could say a single word, he was running, barely avoiding collisions with the low, darkwood furniture. Rounding the corner he stopped suddenly and stared at the woman standing in the doorway. For a second his only expectation was shattered. Each time he saw her she was smaller, with each passing of months her chin became more level, her shoulders less stooped as she bent to speak to him. But this time she was completely shrunken!

He gasped. Had she been sick? Had she been dying and been afraid to tell him? No, that couldn't be it, he told himself. She looked too good. Beautiful, he corrected. Her hair was dark this time, almost black as a crow's feathers, but fluffy instead of stiff. Her make-up was on with a lighter hand than he had ever seen before, yet the crystal-blue of her eyes burst forth brighter than ever. She was dressed the way he liked her: snug dungarees and checked flannel shirt. Barefoot.

Quickly she stepped from between the massive beams of the doorjamb and instantly her tiny form took on some mass. But not much; it had been too long a time. Able to move again he flew toward her and they leapt into each other's arms.

"Oh, Ant, darling," she whispered into his hair. "I'm so glad to see you."

"Mom," he said again. "Mom, I've missed you." He hugged her tighter once more, rubbing his face into the softness of her unheld breasts, and reluctantly stepped back to let her look at him. Her hands still gripped at his shoulders.

The excitement was exploding within him, pushing out words in a mad rush to beat the time clock he knew was wasting away the hours somewhere: "When did you get here? Greg said that you wouldn't be able to get here until maybe Christmas. How long can—"

A smooth, yet insistent, voice like a bassoon interrupted him, shutting his mouth, then making it gape open wide in astonishment. "Hey, what about me?" it said. "Don't I get to say hello or something?"

"Dad!"

Twisting from his mother's tightening grip, he crammed his way past her and dove at the legs of the tall man in the vested suit. Wrapping his arms fiercely around the thighs, Ant spun sideways, bringing his father down to the brick-tiled floor and jumped on top of him before he could rise.

"Pile on," he hollered, squirming all over the man like a live fishnet. "Grizzlies 14, Dads nothing!"

Gradually Ant's frenzied spinning and climbing slowed until he was lying there next to his father, the both of them laughing hard enough to curl them in over their stomachs. A tickling jab was aimed at his ribs and he tried none-too-hard to push the arm away. Their bodies wrestled for a moment, then little by little they began to meld. The laughter was gone now for both of them. For the first time in almost two years, Anthony Walker hugged his father.

And his father hugged back.

Over them, a strong and larger woman with crowblack hair glared down.

"Jonathan, get the hell—"

"Hey, come on, you two," Greg said, gently cutting her off. "Or Marilyn will have to sweep you both out the door with the rest of the dirt." He smiled expansively and winked at the short, blond woman standing by the yellow enameled stove.

"Homemade scrapple and eggs, Ant," she said turning back to the pans sizzling on the burners, a blushing grin on her own face.

Ant craned his head up past his father's shoulder and

smiled at her. "Great," he said. His voice was a trifle hoarse. Giving his dad one last squeeze he clambered to his feet, tugging him from the floor, and added, "Come on, Dad. Let's eat. Marilyn"—Jonathan Walker squinted at him and he corrected himself—"Mrs. Tammaris makes the best scrapple in the world. And I picked the eggs myself from Mr. Bosely's coop. That's on the other side of town."

Since the adults had had breakfast hours earlier, Ant was the only one eating. Looking only at him, his parents sat across from each other at his sides. Greg took a seat at the far side of the kitchen table, glancing every once in a while to his wife at the sink. It seemed as if each bit of food brought forth cascading rivulets of stories about the town and his friends. He told them about the leaf collection he had constructed and matted for his science class, about the cold glacial ponds he and Greg had swum in on their camping trips over the summer, about how he had been chosen quarterback for his midget football team, and about the games they had won. And grudgingly admitted to having lost just a few. He talked for what seemed like hours, cramming the weeks and months into each sentence. Losing them.

Finally he quieted. A puzzled expression filled his face as he tried to remember something. He scanned his parents' faces, first one, then the other, as if it might have something to do with them, but it didn't help. The memory only faded farther away. For the first time since they had sat down, Ant saw his mother look to her husband. The communication needed no words; half command, half plea, it said: *Do something, damnit.*

But as Jonathan began to open his mouth, Greg broke the silence. Again, easing the tension from without. "Tell them about your eyes, Ant."

The older man sat back, attentive. But Kathryn Walker shot a fearful glance to her son before turning back to Greg. "What do you mean? What's wrong with his eyes?"

Ant came out of his lethargy, and gave a playful moan. "Oh, Mom," he whined. "Nothing's *wrong* with my eyes. They change colors, that's all."

She was not put at ease. "What do you mean, honey?" Her tone was very tight though she tried to make the question sound light. "How can they change color?"

"They just do," he insisted. Greg had never questioned him about it. Neither had the guys on the team. They just accepted it, as he did. "They change from blue to green. And back again."

"When did you first notice them change?" his father asked.

Kathryn relaxed back into her chair. He turned to Greg and said, "It was during the first week of practice, wasn't it?"

Tammaris nodded. "Yeah, last August."

Ant shifted his gaze back to the older man and continued. "When I was trying out for quarterback I kept throwing really great passes. I could put them right into my man's stomach, or right over his shoulder, or anywhere. The coach said he never saw anyone start off so good right off the bat." He grinned proudly, matching his father's response. "And they made me quarterback. My eyes were green then," he finished in complete frankness.

"How do you know that?"

"I could feel it." A look of doubt dampened his father's smile, so he tagged on a slight lie. "I even checked my reflection in the water bucket, and they were still green. I could just *feel* it."

"Okay, okay." His father laughed at his vehemence. "Was that it? Or did anything else happen?"

"No, it got better and better," he said, brightening. "By the first time we played a real game, I could do other stuff, too."

"Like what?" Walker was obviously enjoying himself, and Ant was eager to please so he added in all the details he could think of.

"After a while I could run plays or keep the ball myself and still see if they would work or not. If my eyes were green we'd always make the play; we wouldn't fumble or lose yards and we would get the first down." Ant crouched and spun out of his chair, his arms folded over his stomach as if protecting a football from sight after a fake hand-off. Once on his feet he hid behind the chair back, taking little dancing jumps from side to side. "I even ran the ball myself for touchdowns. Four times!"

"Fantastic," exclaimed Jonathan. "That's great!" He looked over at Tammaris and smiled broadly, sharing the pleasure he felt in his son. "How many points did you rack up during the whole season?" he asked Ant. The boy shrugged and regained his seat. He was slightly disappointed at the remark. What did it matter how many points he had gotten? He was the quarterback, he had made touchdowns all on his own, he could remember every single one of them. How he ran, how the greened bodies fell before him, and rose only to fall again. Somehow he couldn't put it all together into numbers and totals. It was just him: what he was, and what he could do.

When he saw an answer was not coming from Ant, Walker glanced back at Greg, who only mirrored the boy's shrug, though with far more concern. Frowning, Walker looked away.

"And what about when they're blue?" he asked. No hint of the smile or his pleasure remained, as if they had been reward enough for one day. "What happens then?"

Ant stared glumly down at his empty plate. "Nothing," he said quietly. "My receivers all have butter-fingers. They drop the ball, or it bounces off their helmets, or I get tackled before I can even throw the ball." It pained him to think about this part of it, especially to have to tell his dad about it. "Sometimes it happens for a whole quarter." He swallowed hard and admitted, "Once for almost a whole game." He paused. "We got shut-out."

"You mean it usually doesn't last that long?"

"Uh-uh." Summoning up the nerve at last to look up from the table again, he explained, "It changes all the time now, even in the middle of a play sometimes." He hesitated for a moment, hoping to find a way out of this part of the conversation, then finally added, "Sometimes it doesn't happen at all; my eyes stay just like they are now. Regular."

They were all quiet now. Marilyn had moved from the sink to stand behind her husband, her hands braced along the back of his chair. She had been listening to the entire conversation with interest. Ant rarely talked about anything in such detail, and the expression on his face must have shown her that something vague and unruly was troubling him. Normally, a shy, quiet woman, even with Anthony, she forced out the words, "What did you see yesterday, Ant?"

The question took them all aback, so that the Walkers and Greg, twisting around in his chair to look up, all turned to stare at her, incredulous. From the corners of his eyes, Ant saw his mother stiffen, his father ease forward, like opposite ends of the same seesaw. But before anyone else could speak, Ant gently filled the stillness. "I felt them change," he said softly. "Not like before; not blue or green. The sky changed color." His eyes came up to meet hers. They were ridden with such sorrow she flinched visibly. From across the table, he whispered to her, "It was purple."

His mother was the only one to move, and she did so smoothly. Resting a small and gentle hand on his arm, she said, "But Ant, honey, none of it's your fault. You don't *do* anything. You just see the colors; the blues, the greens. They don't make the passes, or the fumbles. You do." She was speaking in little rhythms, convincing him by memorization, without truth, without facts. "You aren't responsible for what happened to Donnie," she singsonged.

But somehow Ant knew better. And tried to tell her so with his eyes.

The next few days were a mixture of loss and acceptance for Ant. From the moment he saw them both, he knew that their time together would be short. It always was. Nevertheless, he had long ago reconciled that as a fact of life. True, there were two differences this time, but he also knew better than to take any special meaning from them: This was the first time in his life that he could recall his parents being with him at the same time on their occasional visits (let alone for something as important as the pending Thanksgiving Day game), and that—he was acutely aware of their mutual loathing for one another.

As the week wore slowly on he began to notice things. He

was painfully aware that they did not sleep together as Greg and Marilyn did; his parents each occupied a separate small bedroom to the rear of the second floor. They did not talk to each other in his presence, and the bitterness he heard in their screeching arguments through his ceiling at night made him thankful for that. Worst of all—since they each wanted to be with him constantly—they would not tolerate the other's invasion of the same room, and he was thus left alone most of the time, each seeking to avoid the other. Like vampires, he thought. Afraid to see themselves in the mirror of the other.

Keenly, yet forever lessening, he felt the loss of them, of their bond. They had not lived together for so long as he could remember, each away on business that could not be concluded without their spouse's consent. But he did not really understand the strain and the hatred that those conditions brought upon them. His mother came to him every six months or so; his father irregularly, this last space the longest. Yes, he accepted their loss, their hatred of each other, and gradually his own resentment of them both.

And on Wednesday, he accepted the loss of Donnie as they put him in the ground.

Turkey Day.

Even without the coach having to add it to his pep talk, every boy on the Grizzlies knew they would be playing this game for Donnie. "Win one for the Gipper," one of the linesmen's father kept shouting from the stands, but no one knew what he meant. All they understood was that they had lost Donnie; they didn't want to lose the game, too.

Ant played to win, like he always did, but the first half was almost entirely blue. He fumbled the ball twice and threw two interceptions. His teammates jeered him, and he cried a little when he heard someone say, "We'd be winning if we had Donnie here." He meant to keep the ball that time, he wanted to tell them, he really did, but when he looked for who had said it no one was there.

During the second half he kept his eyes closed much of the time. He did not want to see the blues anymore, and even though the sky was heavily overcast he never raised his vision from the ground. He would not let his eyes mix with the blue that lay behind the clouds, not for anything. Including Donnie.

Finally, it was over. They had lost the game, too. 35–6.

They were all silent in the car on the way back to the house. Greg drove the old station wagon and Marilyn sat close beside him, as close as Ant leaned against his father in the back seat. His mother followed in her own car.

As they emerged from the cars before the cedar-shingled structure, Jonathan Walker slid a comforting hand down his son's arm. Ant had been fighting tears all the way home, and when his father said, "Don't worry about it, Ant; you did your best," he broke from his hold and ran around the house, toward the woods. Immediately, Greg started to follow. "No," called Walker. "I'll go after him." Tammaris stared uncertainly at him. "I should," he mumbled, and trotted away around the corner.

Ant stopped right at the back yard when he heard his father call to him. He did not turn around, but heard the large steady footfalls crushing the leaves behind him. Like the bodies that did not fall anymore, that he wanted to fall very badly. Fried and burnt humus wafted through his nostrils and the world grew a shade darker.

Slowly he shifted to look up at his father and whimpered softly when he saw his tears matched in the man's eyes. "I'm sorry," his father said. "Oh, Ant, I'm so sorry." Then he was on his knees, holding him, crying out a pain Ant did not know was within him. He was lost for a moment in the clamped arms and chilled-sweat smell of the man who was his father, then a voice pulled him away.

"What's the matter with the two of you. It was only a game."

Only a game, he thought.

Donnie.

As his father's hug eased around him, Ant stepped back and stared at him, at the pain on his face. Slowly he rose from his knees and weakly staggered toward the line of trees where the woods began. Ant watched him, wanting desperately to look away, but somehow could not. The pain, the utter miserable hurt on his father's face drew his gaze even after he had turned away.

"Ant," he heard his mother call sternly from somewhere behind. "What was the matter with you today? I thought you were supposed to be so good out on that field." Shut up, he thought. "And now I find you back here having a crying party with *him*." His gaze still followed his father. "Ant! What the hell is the matter with you?"

She grabbed at his shoulder, trying to pull him around to face her. Her nails dug through the soft down and nylon of his jacket, into his muscle, reminding him of his own pain. Jerking his body sharply, he pulled from her grip, agonizingly maintaining his watch. His father had reached the trees now and had wrapped his arms around the trunk of a poplar. Dull, distant sobs came through the chill afternoon air; bursts of white frostbreath sharp around the bole, choked into the bark.

All the remembrances of pain.

"Ant!" His mother was screaming at him now, stepping around in front of him. "Damnit, answer me when I speak to you. Never mind him. *I'm* speaking to you now." With one last step, she moved in front of him, directly blocking his gaze at the man crying into the treebark.

He didn't know why she was angry. Or why he was hurt. It could just as easily have been the other way around.

She seized his chin in her firm fingers and raised his face to her. The world darkened even more. He looked at her but with no difference. As they stared at each other, the anger gradually left her face, her eyes opened wide from the terrible slits of her hate. Her face went blank, until she accepted.

She smiled and let go of his chin, and struck him hard across the cheek.

Then, slowly, like twin blood-burning coals, Ant's eyes began to turn a deeper red.

And gracefully, she stepped out of the way and let him look back at his father.

Fall. A body.

Introduction

Alan Ryan has had short fiction published in The Magazine of Fantasy and Science Fiction, *and in several volumes of the* Chrysalis *series. His first novel,* PANTHER! *will appear from Signet about the time this book sees print. As if that isn't enough, he also writes book reviews and satire for the New York* Times, *the Washington* Post, *and the Los Angeles* Times.

It's also worth mentioning that a good deal of this story is true. But, as with a shadow, the problem lies in knowing where the dark begins and the reality ends.

TELL MOMMY WHAT HAPPENED

by Alan Ryan

His parents knew Robbie was strange. And just a little scary. Robbie . . . saw . . . things.

At three, he had not yet mastered enough language to express or describe with any clarity the odd things he saw, the distant images or scraps of ideas that entered his mind unbidden, unsought, like leaves drifting on a breeze. Nor did he have the age or insight to recognize the images or ideas as strange. Children's minds are not like ours. And Robbie's mind was not like other children's. Not at all.

He was the loveliest child to look at. Light brown hair curled like wisps of fragile silk around his head. His porcelain ears were so perfectly formed—the whorls like those of the rarest seashell—that their intricacy was almost a proof for the existence of God. His skin glowed pink with an inner light that seemed to mold the baby flesh with health. A lovely child to look at.

Margaret Lockwood adored her son. She loved him all the more for having lost two children in miscarriages before him.

She had invested four months flat on her back in bed to give Robbie life. Oh, she loved him.

David Lockwood, as often as he smiled at the beauty and perfection of his tiny son, even more often stared in wonder at him: How could such a beautiful thing exist? How could they have made such a thing? How? And in the stillness of the nighttime house, his hand would grope in the nursery's half light for the hand of his wife and squeeze, squeeze. Imagine! Just look at him!

But there were other times, too, when Margaret and David Lockwood stared at Robbie. In silence. With a different kind of wonder.

Robbie saw things. Things other people did not see. Things he could know nothing about. It was very strange how Robbie could see things.

As far as Margaret and David Lockwood could determine, Robbie began to see things about the time he first began to talk. It was, of course, possible that he had been seeing things before that. There was no way to tell for sure; he may have been simply unable to articulate the things he saw. They preferred—without actually discussing the matter at any great length—not to examine the question too closely. It made them uneasy. And Robbie was too perfect a child to think of in odd terms.

But when he began to talk, the odd things were there.

As Margaret Lockwood was putting Robbie to bed one evening, he suddenly squirmed in her arms. She almost dropped him and had to set him quickly on his feet before he fell. As soon as he was on the floor, Robbie looked up into her face and smiled happily.

"Daddy," he said. "Flashlight."

Margaret Lockwood crouched in front of her lovely son and put her hands gently on his shoulders to hold him in place.

"What, Robbie?" she said.

"Daddy," Robbie said again, his smile widening, lighting up his face. "Daddy have flashlight."

Then he turned and scampered off to his room.

His mother rose and followed him into the nursery. While she was geting him ready for bed, she said again—gently, lightly, coaxingly, "Does Daddy have a flashlight?" She kept smiling.

Robbie ignored her and amused himself by trying to pull the sheet loose from the mattress.

"Robbie, does Daddy have a flashlight?"

But Robbie's mind was far away, his ears deaf to her question. Margaret Lockwood was certain that Robbie knew nothing of any flashlight Daddy might have at the moment. She was uncertain if Robbie had ever used the word "flashlight" before. She thought not.

David Lockwood was a fireman and that week he was working the night shift. When he worked nights, it was his habit to call Margaret from the firehouse around midnight—timing it carefully not to interrupt her 11:00 news or Johnny Carson's monologue—to let her know that everything was all right, and to say good night. They missed each other when he had to work nights.

When David called that night, Margaret was dozing on the couch while the television chuckled at her. The phone startled her awake. She had it to her ear before she realized it was David making his nightly call.

"Quiet tonight," David said. "We only had one alarm all evening. Some old lady's frozen pizza went up in smoke in her oven. Only took us about ten minutes."

"Oh, good, David," Margaret said. She was yawning.

"What took time was getting back to the house. The damn truck broke down and yours truly ended up squiggling around underneath it for half an hour. And that truck's not exactly built like the Volks. But I got it—"

"Your truck broke down?"

"Yeah. But relax, honey, it was no big deal. We lost a hose, that's all. The only problem I had was getting at the damn thing. Took me—"

"Where were you when it happened?"

"Where? Oh, somewhere on Route 18. We were on our way back."

Margaret had stopped yawning. "Was it dark?"

David laughed. "Nah, the sun came out and shone right on the bottom of the truck. Honey, of course it was dark. And just for good measure, two of the flashlights went dead."

"But you had one? I mean, *you* had one?"

"Yes, I had one. Margaret? Is something wrong? You sound strange."

When David returned home a little after 4:30, he found Margaret asleep on the couch instead of in bed. The television was still on, the voices turned down to a distant blur of human sound, just enough to keep her company in the night.

It was just an odd coincidence, they decided in the morning.

But it was not. In the next few months they realized that Robbie really did *see* things. Odd things.

A few months after this third birthday, Robbie began talking to an imaginary playmate called Alec. He would sit out on the lawn or the front steps or in the back yard and mumble away happily to himself for hours on end, apparently chatting with the invisible Alec. When Margaret's girl friends and neighbors came in for coffee, they commented, smiling, and Margaret would laugh with them. Oh, she would say, Alec was a godsend, she didn't know what she would do without him. He kept Robbie busy for hours at a time without a grumble. Better than television for keeping him occupied and out of her hair. He was the best baby-sitter in the world. And the price was right. And he didn't have to be driven home afterwards.

Occasionally she would notice on Robbie's face a look of rapt attention as he appeared to be listening to Alec. She assumed it was Alec. There were moments when it bothered her a bit. But her girl friends' children had imaginary playmates too. Some of them did. A few of them.

But it really didn't bother Margaret Lockwood a great deal. At least it didn't bother her anymore than Robbie's *seeing* things. In fact, the only thing that bothered her at all was the fact that Alec, it seemed, never came into the house. And the only reason that fact got even that much of her attention was that she could have used his help sometimes in the evening to keep Robbie company. The boy was now at an age where he was constantly on the move, exploring, poking into everything, his curiosity and his imagination both working overtime. By evening, Margaret was often exhausted. She wanted Robbie in bed and the evening to herself, especially when David was working nights. In fact, with Robbie at this active stage, she welcomed the evenings alone. After dinner, she would kiss David good-bye and put Robbie to bed and actually look forward to spending the evening alone, relaxing with a magazine or dozing in front of the television. On those evenings, she seemed to sleep so much better on the couch than she ever did in bed. And she still got a normal night's sleep.

But Robbie, refreshed from an afternoon nap, was often a bundle of energy in the evenings. Or, even without the nap, he was too excited, too overactive, too overtired, too *something,* to fall asleep immediately.

On those evenings, Margaret wished Alec would come inside. She would try to coax Robbie into imagining the invisible friend right there in the nursery, right there beside him. But Robbie wouldn't have it. She had no luck. Alec, it seemed, would not set foot—if that was the right word for it—inside the house. No Alec. And little rest for Margaret Lockwood that night.

On those evenings, she wished fervently that Robbie would *see* Alec inside the house.

But he would not.

One day Robbie was standing in the middle of the back yard and his mother thought there was something odd about the way he was standing and . . . looking? She couldn't be sure. She started outside, then grabbed quickly at the screen door to keep it from slamming behind her. Robbie's back was turned. He was staring at the fence at the back of the yard and had no idea his mother was watching him. It was the angle of his head that had caught her eye. It was cocked curiously to one side with the unabashed honesty of children.

He just stood, feet apart at an awkward angle, as if he had been running and had been forced to a sudden halt. By what? His body was still, frozen, head tilted to one side. Margaret Lockwood watched her son. She knew that Robbie was *seeing* something. Suddenly Robbie whirled and ran back toward the house. His eyes were wide. They flew open wider as he spotted her in the doorway. His little legs pumped hard across the manicured grass of the yard, up the brick steps, into the waiting arms of his mother.

"Did something frighten you, Robbie?" she said, her voice already crooning, comforting, accustomed to banishing the fears of childhood.

Robbie stood stiffly in her arms, his body leaning back and away from her slightly.

"Alec . . ." he said. And stopped.

She touched the back of his head, the back of his neck.

"What about Alec, honey?"

Robbie's eyes widened in childish astonishment.

"He walked through the wall."

Margaret Lockwood looked into her son's face.

"He walked through the wall," Robbie said again. His voice expressed amazement as only a child's can: amazement unparalleled and beyond a child's powers to feign.

"He walked through the wall?" his mother said, her voice flitting between disbelief, encouragement, and fright.

Robbie's head bobbed up and down. "Yup," he said, "right through the wall."

Three weeks after Robbie saw Alec walk through the wall, the boy came running inside to his mother shortly after she had sent him out to the yard to play. She was sitting at the kitchen table, having another cup of coffee and listening to the radio as Robbie came crashing into the house. She spilled coffee all over the table and had to grab at the boy to keep him from being splashed and burned.

"Mommy! Mommy!"

He had to catch his breath before he could tell her why he was so excited.

"Robbie, what is it?"

His eyes were gleaming. "Alec . . ." he said.

He stood there, panting heavily.

"Robbie!"

He took a step backward, away from his mother.

"Robbie, what's wrong? Robbie!"

The boy was solemn-faced now, his eyes openly gazing at her. With curiosity? If Robbie had been older, his mother would have described the look on his face as "speculative," as if he were weighing possibilities, making some sort of judgment. But Robbie was only three, too young for anything like that. Much too young.

"Nothing," he said. And he was gone, the kitchen door left to slam loudly behind him.

Margaret Lockwood jumped from the table to follow her son. As she moved, she spilled the remaining coffee from her cup. She swore, hesitated, stopped to wipe it up quickly. By the time she got to the back yard in search of Robbie, the boy was playing with one of his trucks. It was a big red fire engine, made of heavy-gauge steel and weighing, Margaret Lockwood often thought when she had to move it, almost as much as Robbie himself. Its value, David had explained when he brought it home, was in the authenticity of the details. It was fitted with a little seat on top and could be wheeled, slowly, by a boy of Robbie's age and strength. Robbie was sitting on it now, leaning forward, fingers gripping the cab of the truck, knees and legs straining to push it through the grass of the yard. The boy didn't see her; the truck and its weight absorbed all his attention.

Margaret Lockwood stood in the doorway for a moment, watching him, then let the door close silently. Through the screen she continued to watch her son. After a while she decided not to go outside. Robbie was lost in his play with the truck. He would push it a foot or so—two good shoves with his sturdy legs—then stop to rest. Each time he stopped, he would look back over his shoulder, as if he were looking up into somebody's face, almost as if he were seeking approval for how he had moved the heavy truck. Each time he did it, Margaret Lockwood could see his lips move, but she couldn't hear what he was saying. Of course it didn't matter. Robbie was talking to Alec.

That evening she spoke to her husband about Robbie. She told him about the episode that morning. She told him about some of the other strange things that had happened in recent months, as many as she could remember, ones that she had not mentioned to him at the time they occurred. She told him some things that might not have been episodes at all, just little things that, for some reason, had made her uneasy for a moment. She told him everything she could think of about Robbie that had struck her, even for an instant, as strange. She told him about Alec, about Alec walking through the wall, and how she believed it, believed it because Robbie himself had been genuinely puzzled, about how Robbie talked to Alec when he rode the fire truck, about how Alec would not come into the house, no matter how much she coaxed. She told David everything.

He did not exactly make light of it but he saw no cause for concern either. Children have incredible imaginations, he said, remember that. And Robbie's imagination is more vivid than most kids', remember that too. And lots of kids have an imaginary playmate. Kids are different, he said, they have no control over their imaginations, they see things, hear things, stuff like that, and theres' no reason anything like that should ever bother you. And besides, he'll grow out of it.

Margaret said she guessed he was right. They were standing side by side at the stove, both of them putting dinner on the table. Robbie was in the living room.

"And, you know," David said, "you're beginning to talk about this Alec as if you really did believe in him."

Margaret, relieved at having gotten it all out, told it all out loud, laughed and said, "No Alec, huh?"

"No Alec."

She shrugged. "Okay, then," she said. "No Alec."

That was on Friday.

On Monday, David went back to working the night shift for a week.

On Monday evening, Margaret fed husband and son, then sent David off to work with a kiss. She stayed at the door until she saw the car disappear around the corner. Then she went inside to put Robbie to bed. She was relieved when he seemed to fall asleep at once.

When she returned to the kitchen, it was beginning to rain. She flicked on the yard lights for a second to see what had been left outside that might rust. Her eyes swept the yard. There was nothing. She took her time cleaning up after dinner. No rush tonight. Robbie was already asleep. Before she settled in front of the television with a bowl of Jell-O, she went around the house and made sure all the windows were closed. It was raining hard now.

The crash and scream from the bedroom sent her leaping off the couch. The glass bowl flew out of her hand. Her knee caught the edge of the coffe table. Pain shot through her leg.

Robbie!

She ran for the bedroom, stumbling against the wall, her injured knee barely supporting her.

"Robbie?!"

The boy was standing in the crib, his hands gripping the top of the side, fingers curled tightly around the bar. He was looking past her, his gaze fixed.

"Robbie!"

She ran for him, swept him up out of the crib into her arms. She almost had to pull his hands free from the railing. As she gathered him in close to her pounding heart, his head swung away from her. He was still staring into the corner of the room beside the door.

Margaret patted him on the back, stroked him, soothed him.

"What happened, baby? What happened? Tell Mommy what happened?"

She turned from the crib to walk up and down the room with him, as she had done when he was an infant.

"Tell Mommy what happened." She repeated the words over and over. "Tell Mommy what happened." She kept her face close to the boy's silken hair. "Tell Mommy what happened."

"Alec came inside," Robbie said at last.

Margaret's knee hurt more now. She had forgotten it the instant Robbie was safely in her arms, but now the pain burned through her leg, shot down through the bone. She stumbled and had to tighten her grip on the boy as she turned toward the door. Robbie was squirming in her arms. She lost her balance and bumped her shoulder against the doorframe.

She carried Robbie out to the living room. He was stiff in her arms for a moment, as if reluctant to come, but he began to relax when she settled him on the couch beside her. She couldn't hold him in her lap the way she wanted because of the pain in her leg. She thought she could feel the knee already beginning to swell. She tried but she could coax nothing out of Robbie about what had happened, what the noise was, what had made him scream. His only response was a shrug. She felt him all over, his arms and legs, and looked in his eyes, felt his forehead. He was fine. But her examination of him made her realize even more strongly how much her own leg was hurting. It was more than half an hour now since she had struck it and the swelling was now painful itself.

It was almost another half hour before Robbie finally grew drowsy and Margaret felt it was safe to leave him alone on the couch. She made sure he wasn't going to wake up, then hobbled off to the kitchen for ice. She improvised an ice pack with a dish towel and started back to the living room.

But what had happened? She was sure she had heard a crash at the same instant Robbie had screamed. Or had she dreamed it? The rain was still lashing at the windows. She could hear the trees whipping in the wind. Maybe a branch had snapped outside. She'd been distracted by the television when it happened. Maybe her mind had joined all the sounds together.

Robbie was safely asleep on the couch. Margaret supported herself against the wall for a moment, then hobbled slowly down the hall to take one more look in the bedroom, just to be sure.

She flipped on the bright overhead light. Her gaze swept carefully around the room, cataloguing everything in its place, until she came to the corner at her left side.

The red fire truck was in the corner, the front end of it crushed against the wall. The wall itself was split with the impact. The ladders had flown off the truck and lay nearby. One of the wheels had come off. Another was bent askew on its axle and the remains of the truck leaned sideways. The front cab was mangled on one side, crushed almost flat on the other. A red stain soaked the rug beneath it.

"Oh my God!" Margaret said.

Alec came inside.

Then she heard the doorbell ring.

Introduction

Steve Rasnic Tem is a poet, short story writer, and newlywed. I must say that those marble town halls with those long, door-studded corridors, have always held a certain morbid fascination for me. I don't know why. And this piece doesn't help me feel any easier about it.

AT THE BUREAU

by Steve Rasnic Tem

I've been the administrator of these offices for twenty-five years now. I wish my employees were as steady. Most of them last only six months or so before they start complaining of boredom. It's next to impossible to find good help. But I've always been content here.

My wife doesn't understand how I could remain with the job this long. She says it's a dead end; I'm at the top of my pay scale, there'll be no further promotions, or increase in responsibilities. I've no place to go but down, she says. Her complaints about my job always lead to complaints about the marriage itself, of course. No children. Few friends. All the magic's gone, she says. But I've always been content.

When I started in the office we handled building permits. After a few years we were switched to peddling, parade, demolition licenses. Two years ago it was dog licenses. Last year they switched us to nothing but fishing permits.

Not too many people fish these days; the streams are too polluted. Last month I sold one permit. None the two months before. They plan to change our function again, I'm told, but a final decision apparently hasn't been made. I really don't care, as long as my offices continue to run smoothly.

A photograph of my wife taken the day of our marriage has

sat on my desk the full twenty-five years, watching over me. At least she doesn't visit the office. I'm grateful for that.

Last week they reopened the offices next door. About time, I thought; the space had been vacant for five years. Ours was the last office still occupied in the old City Building. I was afraid maybe we too would be moved.

But I haven't been able as yet to determine just what it is exactly they do next door. They've a small staff, just one lone man at a telephone, I think. No one comes in or out of the office all day, until five, when he goes home.

I feel it's my business to find out what he does over there, and what it is he wants from me. A few days ago I looked up from my newspaper and saw a shadow on the frosted glass of our front door. Imagine my irritation when I rushed out into the hallway only to see his door just closing. I walked over there, intending to knock, and ask him what it was he wanted, but I saw his shadow within the office, bent over his desk. For some reason this stopped me, and I returned to my own office.

The next day the same thing happened. Then the day after that. I then refused to leave my desk. I wouldn't chase a shadow; he would not use me in such a fashion. I soon discovered that when I didn't go to the door, the shadow remained in my frosted glass all day long. He was standing outside my door all day long, every day.

Once there were two shadows. That brought me to my feet immediately. But when I jerked the door open I discovered two city janitors, sent to scrape off the words "Fish Permits" from my sign, "Bureau Of Fish Permits." When I asked them what the sign was to be changed to, they told me they hadn't received those instructions yet. Typical, I thought; nor had I been told.

Of course, after the two janitors had left, the single shadow was back again. It was there until five.

The next morning I walked over to his office door. The lights were out; I was early. I had hoped that the sign painters had labeled his activity for me, but his sign had not yet been filled in. "Bureau Of . . ." There were a few black streaks where the paint had been scraped away years ago, bare fragments of the letters that I couldn't decipher.

I'm not a man given to emotion. But the next day I lost my temper. I saw the shadow before the office door and I exploded. I ordered him away from my door at the top of my voice. When three hours had passed and he still hadn't left, I began to weep. I pleaded with him. But he was still there.

The next day I moaned. I shouted obscenities. But he was always there.

Perhaps my wife is right; I'm not very decisive, I don't like to make waves. But it's been days. He is always there.

Today I discovered the key to another empty office adjacent to mine. It fits a door between the two offices. I can go from my office to this vacant office without being seen from the hallway. At last, I can catch this crazy man in the act.

I sit quietly at my desk, pretending to read the newspaper. He hasn't moved for hours, except to occasionally peer closer at the frosted glass in my door, simulating binoculars with his two hands to his eyes.

I take off my coat and put it on the back of my chair. A strategically placed flower pot will give the impression of my head. I crawl over to the door to the vacant office, open it as quietly as possible, and slip through.

Cobwebs trace the outlines of the furniture. Files are scattered everywhere, some of the papers beginning to mold. The remains of someone's lunch are drying on one desk. I have to wonder at the city's janitorial division.

Unaccountably, I worry over the grocery list my wife gave me, now lying on my desk. I wonder if I should go back after it. Why? It bothers me terribly, the list unattended, unguarded on my desk. But I must push on. I step over a scattered pile of newspapers by the main desk, and reach the doorway leading into the hall.

I leap through the doorway with one mighty swing, prepared to shout the rude man down, in the middle of his act.

The hall is empty.

I am suddenly tired. I walk slowly to the man's office door, the door to the other bureau. I stand waiting.

I can see his shadow through the office door. He sits at his desk, apparently reading a newspaper. I step closer, forming my hands into imaginary binoculars. I press against the glass, right below the phrase, "Bureau Of," lettered in bold, black characters.

He orders me away from his door. He weeps. He pleads. Now he is shouting obscenities.

I've been here for days.

Introduction

Chelsea Quinn Yarbro lives in Albany, California, is currently working on an opera about Dracula, and is fascinated with a scholar's devotion with the occult. Her science fiction has been widely praised, but it is her fantasies that allow Quinn to give release to her best, most carefully constructed writing.

For those of you who are familiar with HOTEL TRANSYLVANIA, THE PALACE, *and* BLOOD GAMES . . . *welcome to Cabin 33; and for those who are not . . . read this first, then go buy the books.*

CABIN 33

by Chelsea Quinn Yarbro

In the winter there were the skiers, and in the summer the place was full of well-to-do families escaping to the mountains, but it was in the off-seasons, the spring and the fall, when Lost Saints Lodge was most beautiful.

Mrs. Emmons, who always came in September, sat at her table in the spacious dining room, one hand to her bluish-silver hair as she smiled up at the Lodge's manager. "I do so look forward to my stay here, Mr. Rogers," she said archly, and put one stubby, beringed hand on his.

"It's good of you to say so," Mr. Rogers responded in a voice that managed to be gracious without hinting the least encouragement to the widow.

"I hear that you have a new chef." She looked around the dining room again. "Not a very large crowd tonight."

Mr. Rogers followed her glance and gave a little, eloquent shrug. "It's off-season, Mrs. Emmons. We're a fifth full, which is fine, since it gives us a breather before winter, and allows us a little time to keep the cabins up. We do the Lodge itself in the spring, but you're not here then."

"I'm not fond of crowds," Mrs. Emmons said, lifting her head in a haughty way it had taken her years to perfect.

Nor, thought Mr. Rogers, of the summer and winter prices. He gave her half a smile. "Certainly off-season is less hectic."

She took a nervous sip from the tall-stem glass before her. Mrs. Emmons did not like margaritas, and secretly longed for a side car, but she knew that such drinks were considered old-fashioned and she had reached that point in her life when she dreaded the reality of age. "Tell me," she said as she put the glass down, "is that nice Mr. Franciscus still with you?"

"Of course." Mr. Rogers had started away from the table, but he paused as he said this, a flicker of amusement in his impassive face.

"I've always liked to hear him play. He knows all the old songs." There was more of a sigh in her tone than she knew.

"He does indeed," Mr. Rogers agreed. "He'll be in the lounge after eight, as always."

"Oh, good," Mrs. Emmons said, a trifle too brightly before she turned her attention to the waiter who had appeared at her elbow.

Mr. Rogers was out of the dining room and half way across the lobby when an inconspicuous door on the mezzanine opened and a familiar voice called his name. Mr. Rogers looked up swiftly, and turned toward the stairs that led to the mezzanine.

The door opened onto a small library comfortably furnished in dark-stained wood and substantial Victorian chairs uphol-stered in leather. There was one person in the room at the mo-ment, and he smiled as Mr. Rogers closed the door. When he spoke, it was not in English.

"I just saw Mrs. Emmons in the dining room," Mr. Rogers said with a tinge of weariness. "She's looking forward to see-ing that 'nice Mr. Franciscus.'"

"Oh, God," said Mr. Franciscus in mock horror. "I suppose that Mrs. Granger will be here soon, too?"

"She's due to arrive on Wednesday." Both men had been standing, Mr. Franciscus by the tall north-facing windows, Mr. Rogers by the door. "I've given them cabins A28 and A52, back to back over the creek."

"And if the water doesn't bother them, they'll have a fine time," Mr. Franciscus said. "I didn't have time to tune the harpsichord, so I'll have to use the piano tonight." He came away from the windows and sank into the nearest chair.

"I don't think anyone will mind." Mr. Rogers turned the chair by the writing table to a new angle as he sat.

"Perhaps not, but I should have done it." He propped his elbows on the arms of the chair and linked his fingers under his chin. His hands were beautifully shaped but surprisingly small for a pianist. "There's part of the ridge trail that's going to need reinforcement before winter or we'll have a big wash-out at the first thaw."

"I'll send Matt out to fix it. Is that where you were this afternoon? Out on the trails?" There was a mild interest but his questions were calmly asked and as calmly answered.

"Part of the time. That ranger . . . Jackson, Baxter, something like that, told me to remind you about the fire watch."

"Backus," Mr. Rogers said automatically. "Ever since that scare in Fox Hollow, he's been jittery about fire. He's the one who put up all the call stations on the major trails."

"It's good that someone is concerned. They lost sixteen cabins at Fox Hollow," Franciscus responded with a touch of severity. "If we had the same problem here, there's a great deal more to lose—and one hundred twenty-four cabins would be a major loss."

Mr. Rogers said nothing, watching Franciscus levelly.

"We're going to need some improvements on the stable. The roof is not in good repair and the tack room could stand some sprucing up. The hay-ride wagon should be repainted. If we can get this done before winter it would be helpful." He brushed his black jeans to rid them of dust. His boots were English, not Western, made to order in fine black leather. There was an elegance about him that had little to do with his black clothing. He stared at Mr. Rogers a moment. "Are there any disturbances that I should know about? You seem apprehensive."

"No," Mr. Rogers said slowly, after giving the matter his consideration. "It's just the usual off-season doldrums, I guess. We're a little fuller than we were last fall. There's a retired couple from Chillicothe, name of Barnes in cabin 12, they're new; a couple from Lansing with a teen-aged daughter in cabin 19. I think the girl is recovering from some sort of disease, at least that's what her mother told me—their name is Harper. There's a jumpy MD in cabin 26, Dr. Muller. Amanda Farnsworth is back again. I've put her in cabin A65."

"It's been—what?—three years since she was here last?" Franciscus asked.

"Three years," Mr. Rogers nodded. "There's also a new fellow up in cabin 33."

"Cabin 33? Isn't that a little remote?" He glanced swiftly toward the window and the wooded slope beyond the badminton courts and swimming pool. A wide, well-marked path led up the hill on the far side of these facilities, winding in easy ascent into the trees. Cabin 33 was the last cabin on the farthest branch of the trail, more than a quarter mile from the lodge and dining room.

"He requested it," Mr. Rogers said with a slight shrug. "I told him he would find it cold and quite lonely. He said that was fine."

"If that's what he wants . . ." Franciscus dismissed the newcomer with a turn of his hand. "What about the regulars? Aside from Mrs. Emmons, God save us, and Mrs. Granger?"

"We'll have the Blakemores for two weeks, starting on the weekend. Myron Shire is coming to finish his new book, as usual. Sally and Elizabeth Jenkins arrive next Tuesday. Sally wrote to say that Elizabeth's been in the sanitorium again and we are not to serve her anything alcoholic. We'll have all four Lellands for ten days, and then they'll go on to the Coast. Harriet Goodman is coming for six weeks, and should arrive sometime today. Sam Potter is coming with his latest young man. The Davies. The Coltraines. The Wylers. The Pastores. Professor Harris. Jim Sutton will be here, but for five days only. His newspaper wants him to cover that murder trial in Denver, so he can't stay as long as usual. The Lindholms. He's looking poorly and Martha said that he has had heart trouble this year. Richard Bachmere and his cousin, whose name I can never remember . . ."

"Samuel," Franciscus supplied.

"That's the one. The Muramotos won't be here until Thanksgiving this year. He's attending a conference in Seattle. The Browns. The Matins. The Luis. Tim Halloran is booked in for the weekend only, but Cynthia is in Mexico and won't be here at all. And that's about it." Mr. Rogers folded his hands over his chest.

"Not bad for fall off-season. What's the average stay?" Franciscus inquired as he patted the dust from his pant-leg, wrinkling his nose as the puffs rose.

"No, not bad for off-season. The average stay is just under two weeks, and if this year is like the last three years, we'll pick up an odd reservation or two between now and the skiers. We'll have a pretty steady flow from now until Thanksgiving. We're underbooked until just before Christmas, when we open the slopes. But those twelve cabins still have to be readied."

Franciscus nodded. "Before the skiers." He stared at his boot where his ankle was propped on his knee. "We'd better hire that band for the winter season, I think. I don't want to be stuck doing four sets a night again. Have you asked around Standing Rock for winter help?"

"Yes. We've got four women and three men on standby." He consulted his watch. "The restaurant linen truck should be here in a few minutes. I'd better get over to the kitchen. What time were you planning to start this evening?"

Franciscus shrugged. "Oh, eight-thirty sounds about right for this small crowd. I don't imagine they'll want music much after midnight. We can let Ross do a couple late sets with his guitar if there's enough of an audience. If not, then Frank can keep the bar open as long as he wants. How does that sound to you?"

"Good for the whole week. Saturday will be busier, and

we'll have more guests by then. We'll make whatever arrangements are necessary." He rose. "Kathy's determined to serve chateaubriand in forcemeat on Saturday, and I'm afraid I'm going to have to talk her out of it. I know that the chef's special should live up to its name, but the price of beef today . . ." He rolled his eyes up as if in appeal to heaven.

"Why not indulge her? It's better she make chateaubriand in forcemeat for an off-season crowd than for the skiers. Let her have an occasional extravagance. She's a fine chef, isn't she?" Franciscus leaned back in his chair.

"So they tell me," said Mr. Rogers, switching back to English.

"Then why not?" He reached for his black hat with the silver band. "Just make sure she understands that you can't do this too often. She'll appreciate it." He got to his feet as well. "I want to take one more look through the stable before I get changed for tonight. We've got six guest stalls ready. The Browns always bring those pride-cut geldings they're so proud of. I'll get changed about the time you start serving dinner."

"Fine." Mr. Rogers held the door open and let Franciscus leave ahead of him. "I'll tell Mrs. Emmons."

Franciscus chuckled. "You've no pity, my friend. If she requests 'When the Moon Comes Over the Mountain,' I will expire, I promise you."

The two men were still smiling when they reached the lobby once more. A tall, tweedy woman in her early forties stood at the registration desk and looked around as Mr. Rogers and Franciscus reached the foot of the stairs. "Oh, there you are," she said to the men and gave them her pleasant, horsey grin.

Mr. Rogers said, "Good afternoon, Ms. Goodman" at the same time that Franciscus said, "Hello, Harriet."

"Mr. Rogers. Mr. Franciscus." She extended her hand to them, taking the manager's first. There were three leather bags by her feet and though she wore no makeup beyond lipstick, she now, as always, smelled faintly of *Joy*.

As he slipped behind the registration desk, Mr. Rogers

found her reservation card at once and was filling in the two credit lines for her. "Six weeks this time, Ms. Goodman?"

"Yes. I'm giving myself some extra vacation. I'm getting tired. Six years on the lecture circuit is too wearing." She looked over the form. "Cabin 21. My favorite," she remarked as she scribbled her name at the bottom of the form. "Is Scott around to carry my bags?"

"I'm sorry. Scott's off at U.S.C. now," Mr. Rogers said as he took the form back.

"U.S.C.? He got the scholarship? Well, good for him. He's a very bright boy. I thought it was a shame that he might lose that opportunity." She held out her hand for the key.

"He got the scholarship," Mr. Rogers said with a quick glance at Franciscus.

"I'll be happy to carry your bags, Harriet," Franciscus volunteered. "I'm curious to know how your work's been going."

Her hazel eyes were expressive and for a moment they flickered with a pleasant alarm. Then it was gone and her social polish returned. "Thank you very much. I don't know the etiquette for tipping the musician-cum-wrangler, but . . ."

"No tip," Franciscus said rather sharply. "Call it a courtesy for a welcome friend." He had already picked up the smallest bag and was gathering up the other two.

"I must say, I envy the shape you're in. Lugging those things around wears me out. But look at you. And you must be at least my age." She had started toward the door and the broad, old-fashioned porch that led to the path to cabin 21.

Franciscus was a few steps behind her. "I'm probably older than you think," he said easily. He was walking briskly, his heels tapping smartly on the flagging.

They were almost to cabin 21 when a frail-looking teenager in an inappropriate shirtwaist dress stepped out onto the path. Franciscus recognized her from Mr. Rogers' description of the new guests in cabin 19.

"Excuse me," she said timorously, "but could you tell me where the nearest path to the lake is?"

Harriet Goodman gave the teen-ager a quick, discerning

glance, and Franciscus answered her. "You'll have to go past the lodge and take the widest path. It runs right beside the badminton courts. You can't miss it. There's a sign. But I'm afraid there's no lifeguard, so if you want to swim, you should, perhaps, use the pool. We haven't got the canoes and boats out yet, either. Two more days and they'll be ready."

"It's all right," she said in a quick, shaky voice. "I just want to walk a bit." She clutched her hands nervously, then moved sideways along the path away from them.

"That's one jumpy filly," Harriet Goodman said when the girl was out of earshot. "Who is she?"

"She's new," Franciscus said, resuming the walk to Harriet's cabin. "Mr. Rogers said that she's apparently recovering from an illness of some sort." Having seen the girl, he doubted that was the real problem, but kept his opinion to himself.

Harriet had made a similar assessment. "Recovering from an illness, my ass."

There were five wooden steps down to the door of cabin 21 which was tucked away from the rest on the path, the last one of the twelve on this walk. Harriet Goodman opened the door. "Oh, thank goodness. You people always air out the cabins. I can't tell you how much I hate that musty smell." She tossed her purse on the couch and went to the bedroom beyond. "Everything's fine. Let me check the bathroom." She disappeared and came back. "New paint and fixtures. You're angels."

"The owner doesn't like his property to get run-down," Franciscus said, as he put the bags on the racks in the bedroom.

Harriet Goodman watched him, her hands on her hips. "You know, Franciscus, you puzzle me," she said with her usual directness.

"I do? Why?" He was faintly amused and his fine brows lifted to punctuate his inquiry.

"Because you're content to remain here, I guess." There was a puckering of her forehead.

"I like it here. I value my privacy."

"Privacy?" she echoed, not believing him. "In the middle of a resort."

"What better place?" He hesitated, then went on. "I do like privacy, but not isolation. I have time for myself, and though there are many people around me, almost all of them pass through my life like, well, shadows."

"Shadows."

He heard the melancholy in her voice. "I said *almost* all. You're not a candidate for shadow-dom, Harriet. And you know it."

Her laughter was gently self-deriding. "That will teach me to fish for compliments."

Franciscus looked at her kindly before he left the cabin. "You're being unkind to yourself. What am I but, as you call it, a musician-cum-wrangler?" He nodded to her and strolled to the door.

Her eyes narrowed as she stared at the door he had closed behind him. "Yes, Franciscus. What are you?"

He preferred playing the harpsichord to the piano, though the old instrument was cantankerous with age. He had his wrenches laid out on the elaborately painted bench and was busy with tuning forks when the teen-ager found him at work.

"Oh! I didn't mean . . ." She turned a curiously mottled pale pink. "You're busy. I heard music and I thought . . ."

"Hardly music," Franciscus said as he jangled a discordant arpeggio on the worn keys.

"I think it's pretty." Her eyes pleaded with him not to contradict her.

His curiosity was piqued. "That's kind of you to say, but it will sound a great deal better once I get it tuned."

"May I watch? I won't say anything. I promise." Her hands were knotting in the nervous way he had noticed before.

"If you wish. It's boring, so don't feel you have to stay." His penetrating dark eyes rested on her cornflower blue ones, then he gave his attention to the harpsichord again. He used his D tuning fork, struck it and placed it against the raised lid of the instrument for resonance. He worked quickly, twisting the metal tuning pegs quickly. Methodically he repeated the process with all the Ds on the keyboard.

"Is that hard, what you're doing?" she asked when he had worked his way up to F#.

"Hard? No, not when I've got my tuning forks. I can do it without them, but it takes longer because I have difficulty allowing for the resonances, the over and under tones, in my mind." He did not mind the interruption, though he did not stop his task. He selected the G fork and struck it expertly.

"You have perfect pitch?" She found the idea exciting. "I've never known anyone with perfect pitch."

"Yes." Franciscus placed the vibrating fork against the wood, and the note, eerily pure, hummed loudly in the room. "That's the resonant note of this instrument, which is why it's so much louder than the others."

The teen-aged girl looked awed. "That's amazing."

"No, it's physics," he corrected her wryly. What was wrong with that child? Franciscus asked himself. From her height and the shape of her body, she had to be at least sixteen, but she had the manner of a much younger person. Perhaps she had truly been ill. Or perhaps she was recovering from something more harmful than illness. "All instruments have one particular resonant note. In the ancient world, this was attributed to magic," he went on, watching her covertly.

"Did they? That's wonderful." She sounded so forlorn that he worried she might cry.

"Is something the matter, Miss . . ."

"Harper," she said, with an unaccountable blush. "Emillie Harper."

"Hello, Miss Harper. I'm R. G. Franciscus." He offered her his right hand gravely.

She was about to take it when a stranger came into the room. He was a tall, lean man dressed, like Franciscus, predominantly in black, but unlike Franciscus, he wore the color with an air of menace. There was a flamboyance, a theatricality about him: his dark hair was perfectly silvered at the temples and there was a Byronic grandeur in his demeanor. His ruddy mouth curved in a romantic sneer, and though he was certainly no older than Franciscus, he gave the impression of world-weariness that the other, shorter man conspicuously lacked.

"I didn't mean to interrupt," he announced for form's sake, in a fine deep voice that oozed ennui.

"Quite all right," Franciscus assured him. "I'm almost finished tuning, and Miss Harper and I were discussing resonance. Is there anything I can do for you? Dinner service began a quarter hour ago, if you're hungry."

The stranger gave a slight shudder. "Dinner. No. I'm looking for the manager. Have you seen Mr. Rogers?" His soulful brown eyes roved around the lounge as if he suspected the man he sought to be lurking in the shadows.

"He should be with the chef. He usually is at the start of dinner," Franciscus told him with unimpaired good humor. "Give him another ten minutes and he'll be out."

"I need to see Mr. Rogers at once," the stranger stated with great finality. "It's urgent."

Emillie Harper clenched her hands tightly and stared from one man to the other. Her blue eyes were distressed and she moved in quick, fluttery starts, as if attempting to flee invisible shackles.

"Miss Harper," Franciscus said calmly, "I'm going to the kitchen to get Mr. Rogers for this . . . gentleman. Would you like to come with me?" He took his black wool jacket from the bench and began to roll down his shirt sleeves. With a twitch he adjusted the black silk ascot at his neck before shrugging on the jacket.

The depth of gratitude in the girl's eyes was pathetic. "Oh, yes. I would. Please."

Franciscus regarded the tall interloper. "If you'll be good enough to wait at the registration desk, Mr. Rogers will join you shortly. It's the best I can do, Mr. . . ."

"Lorpicar," was the answer. "I'm in cabin 33."

"Are you." Franciscus had already led Emillie Harper to the door of the lounge. He sensed that Mr. Lorpicar wanted him to look back, and for that reason, he did not, although he felt a deep curiosity possess him as he led the frightened girl away.

Jim Sutton walked into the lounge shortly after ten the next evening, while Franciscus was doing his second set. The reporter was dressed with his usual finicky elegance in contrast to his face which held the comfortable appeal of a rumpled bed. He waved to Franciscus and took a seat at the bar, waiting for the buzzy and unobtrusive sounds of the harpsichord to cease.

"It's good to see you again, Mr. Sutton," the bartender said as he approached. "Cruzan with lime juice, isn't it?"

"Good to see you again, Frank. You're right about the drink." He had often been amused by the tales he had heard of reporters and Bourbon: he had never liked the stuff. Rum was another matter. He put a ten dollar bill on the highly polished mahogany of the bar as Frank brought him one of the neat, square glasses used at Lost Saints Lodge with little ice and a fair amount of rum. "When eight of this is gone, you tell me."

"Sure thing, Mr. Sutton," said the bartender in his faded southern accent as he gave the reporter an indulgent smile before answering the imperious summons of Mrs. Emmons at the far end of the bar.

Jim Sutton was into his second drink when Franciscus slipped onto the stool beside him. "I liked what you were playing," he said by way of greeting.

Franciscus shrugged. "Hayden filtered through Duke Ellington."

"Keeps the peasants happy." He had braced his elbows on the bar and was looking over the lounge. It wasn't crowded but it was far from empty. "You're doing well this year. Rogers said that business was up again."

"It is." Franciscus took the ten dollar bill and stuffed it into Jim Sutton's vest pocket. "Frank, Mr. Sutton is my guest tonight. Present me with a tab at the end of the evening."

"Okay, Franciscus," came the answer from the other end of the bar.

"You don't use any nicknames?" Jim Sutton asked.

"I don't encourage them." He looked at the reporter and thought there was more tension in the sardonic, kindly eyes than he had seen before. "How's it going?"

"I wish I had more time off," Sutton muttered as he finished his drink and set the square glass back on the bar. "This last year . . . God! The mass murders in Detroit, and that cult killing in Houston, and the radiation victims in St. Louis, and now this trial in Denver. I thought I was through that when I came back from Viet Nam. I tell you, it's getting to me."

Franciscus said nothing, but he hooked the rather high heels of his custom-made black shoes over the foot brace of the stool and prepared himself to listen.

It was more than five minutes later that Jim Sutton began to speak again. "I've heard all the crap about reporters being cold sons-of-bitches. It's true of a lot of them. It's easier if you can do it that way. What can you say, though, when you look at fourteen bodies, neatly eviscerated, after two weeks of decomposition in a muddy riverbank? What do you tell the public about the twenty-six victims of a radiation leak at a reactor? Do you know what those poor bastards looked like? And the paper's managers, who know nothing about journalism, talking about finding ways to attract more advertisers! Shit!" Frank had replaced the empty glass with another. Jim Sutton looked at it, and took it with a sigh. "I've been going to a shrink. I used to scoff at the guys who did, but I've had to join them. Lelland University has offered me a post on the faculty. Three years ago I would have laughed at them, but I'm thinking about it."

"Do you want to teach?" It was the first question that Franciscus had asked and it somewhat startled Jim Sutton.

"I don't know. I've never done it. I know that my professors were blithering incompetents, and much of what they told me wasn't worth wiping my ass with. Still, I tell myself that I could make a difference, that if I had had the kind of reporter I am now for a teacher, I would have saved myself a lot of grief. Or maybe I'm just running away, and in a year, I'll be slavering to be back on the job." He tasted the drink and set it aside.

"Why not try teaching for a year, just to find out if you want to do it, and then make up your mind? Your paper will give you leave, won't it?" His suggestion was nonchalant and he said it in such a way that he did not require a response.

Jim Sutton thought about it a moment. "I could do that. It gives me an out. Whether it works or it doesn't, there is a way for me to tell myself I made the right decision." He made a barking sound that was supposed to be a laugh.

"I've got another set coming up," Franciscus said as he got off the stool. "Any requests?"

"Sure." This had become a challenge with them in the last three years. "The ballet music from Tchaikovsky's *Maid of Orleans*." He said it with a straight face, thinking that this was sufficiently obscure, as he himself had only heard it once, and that was a fluke.

Franciscus said, "The court scene dances? All of them?" He was unflustered and the confident, ironic smile. "Too easy, Jim; much too easy."

Jim Sutton shook his head. "I should have known. I'll stump you one day." He took another sip of the rum, and added, "Here's a bit of trivia for you—Tchaikovsky collected the music of the Count de Saint-Germain. Do you know who he was?"

"Oh, yes. I know." He had stepped back.

"Yeah, well . . ." Before he could go on, he was interrupted by Mrs. Emmons at the end of the bar who caroled out, "Oh, Mr. Franciscus, would you play 'When the Moon Comes Over the Mountain' for me?"

Emillie Harper was noticeably pale the next day as she sat by the pool in her tunic swimsuit with ruffled neck and hem. She gave a wan smile to Harriet Goodman as the older woman came through the gate onto the wide, mosaiced deck around the pool.

"Good morning," Harriet called as she saw the girl. "I thought I was the first one out."

"No," Emillie said hastily. "I haven't had much sun, so mother said I'd better do my swimming in the morning and evening."

"Good advice," Harriet concurred. "You won't be as likely to burn."

"I was hoping there might be swimming at night," she said wistfully. "I heard that Mr. Rogers has night swimming in the summer."

"Talk to him about it," Harriet suggested as she spread her towel over the depiction of a Roman bireme. She had often been struck with the very Roman feel of the swimming pool here at Lost Saints Lodge. For some reason it did not have that phony feel that so many others had. The mosaics were part of it, but that was not it entirely. Harriet Goodman had a nose for authenticity, and she could smell it here and wondered why. It was cool but she did not deceive herself that her frission came from the touch of the wind.

"Pardon me," Emillie said a bit later, "but haven't I seen you before? I know that sounds stupid," she added, blushing.

Harriet had cultivated her considerable charm for many years, and she used it now on the distressed girl. "Why, not at all—it's very kind of you. I do occasional television appearances and I lecture all over the country. If I made enough of an impression for you to remember me, I'm flattered."

Emillie's face brightened a little, though on someone as apprehensive and colorless as the teen-ager was, enthusiasm was difficult to perceive. "I did see you. A while ago," she added guiltily.

"Well, I've been around for quite a time," Harriet said as she lay back on the towel. What was bothering the girl? she wondered.

"I'm sorry, but I don't remember what it was you talked about." Emillie was afraid she had insulted the older woman, and was trying to keep from withdrawing entirely.

"Child abuse. I'm a psychiatrist, Miss Harper. But at the moment, I am also on vacation." Her voice was expertly neutral, and she made no move that would suggest disapproval.

"A psychiatrist?" She repeated the word as if it were contaminated.

Harriet had experienced that reaction too many times to be disturbed by it. "Yes, more Jungian than Freudian. I got into child abuse by accident." She had a rich chuckle. "That does sound ominous, doesn't it? What I meant to say, though Freud would have it that my sloppy grammar was hidden truth, is that I became interested in studying child abuse unintentionally. Since I'm a woman, when I first went into practice I had a few male patients. A great many men don't feel comfortable with a woman analyst. After a while, I discovered that a fair number of my women patients were either child abusers themselves or were married to men who were." She raised her head and glanced over at the demure girl several feet away. "Now it's you who should forgive me. Here I've told you I'm on vacation and the next thing, I'm starting shop talk."

"It's all right," Emillie said in a politely gelid tone.

They had been there quite the better part of half an hour when the gate opened again. Mrs. Emmons, in a lavish flowered purple bathing suit and outrageous rhinestoned sunglasses sauntered up to the edge of the pool. "Oh, hello, girls," she called to the others. "Isn't it a beautiful morning?"

"Christ!" Harriet expostulated, and lay back in the sun.

A little bit later, Mrs. Granger arrived, wearing an enormous flowered hat and a beach robe of such voluminous cut that the shrunken body it covered seemed like illicit cargo. By that time Mrs. Emmons was splashing in the shallow end of the pool and hooting with delight.

Pink more with embarrassment than the sun, Emillie Harper gathered up her towel, mumbled a few words that might be construed as excuses, and fled. Harriet propped herself on her elbow and watched Emillie go, scowling, her senses on the alert.

There was a low rock at the tip of the point, and Jim Sutton sat on it, fishing rod at the ready, gazing out over the lake to the steep slope rising on the western bank. A discarded, half-eaten sandwich had already begun to attract ants to the side of the rock.

"Hello, Jim," Harriet said as she came up behind him.

"Hi," he answered, not turning. "There's a spurious rumor that this lake has been stocked with trout."

"But no luck," she inferred.

"No luck." He reeled in the line and cast again. "I got four eighteen-inchers last year."

"Maybe it's the wrong time of day." She had the good sense to stay back from the rock where he sat, though only part of her reason had to do with fishing. "I hear that you'll have to make your stay short this year. There's that trial in Denver . . ."

"There is indeed." He looked down and saw the remains of his sandwich, which he kicked away.

"Mustn't litter," Harriet admonished him lightly.

"Who's littering? I'm supporting the ecological chain by providing a feeding niche," he shot back. "I don't know why I bother. Nothing's going to bite today."

Harriet selected the least-rough part of a fallen log and sat on it, rather gingerly, and was pleased when it held. So much fallen wood was rotten, no matter how sound it appeared. "I'll buy you a drink if you'd like to come back to the Lodge with me."

"A very handsome offer. How can I refuse." He began to reel in his line. "You in cabin 21?"

"As usual. And you?"

"Cabin A42. As usual." He caught up his leader and held it carefully, inspecting his hook and bait before turning to her.

"Then we're almost neighbors." That was a polite fiction: a steep pathway connected the two wider trails on which their cabins were located, and the distance required a good ten minutes after dark.

"Perhaps you'd like to come by." She was careful not to sound too wistful.

"Sounds good." He faced her now, and came up beside her. "Don't worry about me, Harriet. I do take a reasonable amount of care of myself. We're neither of us children, any-more."

She put an arm across his back. "No, we're not children." They were much the same height, so their kiss was almost too easy. "I miss that."

"So do I." They started up the trail together, walking side by side. "Anyone new in your life?"

"No one important," she said with a shrug. "And you?"

"There was one woman, very sensual, but . . . I don't know. Like covering a disaster. Everything afterward is an anticlimax."

They had reached the first turning in the road and were startled to see the strange guest from cabin 33 coming toward them. Mr. Lorpicar nodded to both Harriet and Sutton, but did not speak, continuing down the path with an expression at once determined and abstracted.

"That's one strange duck," Harriet said as they resumed their walk.

"He's the one in cabin 33, isn't he?" Jim Sutton asked, giving the retreating figure a quick look over his shoulder.

"I think so." She dug her hands deep into the pockets of her hiking slacks, watching Jim Sutton with covert concern.

"I saw him after lunch with that Harper girl. I've seen her before, I know I have. I just can't place her . . ." They were at the crest of a gentle rise and through the pines they could see the back of the Lodge. "I hate it when I can't remember faces."

Harriet smiled gently. "You'll think of it. Probably it isn't this girl at all, but another one, equally colorless. Both her parents look like frightened hares." She thought about this as they approached the Lodge. "You'd think one of them would be a tyrant to have the daughter turn out that way. I thought that one of them might be pious or invalidish, but they're as painfully ordinary as the girl is."

"Such language for a psychiatrist," Jim Sutton admonished her, and then they went up the steps into the Lodge, into the lounge, and they did not talk about Emillie Harper or the peculiar Mr. Lorpicar any more.

Nick Wyler was a hale sort of man, whose body and gestures were always a little too large for his surroundings. He enjoyed his own flamboyance, and was sincerely upset if others did not enjoy it, too. His wife, Eleanore, was a stately woman, given to wearing long skirts and Guatemalan peasant blouses. They had taken cabin A68, right on the lake, one of the largest and most expensive cabins at Lost Saints Lodge.

"Rogers, you're outdoing yourself," Nick Wyler announced as he came into the dining room. "I'm impressed, very impressed."

Mr. Rogers made a polite gesture which was very nearly a bow. "It's good of you to say so."

"That mysterious owner of yours does things right. You may tell him I said so." He gave a sweeping gesture that took in the entire dining room and implied the rest of the building. "Really beautiful restoration. None of the schlock that's turning up all over the place. I'd bet my eye teeth that the lowboy in the foyer is genuine. English, eighteenth century." He beamed and waited for his expertise to be confirmed.

"Actually, it's Dutch," Mr. Rogers said at his most apologetic. "It was built at the Hague in 1761." Before Nick Wyler could take issue with this, or embark on another round of compliments, Mr. Rogers had turned away and was leading Mrs. Emmons and Mrs. Granger to their table by the window.

"The chef's special this evening, ladies, is stuffed pork chops. And in addition to the usual dessert menu, the chef has prepared a custard-filled tart. If you'll simply tell the waiter, he'll see that your selections are brought promptly."

"I like him," Mrs. Granger confided in a loud, gravelly voice. "He knows what service means."

Mr. Rogers had signaled for the waiter and was once again at the door of the dining room. All three Harpers were waiting for him, and smiled ingratiatingly, as if they were the inferiors. Mr. Harper was solicitous of his wife and daughter and respectful to Mr. Rogers.

"Our table there, Doris, Emillie. Mr. Rogers will lead the way." He was so eager to behave properly that he was infuriating.

As Mr. Rogers held the chair for Doris Harper, he saw, with real pleasure, Harriet Goodman and Jim Sutton come in from the lounge. He hastened back to them. "A table together, I assume?"

"Why make more work than's necessary?" Jim asked magnanimously. "Harriet's got the nicer table, anyway." His voice dropped and he stared once more at the Harpers. "I know I've seen that girl. I know it."

"It'll come to you," Harriet told him patiently as they followed Mr. Rogers. She was growing tired of hearing him speculate. They saw each other so rarely that she resented time lost in senseless preoccupation with others.

Franciscus appeared in the door to the lounge and motioned to Mr. Rogers, and when the manager reached him, he said, "Where's Lorpicar? I saw him out on the trails today. Has he come back?"

"I haven't seen him," Mr. Rogers said quietly. "Oh, dear."

"I'll go have a look for him if he hasn't turned up by the end of dinner." He was dressed for playing in the lounge, not for riding at night, but he did not appear to be put out. "I saw the Blakemores come in this afternoon. I think he might be willing to play a while, and he's a good enough pianist for it."

"Last year he did an entire evening for us," Mr. Rogers recalled, not precisely relieved. "I'll make a few inquiries here, in case one of the other guests have seen Lorpicar." He watched Franciscus return to the lounge, and then went to seat the Browns and the Lindholms, who waited for him.

Dinner was almost finished and Mr. Rogers had discovered nothing about the reclusive man in cabin 33. He was about to return with this unpleasant piece of information when he saw the stranger stride through the doors into the foyer.

"Mr. Lorpicar," Mr. Rogers said as he came forward. "You're almost too late for dinner."

The cold stare that Mr. Lorpicar gave the manager was enough to silence a lesser man, but Mr. Rogers gave his blandest smile. "We were concerned when you did not return."

"What I do is my own business," Mr. Lorpicar declared, and stepped hastily into the dining room and went directly to the Harpers' table.

At the approach of Mr. Lorpicar, Emillie looked up and turned even paler than usual. "Gracious," she murmured as the formidable man bore down on her.

"I wonder who this is supposed to impress?" Harriet said very softly to Jim.

"Shush!" was the answer, with a gesture for emphasis. The rest of the dining room buzzed with conversation, and then fell silent as many eyes turned toward the Harper table.

"You did not come," Mr. Lorpicar accused Emillie. "I waited for you and you did not come."

"I couldn't," she answered breathlessly.

Mr. Rogers, watching from the door, felt rather than saw Franciscus appear at his elbow.

"Trouble?" Franciscus asked in a low voice.

"Very likely," was the manager's reply.

"See here . . ." Emillie's father began, but the tall, dark-clad man cut him off.

"I am not speaking to you. I am speaking to Emillie and no one else." His burning gaze went back to the girl's face. "I want to see you tonight. I must see you tonight."

The diners were silent, their reactions ranging from shock to cynical amusement to disgust to envy. Jim Sutton watched closely, his face revealing nothing, his eyes narrowed.

"I don't know if I can," she faltered, pushing her fork through the remains of her meal.

"You will." He reached out and tilted her head upward. "You will."

Doris Harper gave a little shriek and stared at her water glass as her husband pressed pleats into his napkin.

"I don't know . . ." Emillie began, but got no further.

"Excuse me," Franciscus said with utmost urbanity. "If Miss Harper wishes to continue what is obviously a private conversation in the lounge, I'll be glad to offer you my company so that her parents need not be concerned. If she would prefer not to talk with you just at present, Mr. Lorpicar, it might be best if you take a seat for the meal or . . ."

Mr. Lorpicar failed to shove Franciscus out of his way, but he did brush past him with a softly spoken curse, followed by a declaration to the room at large. "I'll eat later," and added, in the same breath to Emillie Harper, "We haven't finished yet."

Franciscus left the dining room almost at once, but not before he had bent down to Emillie and said quietly, "If you would rather not be importuned by Mr. Lorpicar, you have only to tell me so." Then he made his way back to the lounge, and if he heard the sudden rush of conversation, there was no indication of it in his manner.

There were five people in the lounge now and Frank was smothering a yawn at the bar.

"I've been meaning to tell you all evening," Harriet said to Franciscus, "that was a masterful stroke you gave in the dining room."

Franciscus raised his fine brows in polite disbelief. "It seemed the best way to deal with a very awkward situation." He looked at Jim Sutton on the other side of the small table. "Do you remember where you've seen the girl yet?"

"No." The admission bothered him; he ground out his cigarette in the fine crystal ashtray.

"You know," Harriet went on with professional detatchment, "it was most interesting to watch Emillie. Most of the people in the room were looking at Lorpicar, but I found Emillie the more interesting of the two. For all her protestations, she was absolutely rapt. She looked at that man as if he were her salvation, or he a god and she his chosen acolyte. Can you imagine feeling that way for a macho nerd like Lorpicar?"

"Is macho nerd a technical term?" Franciscus asked, favoring her with a delighted, sarcastic smile.

"Of course. All conscientious psychiatrists use it." She was quite unrufflable.

"Acolytes!" Jim Sutton burst out, slapping his hand on the table top and spilling his drink. "That's it!"

"What?" Harriet inquired in her best calming tones.

"That girl. Their last name isn't Harper, it's Matthisen. She was the one who caused all the furor when that religious fake in Nevada brought the suit against her for breach of contract. He makes all his followers sign contracts with him, as a way to stop the kind of prosecution that some of the other cults have run into. She, Emillie, was one of Reverend Masters' converts. She was kidnapped back by one of the professional deprogrammers. A man by the name of Eric Saul. He got himself declared persona non grata in Nevada for his work with Emillie. Reverend Masters brought suit against Emillie for breach of contract and against her parents and Eric Saul for conspiracy." His face was flushed. "I read most of the coverage of the trial. Loren Hapgood defended the Matthisens and Saul. Part of the defense was that not only was the girl under age—she was sixteen then—but that she was socially unsophisticated and particularly vulnerable to that sort of coercion." He took his glass and tossed off the rum with a tight, eager smile.

"Didn't Enid Hume serve as expert witness?" Harriet asked, thinking of her illustrious colleague. "She's been doing a lot of that in similar cases."

"Yes, she and that guy from LA. I can't remember his name right off. It's something like Dick Smith. You know the one I mean. The psychologist who did the book a couple years back." He leaned toward Harriet, and both were so caught up in what Jim was saying that they were startled when Franciscus put in a question.

"Who won?" He sat back in his chair, hands folded around the uppermost crossed knee.

"The defense," Jim Sutton said promptly. "The argument was that she was under age and that the nature of the agreement had not been explained to her family. There was also a demonstration that she was more gullible to a con of that sort than a great many others might be."

Harriet pursed her lips. "Enid told me about this, or a similar case, and said that she was worried about kids like Emillie. They're always seeking someone stronger than they are, so that they don't have to deal with their own fears of weakness, but can identify with their master. Reverend Masters is fortunate in his name," she added wryly. "I've seen women who feel that way about domineering husbands, kids who feel that way about parents, occasionally, adults who feel that way about religious or industrial or political leaders. It's one of the attitudes that makes tyranny possible." Harriet had a glass of port she had been nursing, but now she took a fair amount of the ripe liquid into her mouth.

"Reverend Masters," Jim Sutton repeated the name three or four times to himself. "You know, he's a tall man, like Lorpicar. Not the same type. A blond, fallen-angel face, one of those men who looks thirty-five until he's sixty. He's in Arizona or New Mexico now, I think. Some place where the locals aren't watching him too closely."

"And do you think he'll continue?" Franciscus inquired gently of the two.

"Yes," Harriet said promptly. "There are always people who need a person like Masters in their lives. They invent him if they have to. He's a magnet to them."

"That's damn cynical for a woman in your line of work," Jim Sutton chided her. "You make it sound so hopeless."

For a moment Harriet looked very tired and every one of her forty-two years. "There are times I think it is hopeless. It might be just because I deal with child abuse, but there are times I feel that it's not going to get any better, and all the work and caring and heartbreak will be for nothing. It will go on and on and on."

Jim Sutton regarded her with alarm, but Franciscus turned his dark, compassionate eyes on her. "I understand your feeling—far better than you think. Harriet, your caring, your love is never wasted. It may not be used, but it is never wasted."

She stared at Franciscus astonished.

"You know it is true, Harriet," Franciscus said kindly. "You know it or you wouldn't be doing the work you do. And now, if you'll excuse me . . ." he went on in his usual tones, and rose from the table. "I have a few chores I must finish before the bar closes up for the night." He was already moving across the dimly lit room, and stopped only once on his way to speak to the Wylers.

"Well, well, well, what do you know," Jim Sutton observed, a laconic smile curving his mouth. "I'm beginning to see why you have dreams about him. He's got a great line."

"That wasn't a line," Harriet said quietly.

Jim nodded, contrition in his face. "Yeah. I know." He stared into his glass. "Are the dreams like that?"

Her answer was wry but her expression was troubled. "Not exactly. I haven't had one yet this time. I kind of miss it."

"You've got the real thing instead. Your place or mine to-night?" He put his hand on her shoulder. "Look, I didn't mean that the way it sounded. Erotic dreams, who doesn't have them? Franciscus is a good guy."

"I only have the dreams when I'm here," Harriet said, as if to explain to herself. "I wish I knew why." Her laugh was sad. "I wouldn't mind having them elsewhere. Dreams like that . . ."

"It's probably the proximity," Jim Sutton said, and then, sensing her withdrawal, "I'm not jealous of the other men you sleep with, so I sure as hell am not going to be jealous of a dream." He finished his rum and cocked his head in the direction of the door. "Ready?"

"God, yes," she sighed, and followed him out of the lounge into the night.

For the last two days Emillie Harper had wandered about listlessly, oblivious to the stares and whispers that followed her. She had taken to wearing slacks and turtleneck sweaters, claiming she was cold. Her face was wan and her eyes were fever-bright.

"I'm worried about that child," Harriet said to Franciscus as they came back from the stable.

"Victim's syndrome, do you think?" Franciscus asked, his voice carefully neutral.

"More than that. I can't imagine that Lorpicar is a good lay.

Men like that almost never are." She was sore from the ride, since she had not been on a horse in eight months, but she walked energetically, doing her best to ignore the protesting muscles, and reminding herself that if she walked normally now, she would be less stiff in the morning.

"Do you think they're sleeping together?" Franciscus asked. They were abreast of the enclosed swimming pool now and could hear Mrs. Emmons' familiar hoots of delight.

"What else? She drags around all day, hardly eats, and meets him somewhere at night. And I've yet to see him up before dusk." She nodded to Myron Shires, who had set a chair out on the lawn in front of the Lodge and had propped a portable typewriter on his knees and was tapping the keys with pianistic intensity. There was a two-beat pause as he waved an off-handed greeting.

"Why do you think that Lorpicar wants her?" Franciscus persisted.

"Because she's the youngest woman here, because she adores him," Harriet said distastefully. "She likes his foreign air, his domination. Poor kid."

"Foreign?" Franciscus asked, reserving his own judgment.

"He does cultivate one," Harriet allowed, glancing up as a large pickup with a two-horse trailer passed by. "Where would you say he comes from?"

Franciscus laughed. "Peoria."

"Do you say that because you're foreign yourself?" She made her inquiry casually, and added, "Your English is almost perfect, but there's something about the rhythm of it, or the word choice. You don't speak it natively, do you?"

"No, not natively." His answer, though terse, was not critical.

Harriet felt herself encouraged. "I've wondered just where you do come from . . ."

They had started up the wide steps of the porch, heading toward the engraved-glass doors that led into the foyer. There was a joyous shout from inside and the doors flew open.

Franciscus' face froze and then lit with a delight Harriet had never seen before. He stopped on the second step and opened his arms to the well-dressed young woman who raced toward him. They stood embraced for some little time; then he kissed her eyelids and murmured to her, "Ah, *mon coeur,* how good to see you again."

"And you." The young woman was perhaps twenty-two, though her face was a little young in appearance. Her dark hair fell around her shoulders, her violet eyes danced. She was sensibly dressed in a twill pantsuit with cotton shirt and high, serviceable boots. Harriet had seen enough tailor-made clothes in her life to know that this young woman wore such clothes.

"You must forgive me," Franciscus said, recalling himself. "Harriet, this is Madelaine de Montalia, though the *de* is mere courtesy these days, of course." He had stepped back, but he held Madelaine's hand firmly in his.

"A pleasure," Harriet said. She had never before felt herself to be as much an intruder as she did standing there on the steps of the Lodge. The strength of the intimacy between Franciscus and Madelaine was so great that it was a force in the air. Harriet wanted to find a graceful way to excuse herself, but could think of none. She admitted to herself that she was curious about the young woman, and felt an indefinable sort of envy.

"You must not be shocked," Madelaine said to Harriet. "We are blood relatives, Sain . . . Franciscus and I. There are not so many of us left, and he and I have been very close."

You've been close in more ways than blood, Harriet thought to herself, but did not voice this observation. She felt a wistfulness, knowing that few of her old lovers would respond to her now as Franciscus did to Madelaine. "I'm not shocked," she managed to say.

"Harriet is a psychiatrist, my dear," Franciscus explained.

"Indeed?" Madelaine was genuinely pleased. "I am an archeologist."

"You seem fairly young to have . . ." She did not know how to express her feelings, and made a gesture in compensation.

"My face!" Madelaine clapped her free hand to her cheek.

"It is very difficult, Harriet, to look so young. I assure you that I am academically qualified. I've done post-doctoral work in Europe and Asia. You mustn't assume I'm as young as I look." Her dismay was quite genuine and she turned to Franciscus. "You're worse than I am."

"It runs in the family," Harriet suggested, looking from Madelaine to Franciscus.

"Something like that," he agreed. "Harriet, will you forgive me if I leave you here?"

"Certainly. You probably want to catch up on everything." She still felt a twinge of regret, but rigorously overcame it. "I'll see you in the lounge tonight." As she started back down the stairs and along the wooded path toward her cabin, she heard Madelaine say, "I've brought one of my colleagues. I hope that's all right."

"I'm sure Mr. Rogers can work something out with the owner," Franciscus said, and was rewarded with mischievous laughter.

Harriet dug her hands into her pockets and told herself that the hurt she felt was from her unaccustomed riding, and not from loneliness.

The moon was three days past full and one edge was ragged, as if mice had been at it. Soft light illumed the path by the lake where Emillie Harper walked, her face pensive, her heart full of unspoken longing. No one, not even Reverend Masters, had made her feel so necessary as Mr. Lorpicar. A delicious shudder ran through her and she stopped to look at the faint reflection of her form in the water. She could not see the expression of her face—the image was too indistinct for that. Yet she could feel the smile and the lightness of her desires. She had never experienced any feeling before that was as irresistible as what Lorpicar summoned up in her.

A shadow crossed the moon, and she looked up, smiling her welcome and anticipation. In the next instant a change came over her, and her disappointment was almost ludicrous.

"Good evening, Miss Harper," Franciscus said kindly. He

was astride his grey mare, saddle and bridle as English as his boots.

"Hello," she said listlessly.

He smiled at her as he dismounted. "I felt you might be here by the lake. Your parents are very worried about you."

"Them!" She had hoped to sound independent and confident, but even to her own ears the word was petulant.

"Yes, them. They asked me if I'd look for you, and I said that I would. I thought you'd prefer talking to me than to your father."

Emillie's chin rose. "I heard that you had a Frenchwoman come to visit you."

"And so I have," Franciscus said with prompt geniality. "She's a very old friend. We're related in a way."

"Oh, are you French?" she asked, interested in spite of herself.

"No, though I've lived there upon occasion." He was leading the grey now, walking beside Emillie with easy strides, not rushing the girl, but in a subtle way not permitting her to dawdle.

"I'd like to go to France. I'd like to go to Europe. I want to be someplace interesting." Her lower lip pouted and she folded her arms.

Franciscus shook his head. "My dear Emillie, interesting is often another word for dangerous. There is an old Chinese curse to that effect."

Emillie tossed her head and her pale brown hair shimmered in the moonlight. She hoped that Mr. Lorpicar was able to see her, for she knew that her pale hair, ordinarily mousy in the daylight, turned a wonderful shade of lunar gold in bright nights. She did not look at the man beside her. "You don't know what it is to be bored."

"I don't?" His chuckle was not quite kind. "I know more of boredom than you could imagine. But I have learned."

"Learned what?" she challenged, staring along the path with ill-concealed expectation.

He did not answer her question, but remarked, "I don't think that Mr. Lorpicar will be joining you tonight." He did not add that he had gone to cabin 33 earlier and made a thorough investigation of the aloof guest. "You know, Emillie, you're letting yourself . . ." He did not go on. When had such advice ever been heeded, he asked himself.

"Get carried away?" she finished for him with as much defiance as she could find within herself. "I want to be carried away. I want something exciting to happen to me before it's too late."

Franciscus stopped and felt his mare nudge his shoulder with her nose. "Too late? You aren't even twenty."

She glared at him, saying darkly, "You don't know what it's like. My father wanted me to marry Ray Gunnerman! Can you imagine?"

Though Franciscus knew nothing of this unfortunate young man, he said with perfect gravity, "You're hardly at an age to get married, are you?"

"Father thinks I am. He says that I need someone to take care of me, to protect me. He thinks that I can't manage on my own." Her voice had become shrill and she had gone ahead of him on the path.

Privately, Franciscus thought that Mr. Harper might be justified in his conviction, for Emillie Harper was certainly predisposed to harm herself through her desire to be controlled. "You know," he said reminiscently, "I knew a woman, oh, many years ago . . ."

"That Frenchwoman?" Emillie asked so sharply that Franciscus raised his fine brows.

"No, this woman was Italian. She was a very attractive widow, and she wanted new sensations in her life. There always had to be more, and eventually, she ran out of new experiences, which frightened her badly, and she turned to the most rigorous austerity, which was just another form of sensation for her. I'm telling you about her because I think you might want to examine your life now."

"You want me to settle for Ray Gunnerman?" she demanded, flushing in that unbecoming, mottled way.

"No. But you should realize that life is not something that is done to you, but a thing that you experience for yourself. If you always look outside yourself for your definitions, you may never discover what is genuinely your own—your self." He could tell from the set of her jaw that she did not believe him.

"What happened to that Italian woman?" she asked him when he fell silent.

"She died in a fire." Which was no more than the truth. "Come, Emillie. It's time you went back to your cabin. Mr. Lorpicar won't be coming now, I think."

"You just don't want me to see him. That's the second time you said he wasn't coming." She thought he would be impressed with her determination, and was shocked when he smiled gently.

"Of course I don't want you to see him—he's a very dangerous man, Emillie."

"He's not dangerous," she protested, though with little certainty. "He wants to see me."

"I am sure he does," Franciscus agreed dryly. "But you were with him last night and the night before. Surely you can forego tonight, for your parents' peace of mind, if not your own protection."

"Well, I'll go up to see him tomorrow afternoon," Emillie declared, putting her hands on her hips, alarmed to discover that they were trembling.

"Tomorrow afternoon? That's up to you." There was a sad amusement in his dark eyes, but he did nothing to change her mind.

"I will." She looked across the curve of the lake to the hillside where cabin 33 was located. The path was a little less than a quarter mile around the shore, but from where she stood, the cabin was no more than a hundred fifty yards away. The still water was marked by a moon path that lay like a radiant silver bar between her and the far bank where Mr. Lorpicar waited for her in vain. "He has to see me," she insisted, but turned back on the path.

"That's a matter of opinion," Franciscus said and changed the subject. "Are you going to be at the picnic at the south end of the lake tomorrow? The chef is making Mexican food."

"Oh, picnics are silly," she said with the hauteur that only a woman as young as she could express.

"But Kathy is an excellent chef, isn't she?" he asked playfully, knowing that Lost Saints Lodge had a treasure in her.

"Yes," she allowed. "I liked that stuff she made with asparagus and walnuts. I didn't know it could be a salad."

"I understand her enchiladas and chihuahuenos are superb." He was able to speak with complete sincerity.

"I might come for a little while," she said when she had given the matter her consideration. "But that's not a promise."

"Of course not," he agreed gravely as they walked past the bathing beach and pier and turned toward the break in the trees and the path that went from the beach to the badminton courts to the Lodge itself and to cabin 19 beyond, where the Harpers waited for their daughter.

Harriet Goodman was deep in conversation with Madelaine de Montalia, though most of the other guests gathered around the stone fireplace where a large, ruddy-cheeked woman held court while she put the finishing touches on the meal.

"And lots of garlic, comino, and garlic," the chef was instructing the others who stood around her, intoxicated by the smells that rose from the various cooking vessels. "Mexican or Chinese, there's no such thing as too much garlic." She paused. "Most of the time. Now, making Kung-Pao chicken . . ." and she was off on another description.

"I don't know how she does it," Harriet said loudly enough to include Franciscus in her remark.

"She's an artist," Franciscus said simply. He was stretched out under a young pine, his hands propped behind his head, his eyes all but closed.

Mrs. Emmons bustled around the wooden tables setting out the heavy square glasses that were part of the picnic utensils. "I must say, the owner must be quite a surprising man—real glass on a picnic," she enthused.

"He's something of a snob," Mr. Rogers said, raising his voice to call, "Mr. Franciscus, what's your opinion?"

Franciscus smiled. "Oh, I concur, Mr. Rogers."

"Are you going to spend the entire afternoon supine?" Madelaine asked him as Harriet rose to take her place in line for food.

"Probably." He did not look at her but there was a softening to his face that revealed more than any words or touching could.

"Madelaine!" Harriet called from her place in line, "Do you want some of this? Shall I bring you a plate?"

The dark-haired young woman looked up. "Thank you, Harriet, but no. I am still having jet lag, I think."

"Aren't you hungry?" Harriet asked, a solicitous note in her voice.

"Not at present." She paused and added, "My assistant will provide something for me later."

Harriet recalled the cherub-faced Egyptian student who had arrived with Madelaine. "Where's she?"

"Nadia is resting. She will be here later, perhaps." She leaned back against the tree trunk and sighed.

"Nadia is devoted to you, my heart?" Franciscus asked quietly.

"Very." She had picked up a piece of bark and was toying with it, turning it over in her hands, feeling the rough and the smooth of it.

"Good. Are you happy?" There was no anxiety in his question, but a little sadness.

Madelaine's answer was not direct. "You told me many years ago that your life is very lonely. I understand that, for I am lonely, but I would rather be lonely, having my life as it is, than to have succumbed at nineteen and never have known all that I know. When I am with you, I am happy. The rest of the time, I am content, and I am always learning."

"And the work hasn't disappointed you?" His voice was low and lazy, caressing her.

"Not yet. Every time I think that I have truly begun to understand a city or a people, something new comes to light, and I discover that I know almost nothing, and must begin again." She was pulling at the weeds that grew near the base of the tree.

"This doesn't disappoint you?"

"No. Once in a while, I become annoyed, and I suppose if my time were short, I might feel more urgency, but, as it is . . ." She shrugged as only a Frenchwoman can.

A shadow fell across them. "Excuse me," said Mr. Harper, "but have you seen my daughter, Emillie? She went out very early this morning, but I thought surely she'd be back by now." He gave Franciscus an ingratiating smile.

Franciscus opened his eyes. "You mean she isn't here?"

"No. My wife thought that she might have gone swimming, but her suit was in the bathroom, and it's quite chilly in the mornings . . ." He held a plate of enchiladas and chalupas, and he was wearing a plaid shirt and twill slacks that were supposed to make him look the outdoors sort, but only emphasized the slope of his shoulders and the pallor of his skin.

Alert now, Franciscus sat up. "When did you actually see your daughter last?"

"Well, she came in quite late, and Doris waited for her. They had a talk, and Doris left her about two, she says." His face puckered. "You don't think anything has happened to her, do you?"

"You must think so," Franciscus said with an odd combination of kindness and asperity.

"Well, yes," the middle-aged man said apologetically. "After everything the child has been through . . ." He stopped and looked at the food on his plate as if there might be revelations in the sauces.

Franciscus got to his feet. "If it will make you less apprehensive, I'll check out the Lodge and the pool for her, and find out if any of the staff has seen her."

"Would you?" There was a weak, manipulative kind of gratitude in the man's pale eyes, and Franciscus began to understand why it was that Emillie Harper had become the victim of the Reverend Masters.

"I'll go now." He touched Madelaine's hair gently. "You'll forgive me, my heart?"

She smiled up at him, saying cryptically, "The Count to the rescue."

"You're incorrigible," he responded affectionately as he put his black hat on. "I'll be back in a while. Tell Mr. Rogers where I've gone, will you?"

"I'll be happy to." Madelaine patted his leg, then watched as he strode off.

"He seems reliable," Mr. Harper said to Madelaine, asking for reassurance.

"He is," she said shortly, leaned back against the tree and closed her eyes.

Mr. Harper looked at her, baffled, then wandered off toward the tables, looking for his wife.

Kathy had served most of the food and had launched into a highly technical discussion with Jim Sutton about the proper way to cook scallops.

Emillie Harper was not at the Lodge, in the recreation building, at the swimming pool, the badminton courts or the beach area of the resort. Franciscus had checked all those places and had found no trace of the girl. Those few guests who had not gone on the picnic had not seen her, and the staff could not recall noticing her.

At first Franciscus had assumed that Emillie was giving a show of childish petulance—she clearly resented Franciscus' interference in her tryst the night before. As he walked along the shore trail past the small dock, he wondered if he had been hasty, and his steps faltered. He glanced north, across the bend of the lake toward the hillside where cabin 33 was, and involuntarily his face set in anger. Why, of all the resorts in the Rocky Mountains, did Mr. Milan Lorpicar have to choose Lost Saints Lodge for his stay?

A sound intruded on his thoughts, the persistent clacking of a typewriter. The door to cabin 8 stood ajar, and Franciscus could see Myron Shires hunched over on the couch, his typewriter on the coffee table, his fingers moving like a pair of dancing spiders over the keys. Beside the typewriter there was a neat stack of pages about two inches high. The sound stopped abruptly. "Franciscus," Myron Shires said, looking up quickly.

"Good afternoon, Mr. Shires. I thought you'd be at the picnic." He liked the big, slightly distracted man, and was pleased to let him intrude on his thoughts.

"Well, I'm planning to go," he said. "What time is it?"

"After one," Franciscus said, smiling now.

"After one?" Shires repeated, amazed. "How on earth . . ."

"There's plenty of food," Franciscus assured him, not quite smiling at Myron Shires' consternation.

Shires laughed and gave a self-deprecating shrug. "I ought to have a keeper. My ex-wife hated it when I forgot things like this, but I get so caught up in . . ." He broke off. "You weren't sent to fetch me, were you?"

"No," Franciscus said, leaning against the door. "As a matter of fact I was looking for the Harper girl. Her parents are worried because she hasn't shown up for lunch."

"The Harper girl?" Shires said. "Is that the skittish teenager who looks like a ghost most of the time?"

"That's her," Franciscus nodded. "Have you seen her?"

Shires was gathering his pages into a neat stack and did not answer at once. "Not today, no. I did see her last night, walking along the trail on the other side of the beach. She stopped under the light and I thought that she was really quite graceful."

Franciscus almost dismissed this, remembering his encounter with Emillie the night before, but his curiosity was slightly piqued: He wanted to know how long the girl had waited for Mr. Lorpicar. "When was that?" he asked.

"Oh, quite late. Three, three-thirty in the morning. You know me—I'm night people." He had put the pages into a box and was putting his typewriter into its case.

"Three?" Franciscus said, dismayed. "Are you sure?"

"Well, it might have been a little earlier," Shires allowed as he closed the lid of the case. "Not much earlier, though, because I had my radio on until two and it had been off for a time." He caught sight of Franciscus' face. "Is anything wrong?"

Franciscus sighed. "I hope not." He looked at the novelist.

"Do you think you can find your way to the picnic without me?"

Myron Shires laughed. "I'm absentminded, but not *that* absentminded," he said with real joviality. "Kathy's picnics are one of the best draws this place offers." He had put his typewriter aside and was pulling on a light jacket.

"Would you be kind enough to tell Mr. Rogers what you've told me?" Franciscus added as he went to the door.

"That I saw the Harper girl go out late? Certainly." He was plainly puzzled but too courteous to ask about the matter.

"I'll explain later, I hope. And, if you can, contrive that her parents don't hear what you say." He had the door open.

"I'm not a complete boor, Franciscus." He had picked up his key from the ash tray on the end table and turned to address a further remark to Franciscus, but the man was gone.

The path to cabin 33 was well kept. There were rails on the downhill side of it, and neat white stones on the other, and at night the lanterns were turned on, making a pool of light every fifty feet. Franciscus knew the route well, and he walked it without reading any of the signs that pointed the way to the various clusters of cabins. He moved swiftly, though with such ease that his speed was not apparent. The trail turned and grew steeper, but his pace did not slacken.

Cabin 33 had been built eight years before, when all the cabins at the north end of the lake had been added. It was of medium size, with a front room, a bedroom, bath and kitchenette, with a screened porch which was open in the summer but now had its winter shutters in place.

Franciscus made a quick circle of the place, then waited to see if Mr. Milan Lorpicar would make an appearance. The cabin was silent. Coming back to the front of cabin 33, Franciscus rapped with his knuckles. "Mr. Lorpicar?" A glance at the red tab by the doorframe told him that the maid had not yet come to change the bed and vacuum the rugs, which was not surprising with the small staff that the Lodge kept during the off-season. The more remote cabins were serviced in the late afternoon.

A second knock, somewhat louder, brought no response, and Franciscus reached into his pocket, extracting his passkey. He pounded the door one more time, recalling with certain amusement the time he had burst in on a couple at the most awkward of moments, made even more so because the husband of the woman and wife of the man were waiting for their absent partners in the recreation hall. The tension in his neck told him that this occasion would be different.

The door opened slowly onto a perfectly orderly front room. Nothing there hinted that the cabin was occupied. There were no magazines, no papers, no cameras, no clothes, no fishing tackle, nothing except what Lost Saints Lodge provided.

Emillie was in the bedroom, stretched out with only the spread over her, drawn up to her chin. She was wan, her closed eyes like bruises in her face, her mouth slightly parted.

"Emillie?" Franciscus said quietly, not wanting to alarm her. She did not awaken, so he came nearer after taking a swift look around the room to be sure that they were alone. "Emillie Harper," he said more sharply.

The girl gave a soft moan, but her eyes did not open.

Franciscus lifted the spread and saw, as he suspected, that she was naked. He was startled to see how thin she was, ribs pressing against her skin, her hips rising like promontories at either side of her abdomen. There were dark blotches here and there on her body, and he nodded grimly as he recognized them.

"God, an amateur," he said under his breath, and dropped the spread over Emillie.

A quick search revealed the girl's clothes in a heap on the bathroom floor. There was no sign of Lorpicar there, either— no toothbrush, no razor. Franciscus nodded, picked up the clothes and went back to the bedroom. He pulled the spread aside once more, and then, with deft persistence, he began to dress the unconscious Emillie Harper.

"I don't know what's wrong," Doctor Eric Muller said as he stood back from the bed. He smoothed his graying hair nervously. "This isn't my field, you know. Most of my patients are referred to me. I'm not very good at off-the-cuff diagnoses like this, and without a lab and more tests, I really couldn't say . . ."

Franciscus recalled that Mr. Rogers had warned him that the doctor was jumpy, and so he schooled his patience. "Of course. I understand. But you will admit that it isn't usual for a girl, or a young woman, if you prefer, to be in this condition."

"No, not usual," the doctor agreed, refusing to meet Franciscus' eyes. "Her parents ought to get her to an emergency room, somewhere."

"The nearest emergency facility," Franciscus said coolly, "is thirty miles away and is operated by the forest service. They're better suited to handling broken ankles, burns, and snake bites than cases like this."

Dr. Muller tightened his clasped hands. "Well, all I can recommend is that she be taken somewhere. I can't be of much help, I'm afraid."

"Why not?" Franciscus asked. He had hoped that the doctor would be able to tell the Harpers something reassuring when he left this room.

"There aren't lab facilities here, are there? No. And I'm not licensed in this state, and with the way malpractice cases are going, I can't take responsibility. There's obviously something very wrong with the girl, but I don't think it's too serious." Dr. Muller was already edging toward the door. "Do you think Mr. Rogers would mind if I checked out early?"

"That's your business, Doctor," Franciscus said with a condemning lift of his fine brows.

"There'll have to be a refund. I paid in advance." There was a whine under the arrogance, and Franciscus resisted the urge to shout at him.

"I don't think Mr. Rogers would stop you from going," he said with an elegant inclination of his head.

"Yes. Well." The door opened and closed like a trap being sprung.

Franciscus remained looking down at the girl on the bed.

She was in cabin 19 now, in the smaller bedroom, and her parents hovered outside. Harriet Goodman was with them, and occasionally her steady, confident tones penetrated to the darkened room.

There was a knock, and Franciscus turned to see Mr. Harper standing uncertainly near the door. "The doctor said he didn't know what was wrong. He said there would have to be tests . . ."

"A very wise precaution," Franciscus agreed with a reassuring smile. "But it's probably nothing more than overdoing. She's been looking a little washed out the last few days, and all her activity probably caught up with her." It was plausible enough, he knew, and Mr. Harper was searching for an acceptable explanation. "You'll probably want to call the doctor in Fox Hollow. He makes calls. And he will be able to order the right transportation for her if there is anything more than fatigue the matter." He knew that Mr. Harper was wavering, so he added, "Also, it will save Emillie embarrassment if the condition is minor."

Mr. Harper wagged his head quickly. "Yes. Yes, that's important. Emillie hates . . . attention." He came nearer the bed. "Is there any change?"

"Not that I've noticed." It was the truth, he knew, but only a portion of it. "You might like Ms. Goodman or my friend Ms. Montalia to sit with Emillie until she wakes up."

"Oh, her mother and I will do that," Mr. Harper said at once.

Franciscus realized that he had pressed the matter too much. "Of course. But I'm sure that either lady would be pleased to help out while you take dinner, or speak with Dr. Fitzallen, when he comes." It was all Franciscus could do to hold back his sardonic smile. Mr. Harper was so transparently reassured by that very proper name, and would doubtless be horrified when the physician, a forty-two-year-old Kiowa, arrived. That was for later, he thought.

"Did you . . . anyone . . . give her first aid?" Mr. Harper asked in growing distress.

"I know some first aid," Franciscus said kindly. "I checked

her pulse, and breathing, and did my best to determine that no bones were broken." It was a facile lie, and not in the strictest sense dishonest. "Mr. Harper," he went on in sterner tones, "your daughter is suffering from some sort of psychological problem, isn't she?" Though he could not force the frightened father to discuss his daughter's involvement with the Reverend Masters, he felt he had to dispell the illusion that all was well.

"Not exactly," he said, watching Franciscus uneasily.

"Because," Franciscus went on relentlessly, "if she is, this may be a form of shock, and in that case, the treatment might be adjusted to her needs." He waited, not moving, standing by Emillie as if guarding her.

"There has been a little difficulty," Mr. Harper said when he could not endure the silence.

"Be sure you tell Dr. Fitzallen all about it. Otherwise he may, inadvertently, do the wrong thing." With a nod, he left the bedside and went to the door to the sitting room. "Harriet," he said crisply as he started across the room, "get Jim and join me for a drink."

Harriet Goodman was wise enough to ask no questions of him, though there were many of them building up in her as she hastened after him.

"I was *horrified!*" Mrs. Emmons announced with delight as she told Mrs. Granger, who had been asleep with a headache, of the excitement she had missed. "The girl was white as a sheet—I can't tell you." She signaled Frank, the bartender, to send over another round of margaritas, though she still longed for a side car.

At the other end of the lounge, Franciscus sat with Harriet Goodman and Jim Sutton. His face was turned away from the two old women who were now regaling Frank with a catalogue of their feelings on this occasion. "I can't insist, of course," he said to Jim Sutton.

"Let's hear it for the First Amendment," Jim said. "I don't like to sit on good stories, and this one is a beauty." He was drinking coffee and it had grown cold as they talked. Now he made a face as he tasted it. "Christ, this is awful."

Harriet Goodman regarded Franciscus gravely. "That child may be seriously ill."

"She is in danger, I'll concede that," Franciscus responded.

"It's more than that. I helped her mother undress her, and there were some very disturbing . . ." She could not find a word that satisfied her.

"I saw them," Franciscus said calmly, but quietly so that this revelation would not attract the two women at the other end of the lounge.

"Saw them?" Harriet repeated, and Jim Sutton leaned forward.

"What were they like? Harriet hasn't told me anything about this."

Franciscus hesitated a moment. "There were a number of marks on her and . . . scratches."

Jim Sutton shook his head. "That guy Lorpicar must be one hell of a kink in bed."

"That's not funny, Jim," Harriet reprimanded him sharply.

"No, it's not," he agreed. "What . . . how did she get the marks? Was it Lorpicar?"

"Probably," Franciscus said. "She was in his cabin, on his bed, with just the spread over her." He let this information sink in, and then said, "With what Emillie has already been through with that Reverend Masters, she's in no shape for more notoriety. And if this gets a lot of press attention . . ."

"Which it might," Jim allowed.

Franciscus gestured his accord and went on, ". . . then she might not come out of it very well. The family has already changed its name, and that means there was a lot of pressure on them to begin with. If this is added . . ."

"Yes," Harriet said in her calm way. "You're right. Whatever is happening to that girl, it must be dealt with circumspectly. That means you, Jim."

"It means you, too. You can't go putting this in a casebook and getting a big publicity tour for it," Jim shot back, more caustically than he had intended.

"Both of you, stop it," Franciscus said with such assurance

and resignation that the other two were silenced at once, like guilty children. "I'm asking that you each suspend your first inclinations and keep quiet about what is going on here. If it gets any worse, then you'll have to do whatever your professions demand. However, Harriet, with your training, I hope that you'll be willing to spend some time with Emillie once she regains consciousness."

"You seem fairly certain that she will regain consciousness," Harriet snapped.

"Oh, I'm certain. I've seen this condition before. Not here. I hadn't expected to encounter this . . . affliction here." He stared toward the window and the long, dense shadows that heralded night. There were patches of yellow sunlight at the ends of dusty bars of light, and the air was still.

"If you know what it is, why didn't you tell the Harpers?" Jim Sutton demanded, sensing a greater mystery.

"Because they wouldn't believe me. They want to talk to a doctor, not to me. Jorry Fitzallen is welcome to talk to me after he's seen Emillie."

Harriet tried to smile. "You're right about her parents. They do need to hear bad news from men with authority." She stood up. "I want to change before dinner, and I've got less than half an hour to do that. I'll look in on the girl on my way back to the cabin."

"Thank you," Franciscus said, then turned his attention to Jim Sutton. "Well? Are you willing to sit on this story for a little while?"

He shrugged. "I'm on vacation. There's a murder trial coming up in Denver that will keep my paper in advertisers for the next six months. I'll pretend that I haven't seen or heard a thing. Unless it gets bigger. That would make a difference." He raised his glass in a toast. "I must be running out of steam —two years ago, maybe even last year, I would have filed the story and be damned. It might be time to be a teacher, after all." He tossed off his drink and looked away.

The dining room was about to open when Franciscus came through the foyer beside the lobby calling out, "Mr. Rogers, may I see you a moment."

The manager looked up from his stand by the entrance to the dining room. "Why, certainly, Mr. Franciscus. In the library?"

"Fine." Franciscus was already climbing the stairs, and he held the door for Mr. Rogers as he came up.

"It's about Lorpicar?" Mr. Rogers said as the door closed.

"Yes. I've been up to his cabin and checked it out. Wherever he's staying, it's not there. No one is staying there. That means that there are almost a hundred other places he could be. I've asked the staff to check their unoccupied cabins for signs of entry, but I doubt he'd be that foolish, though God knows he's bungled enough so far . . ." He pounded the bookcase with his small fist, and the heavy oak sagged. "We don't even know that he's at the resort. He could be camping out beyond the cabins."

"What about Fox Hollow? Do you think he could have gone that far?" Mr. Rogers asked, and only the slightly higher pitch of his voice belied the calm of his demeanor.

"I doubt it. That ranger . . . Backus, he would have seen something if Lorpicar were commuting." He sat down. "The idiot doesn't know enough not to leave bruises!"

"And the girl?" Mr. Rogers said.

"I think we got her in time. If we can keep Lorpicar away from her for a couple of nights, she'll be all right. Certainly no worse than she was in the hands of Reverend Masters." He laughed once, mirthlessly.

"What are you going to do?" Mr. Rogers had not taken a seat, but watched as Franciscus paced the area between the bookcases and the overstuffed Victorian chairs.

"Find him. Before he makes a worse mistake." He halted, his hand to his forehead. "He could have chosen any resort in the Rockies!"

"And what would have happened to that girl if you had not found her?" He expected no answer and got none.

"Harriet thinks that giving Emillie a crucifix would not be a good idea, considering what she's been through. She's probably right, but it makes our job tougher. Because you can be completely confident that Lorpicar believes the myths." Franciscus looked out the window. "I'll see if Kathy can spare some garlic. That will help."

"I'll tell her that you want some," Mr. Rogers promised.

Suddenly Franciscus chuckled. "I'm being an Uncle . . . what? Not Tom, surely. An Uncle Vlad? Uncle Bela? But what else can I do. Either we stop this rash youngster or Madelaine, and you, and I will be exposed to needless risk." He gave Mr. Rogers a steady look and though Franciscus was quite short, he had a kind of majesty in his stance. "We've come through worse, old friend. I'm not blaming you, I'm miffed at myself for being caught napping."

Mr. Rogers allowed himself to smile. "Thank you for that." He took a step toward the door. "I'd better go down and start dinner seating. Oh." He turned in the open door. "There was a call from Fox Hollow. Jorry Fitzallen will be here by eight."

"Good. By then, I'll have a better idea where we stand."

Franciscus' confidence was destined to be short-lived. He had left the library and had not yet reached the glass doors opening onto the porch when he heard an anguished shout from the area of the lounge and Harriet Goodman started toward him.

"Franciscus!" she called in a steadier tone, though by that time, Mrs. Emmons had turned on her barstool and was watching with undisguised enthusiasm while Nick and Eleanore Wyler paused on the threshold of the dining room to listen to the latest. Eleanore Wyler was wearing a long Algerian caftan with elaborate piping embroidery with little mirrors worked into it, and she shimmered in the dusk.

Assuming a levity he did not feel, Franciscus put his small hands on his hips. "Ms. Goodman, if that frog is still living under your bathtub . . ." It had happened the year before and had become a harmless joke. The Wylers had been most amused by it, and Nick Wyler chortled and began in a loud voice to remind Eleanore of the various methods that were used to rout the offending frog.

Under the cover of this hearty basso, Harriet nodded gratefully. "Thanks. I realized as soon as I spoke that I should have remained quiet. You've got your wits about you, which is more than I do." She put her hand up to wipe her brow, saying very softly, "I'm sorry, but Emillie is missing."

"Missing?" Franciscus repeated, genuinely alarmed.

"I heard Mrs. Harper making a fuss, so I went up the path to their cabin and asked what was wrong. She said she'd been out of Emillie's bedroom for a few moments—I gather from her choice of euphemisms that she was in the john—and when she came back the bedroom door was open and Emillie was nowhere to be seen."

Franciscus rubbed his smooth-shaven face. "I see. Thank you. And if you'll excuse me now . . ." He had motioned to Mr. Rogers, but did not approach the manager. Instead he was out the glass doors in a few seconds, walking swiftly on the east-bound path past the parking lot to the trail leading to the Harpers' cabin 19. His thoughts, which had been in turmoil when Harriet had spoken to him, were now focused and untainted by anger. He had let the matter go on too long, he told himself, but without useless condemnation. He had not supposed that any vampire would be as obvious, as flamboyantly inept as Milan Lorpicar. He lengthened his stride and steeled himself to deal with Doris Harper.

Jorry Fitzallen had required little persuasion—he allowed himself to be put up in one of the best cabins and provided with one of Kathy's special late suppers. He was curious about the girl, he said, and would not be needed in Fox Hollow that night unless an emergency arose. He spent the evening listening to the descriptions of the missing girl from her parents, from Harriet Goodman, from all those who had seen Emillie and all those who had an opinion. From Jim Sutton he got the background of Emillie's disputes with Reverend Masters, and shook his head with distress. He had treated a few of the good Reverend's followers and had some strong words about that cult leader. He was not able to talk to Dr. Eric Muller, for though the physician had examined Emillie Harper, he kept insisting that he was only a dermatologist and had never encountered anything like Emillie's wounds before and did not want to again. At last Jorry Fitzallen abandoned the questions for the pleasure of talking shop with Harriet Goodman.

There was no music in the lounge that night, for Mr. Franciscus was out with half the day staff, searching for Emillie Harper, and for the strange Mr. Lorpicar.

"I *knew* he was not to be trusted," Mrs. Emmons told the Jenkins sisters, Sally and Elizabeth, who had arrived that afternoon shortly before Emillie Harper was reported missing.

"But how could you? What was he like?" Sally asked, watching her sister stare longingly at Mrs. Emmons' margarita.

"Well, *you* know. Men like that—oh, very handsome in a *savage* way. Tall, dark, atrocious manners, and *so* domineering!" Her intended condemnation was wistful. "Anyone could see at once that there would be no discouraging such a man once he made up his mind about a woman."

The Wylers, at the next table, were indulging in more speculation. "If she had bruises all over her, maybe he simply beat her up. Girls like to be treated rough if they're inhibited, and if ever I saw someone who is . . ." Nick Wyler asserted loudly.

"I can't imagine what that poor child must have gone through," Eleanore agreed in a tone that implied she knew what she would want done to her, had Mr. Lorpicar—and everyone was certain that her assailant was Mr. Lorpicar—chosen her instead of Emillie Harper.

The Browns, Ted and Katherine, came in and were instantly seized upon for news. Since they had brought their own horses, they had been out on the trails with Franciscus and two others. Enjoying this moment of attention, they described their meeting with the ranger named Backus who had reluctantly promised to alert his fire patrol to the two missing guests.

"I think," Ted Brown said, his smiling making seams in his face, "that Backus thought those two don't want to be found for a while. He said as much to Franciscus."

There were knowing laughs in answer to this, and listening,

Harriet Goodman was glad that the Harpers had remained in their cabin rather than come to the lounge.

"That Backus sure didn't want to help out," Katherine Brown agreed with playful indignation. "He's worried about fire, not a couple of missing people."

Several diverse points of view were heard, and in this confusion, Ted Brown ordered drinks from the bar.

It was more than an hour later, when the noise in the lounge was greater and the talk was much less unguarded, that Franciscus appeared in the doorway. His black clothes were dusty and his faced was tired. At the back of his dark eyes there was a cold wrath burning.

The conversation faltered and then stopped altogether. Franciscus came across the floor with quick, relentless steps, to where Jorry Fitzallen sat with Harriet Goodman. "I need you," he said to the doctor, and without waiting for a response, he turned and left the lounge.

The Kiowa made no apologies, but followed Franciscus, hearing the talk erupt behind him as he reached the front door.

On the porch, Franciscus stopped him. "We found her. She's dead."

"You're certain?" Jorry asked. "Laymen sometimes think that . . ."

Franciscus cut in sharply. "I've seen enough dead bodies to recognize one, Doctor Fitzallen."

Jorry Fitzallen nodded, chastened, though he was not sure why. "Where is she?"

"In cabin 19. Her parents are . . . distraught. If you have a sedative, a strong one, Mrs. Harper could use it." The words were crisp, and Franciscus' ire was no longer apparent, though Jorry Fitzallen was sure that it had not lessened.

"I'll get my bag. Cabin 19 is on the eastern path, isn't it?"

"Yes. Second from the end on the right." He studied the physician's sharp features. "You will need to be very discreet, Jorry."

Jorry Fitzallen puzzled the meaning of that remark all the way from his car to cabin 19.

Madelaine de Montalia was seated beside Mrs. Harper, her arm around Doris Harper's shoulder, a barrier for the near-hysterical sobs that slammed through her like seismic shocks. Franciscus, who was pouring a third double scotch for the stunned Mr. Harper, gave Jorry Fitzallen a quick glance and cocked his head toward the women on the couch.

With a nod, the doctor put his bag on the coffee table and crouched before Mrs. Harper.

Doris Harper gasped at the newcomer, looking toward her husband in deep distress. "Howard . . ." she wailed.

Franciscus stepped in, letting Mrs. Harper see the full compelling force of his dark eyes. "Yes, you are very fortunate, Mrs. Harper. Dr. Fitzallen came as soon as our message reached him, and he's waiting to have a look at you."

"But Emillie . . ." the woman cried out.

"That will wait," was Franciscus' immediate reply. He laid one beautiful, small hand on her shoulder. "You must be taken care of first." Had that ever happened to this poor, faded, middle-aged woman before in her life? Franciscus thought. He had seen women like her, all his life long. They tried to buy safety and love and protection by putting themselves last, and it had never saved them. He sighed.

"I'm going to give you an injection, Mrs. Harper," Jorry Fitzallen was saying in his most professional tones. "I want you to lie down on the couch afterward. You'll stay with her, will you, Miss . . . ?"

"As long as you think is wise," Madelaine answered at once.

Mrs. Harper gave a little, desperate nod of thanks and gritted her teeth for the injection.

"I think she'll sleep for several hours," the doctor said to Franciscus and Mr. Harper. "But she's already under tension, from what Mr. Franciscus has told me, Mr. Harper, and it would be wise to get her back into familiar surroundings as soon as possible."

"But we sold everything when we moved and changed . . ." He stopped, glancing uneasily from one man to the other.

"Your name, yes," Franciscus said gently. "But now that doesn't matter, and you will have to make certain arrangements. If you have family in another part of the country . . ."

"God help me, the funeral," Mr. Harper said, aghast, and put his hands to his eyes.

Before either Franciscus or Jorry Fitzallen could speak, Madelaine came up beside them. "I think that Mr. Harper would like a little time to himself, gentlemen." With a deft move, she extricated the grieving father from the other two.

"Let's see the body," Jorry Fitzallen said quietly, feeling that same disquieting fatigue that the dead always gave him.

Franciscus held the door and the two passed into the smaller bedroom.

Emillie was nude, and her skin was more mottled than before, though this time the marks were pale. The body had a waxy shine and looked greenish in the muted light.

"Jesus H. Christ," Jorry Fitzallen murmured at the sight of her. "Is there *any* post-mortem lividity?"

"A little in the buttocks. That's about it." Franciscus kept his voice level and emotionless.

"Exsanguination is your cause of death, then. Not that there could be much doubt, given her color." He bent to touch one of the many wounds, this one on the inside of her elbow. "How many of these on her?"

"Sixteen total. Seven old, nine new. It happened before, which is why you were called. She was unconscious." Franciscus had folded his arms and was looking down at the dead girl.

"If her blood loss was as heavy as I think it might have been, no wonder she was out cold." He bent over the girl and examined the wound at the elbow. "What kind of creature makes bites like this? Or is this one of the new torture cults at work?"

"The wounds were made by a vampire; a very sloppy and greedy one," Franciscus stated surely.

"Oh, for the love of God, don't joke!" Jorry Fitzallen snapped. "I'll have to notify the county about this at once. The sheriff and the medical examiner should be alerted." He was inspecting two more of the bites now, one on the curve of her ribs and one just above her hip. "They're not deep. She shouldn't have bled like this."

Franciscus was silent.

"This is going to take a while," Jorry said, rather remotely. "I'm going to have to be very thorough. Will you give the ambulance service in Red Well a call. Tell them it isn't urgent, but they better bring a cold box."

"Of course," Franciscus said, grateful for the dismissal. There were too many things he had to do for him to spend more time with the Kiowa physician.

The Harpers left the next morning, and so did the Barneses, though they had done little but sit in their cabin and play table tennis in the recreation hall.

"She was so close to us," said Mr. Barnes, who had been in the first cabin on the eastern trail. He looked about nervously, as if he thought that death might be lurking around the registration desk.

"I quite understand," Mr. Rogers assured him, and handed him the accounting of the elderly couple's brief stay.

"How many have checked out this morning?" Madelaine asked when the lobby was empty. She had been standing at the mezzanine, watching Mr. Rogers.

"Dr. Muller, the Barneses, the Harpers, Amanda Farnsworth and the Lindholms. As Martha so correctly pointed out, a man with a heart condition does not need to be distressed, and the events of the last two days are distressing." He had closed the huge, leather-bound register.

"But Lorpicar is still here," Madelaine said, her violet eyes brightening with anger.

"Apparently. No one has seen him. He hasn't checked out. He could have decamped without bothering to settle his account, and that would be quite acceptable to me," Mr. Rogers said austerely, but with an understated familiarity.

The lobby doors by the foyer opened and Jim Sutton strode into the room. "Have either of you seen Harriet?" he asked anxiously.

"No, not since breakfast," Mr. Rogers answered. "Miss Montalia?"

"Not this morning."

Jim sighed, tried to look irritated and only succeeded in looking worried. "She was talking some nonsense about that Lorpicar whacko. She said that she could figure out where he was hiding if she could only figure out what his guilt-patterns are. What a time to start thinking like a shrink!" He started toward the door and turned back. "If Franciscus comes in, ask him if he's seen her. It's crazy, I know," he went on in a voice that ached to be reassured. "It's because of that girl. You'd think I'd be used to bizarre deaths by now, wouldn't you? But with Harriet trying to prove a point, damn her . . ." He pushed the door open and was gone.

"Where's the Comte?" Madelaine asked Mr. Rogers quietly.

"Searching the cabins on the north end of the lake. He's already done the southern ones." His face showed no emotion, but he added, "I thank you."

Madelaine tossed her head. "I'll tell him. He likes Harriet." She was down the stairs and almost to the doors. "So do I."

"Next we'll have Mrs. Emmons out skulking in the bushes!" Franciscus burst out when Madelaine had told him about Harriet. "Why couldn't she have waited a bit?"

"For the same reason you didn't, probably," Madelaine said with a sad, amused smile.

He touched her face, a gesture of infinite longing. "I do love you, my heart. The words are nothing. But now, they are all we can share." He took her in his arms briefly, his face pressed against her hair. She was only half a head shorter than he and she was so lonely for him that she gave a little cry, as if in remembered pain.

"Why not you, when I love you best?" she protested.

"You know the answer. It is not possible when you and I are of the same blood. Before, well, since we do not die, we must find our paradise here on earth, and for a time it was ours. My dearest love, believe this. We have had our heaven

together. And our hell," he added, thinking back to the deso-
lation of war.

Their kiss was brief and intense, as if each feared to make it
longer. It was Madelaine who stood back. "We have not
found Harriet," she reminded him.

"And we must do that, if we are to prevent another trag-
edy." He agreed promptly, taking her hand. "You know what
we are looking for. Undoubtedly he will have his box of earth
somewhere near."

"And if he has treated Harriet to the same brutality that he
gave Emillie?" Madelaine asked gently.

Franciscus tried for humor, "Well, we won't be able to keep
Jim Sutton from filing a story on it."

"Don't mock, Saint-Germain."

He sighed. "If he has, we must be very, very cautious. We
must be so in any case." He stopped in the open door of the
empty cabin. "I don't want to sell this place. I like it here.
These mountains remind me of my home, and the life is pleasant. I suppose it is wisest, though."

Madelaine touched his arm. "She may be all right. And a
girl like Emillie . . . there will not be too many questions
asked. You need not give up Lost Saints Lodge."

"Perhaps." He shook off the despondency. "I'll take the
west side of the trail and you take the east. We should be able
to do all the cabins in half an hour."

Harriet was on the floor of a tool shed near the stable.
There were savage discolorations on her throat and wrists,
and one of the rips in her skin still bled sluggishly.

"Good God," Madelaine said in disgust. "Hasn't that man
any sense?"

"The evidence is against it," Franciscus said wryly. He bent
to pick up Harriet. "She'll come out of it, but I think we'd better hold her in the Lodge. There's a room behind my . . .
workshop where I've got a bed. Jorry Fitzallen can check her
over."

"And what will he say?" Madelaine asked, not able to con-
ceal her anxiety.

"My dear, Jorry Fitzallen is a Kiowa. He will be very circumspect. Last year there was a shamanistic killing which he attributed to snakebite, which, if you stretch a point, was true." He carried Harriet easily, as if she were little more than a child. "You'd best make sure that there is no one on the trail. I would not like to have any more rumors flying than we already have to contend with."

Jim Sutton had turned first pale, but now his face was flushed and he stammered as he spoke. "If I get m-my hands on that b-bastard . . ."

"You will endanger yourself and Harriet needlessly," Franciscus said sharply. "It won't work, Jim. It's much better that you stay with Harriet—she will be grateful, you know—than that you waste your energy running around the hills looking for this man."

The room off what Franciscus called his workshop was spartanly simple. There was a narrow, hard captain's bed, a simple writing table and a chair. On the wall were three paintings, two of unremarkable subjects and talents, one, clearly by a more skilled hand, showed a rough-visaged Orpheus lamenting his lost Eurydice.

"This is yours?" Jim Sutton asked as he glanced around. Now that the shock of seeing Harriet had lessened, he was intrigued by his surroundings.

"Yes."

"It's damned austere," he said uncomfortably.

"I prefer it," Franciscus responded.

"That *Orpheus* looks something like a Botticelli," he remarked after staring at it a little while.

"It does, doesn't it?" Franciscus drew the single chair up to the bed where Harriet lay. "Come, sit down. She'll be awake by sunset. I'll have Frank send in an occasional double Cruzan." He waited while Jim Sutton reluctantly sat down. "I would recommend that you open the door only to me and Mr. Rogers. It's true that Lorpicar hasn't been found, but there is a possibility"—he knew it was, in fact, a certainty—"that Lorpicar may try to find Harriet to . . . finish what he started."

Jim Sutton's eyes were too bright. "I'll kill him," he vowed.

"Will you." Franciscus looked at the reporter. "Harriet needs your help. Leave Lorpicar to me."

"You?" There was polite incredulity in his expression.

"I know what I am up against, my friend. You don't. And in this instance, a lack of knowledge might be fatal." He bent over Harriet, his dark eyes keen. "She will recover. I don't think there will be any serious aftereffects."

"God, I hope not," Jim Sutton said quite devoutly.

Franciscus almost smiled. "I'll send you word when we've found Lorpicar. Until then, if you want to stay here, fine. If you'd rather leave, it would be best if you let Mr. Rogers know so that someone else can stay with Harriet."

"Then she isn't safe yet?" he said, catching at Franciscus' sleeve.

"She, herself, is not in any great danger. But Lorpicar is another matter, and he may still try to reach her." He wanted to be certain that Jim Sutton did not underestimate the risk involved. "Harriet is all right now, but if Lorpicar has another go at her . . ."

"Oh, shit." Jim rubbed his face. "The world is full of psychos. I swear it is."

Franciscus said nothing, but before he closed the door, he saw Jim Sutton take Harriet's unresisting hand between his own.

There was little conversation at dinner, though Kathy had outdone herself with the food. Guests drank more heavily than usual, and Nick Wyler had offered to stand guard on the porch with a shotgun, but Mr. Rogers had quickly put an end to that idea, much to the relief of the other guests. By the time the dining room was empty much of the fear had been dispelled, though Mrs. Emmons had declared that she would not sleep a moment for fear she would be the next victim.

Frank kept the bar open until eleven, and Mr. Franciscus sat at the harpsichord in the lounge, playing music no one noticed. But even the most intrepid guests were touched by fear, and the last group bought a bottle of Bourbon and left together, taking comfort from the drink and familiar faces.

"You going to bed, Franciscus?" the bartender called as he finished closing out the register for the evening.

"In a while. Don't mind me." He was playing a Scarlatti sonata now. "Turn off the lights when you go."

The bartender shrugged. "Whatever you say."

Half an hour later, Franciscus sat alone in the dark. The harpsichord was silent. The last pan had rattled in the kitchen some time before and the tall clock in the lobby sounded oddly muffled as its St. Michael's chimes tolled the quarter hour.

An errant breeze scampered through the lounge and was gone. Franciscus waited, alert, a grim, sad curve to his lips.

There was a soft tread in the dining room, the whisper of cloth against cloth, the quiet squeak of a floorboard.

The lounge, at an oblique angle to the foyer and separated from the lobby by an arch, was not touched by the single light that glowed at the registration desk, and the soft footfalls turned to the lounge from the dining room, seeking the haven of darkness.

When the steps were halfway across the room, Franciscus snapped on the light over the keyboard. It was soft, dispelling little of the night around it, but to the black-cloaked figure revealed on the edge of its luminescence, it glowed bright as the heart of a star.

"Good evening, Mr. Lorpicar," Franciscus said.

"You!"

Franciscus watched the tall man draw back, one arm raising as if to ward off a blow. "You've seen too many Hammer films," he remonstrated gently.

Milan Lorpicar chose to ignore this remark. "Do not think to stand in my way."

"Far too many," Franciscus sighed.

Mr. Lorpicar had been treated with fear, with hysteria, with abject adoration, with awe, but never with amused tolerance. He straightened to his full, considerable height. "You cannot stop me."

"But I can, you know." He had not moved from the piano bench. His legs were crossed at the ankle and his neat black-and-white clothes were relieved by a single ruby on a fine silver choker revealed by the open collar of his white silk shirt. Short, stocky, compact, he did not appear to be much of a threat, and Mr. Lorpicar sneered.

"You may try, Franciscus." His posture, his tone of voice, the tilt of his head all implied that Franciscus would fail.

The muted sounds of the lobby clock striking the hour caught the attention of both men in the lounge.

"It is time. I cannot stay," Mr. Lorpicar announced.

"Of course you can," Franciscus replied. He had still not risen, and he had maintained an irritatingly civil attitude. "I can't permit you to go. You have been a reckless, irresponsible barbarian since you came here, and were before, I suspect. But you need not compound your mistakes." A steely note had crept into his voice, and his dark eyes regarded the tall man evenly. There was no trace of fear in him.

Mr. Lorpicar folded his arms. "I will not tolerate your interference, Franciscus."

"You have that wrong," Franciscus said with a glittery smile. "I am the one who will not tolerate interference. You've killed one person here already and you are trying to kill another. I will not allow that."

With a terrible laugh, Mr. Lorpicar moved toward the arch to the lobby. "The woman is in the building. I feel it as surely as I felt the power of night at sunset. I will have her. She is mine."

"I think not." Franciscus raised his left hand. He held a beautiful eighteenth-century dueling pistol.

"You think that will stop me?"

"Would you prefer crucifixes and garlic?"

"If you know that, you know that bullets cannot harm me," Mr. Lorpicar announced as he started forward.

"Take one more step and you will learn otherwise." There was sufficient calm command in Franciscus' manner that Mr. Lorpicar did hesitate, regarding the shorter man with icy contempt.

"I died," he announced, "in eighteen-ninety-six."

"Dear me." He shook his head. "No wonder you believe all that nonsense about garlic and crucifixes."

Now Mr. Lorpicar faltered. "It isn't nonsense."

Franciscus got to his feet. He was a full ten inches shorter than Milan Lorpicar, but he dominated the taller, younger man. "And these last—what?—eighty-four years, you have learned nothing?"

"I have learned the power of the night, of fear, of blood." He had said it before and had always found that the reaction was one of horror, but Franciscus merely looked exasperated.

"God save us all," he said, and as Mr. Lorpicar shrank back at his words, he burst out, "of all the absurdities!"

"We cannot say . . . that name," Mr. Lorpicar insisted.

"Of course you can." He sat down again, though he did not set the pistol aside. "You're a menace. Oh, don't take that as a compliment. It was not intended as one."

"You do not know the curse of this life-in-death." He made an effort to gain mastery of the situation, and was baffled when Franciscus laughed outright.

"None better." He looked at Mr. Lorpicar. "You've been so involved with your posturing and pronouncements that you have not stopped to think about what *I* am." He waited while this sunk in.

"You walk in the daylight . . ." Mr. Lorpicar began.

"And I cross running water. I also line the heels and soles of my shoes with my native earth." He saw the surprise on Mr. Lorpicar's features deepen. "I handle crucifixes. And I know that anything that breaks the spine is deadly to us, so I remind you that a bullet, hitting between the shoulderblades, will give you the true death."

"But if you're vampiric . . ." Mr. Lorpicar began, trying to frame an appeal.

"It means nothing. Any obligation I may have to those of my blood don't extend to those who do murder." It was said pragmatically, and for that reason alone Mr. Lorpicar believed him. "You're an embarrassment to our kind. It's because of you and those like you that the rest of us have been hunted and hounded and killed. Pray don't give me your excuses." He studied the tall cloaked figure at the edge of the light. "Even when I was young, when I abused the power, this life-in-death as you call it, I did not make excuses. I learned the folly of that quickly."

"You mean you want the women for yourself," Mr. Lorpicar said with cynical contempt.

"No. I don't take those who are unwilling." He heard Mr. Lorpicar's incredulous laugh. "It isn't the power and the blood, Mr. Lorpicar," he said, with such utter loneliness that the tall man was silenced. "It is the touching. Terror, certainly, has a vigor, but it is nothing compared to loving."

"Love!" Mr. Lorpicar spat out the word. "You've grown maudlin, Franciscus." He heard the chimes mark the first quarter hour. "You can't do this to me." There was a desperate note in his voice. "I must have her. You know the hunger. I must have her!"

Franciscus shook his head. "It's impossible."

"I want her!" His voice had grown louder and he moved toward the arch once more.

"Stop where you are!" Franciscus ordered, rising and aiming.

Before he could fire there was the crack of a rifle and Mr. Lorpicar was flung back into the lounge to thrash once or twice on the floor.

Aghast, Franciscus looked toward the lobby, and saw in the dimness that Jim Sutton was standing outside the inconspicuous door to the workshop, a .22 in his hand.

"How long have you been there?" Franciscus asked after he knelt beside Mr. Lorpicar.

"Long enough to know to aim for the neck," was the answer.

"I see."

"I thought vampires were supposed to melt away to dust or something when they got killed," Jim Sutton said between pants as he lugged the body of Milan Lorpicar up the trail toward cabin 33.

Franciscus, who had been further up the trail, said quietly as he came back, "One of many misconceptions, I'm afraid. We can't change shape, either."

"Damn. It would be easier to lug the body of a bat up this hill." He stood aside while Franciscus picked up the dead man. It was awkward because Mr. Lorpicar was so much taller than he, but he managed it well. "I don't think I really accept this," he added.

"There aren't any more occupied cabins from here to 33," Franciscus said, unwilling to rise to Jim Sutton's bait.

"What are you going to do?" he asked, giving in.

"Burn the cabin. Otherwise there would be too many questions to answer." He wished it had not happened. As much as he had disliked Lorpicar himself, and abhorred his behavior, he did not want the man killed.

"Why's that?" The reporter in Jim Sutton was asserting himself.

"Autopsies are . . . inadvisable. There's too much to explain."

Jim considered this and sighed. "I know this could be the biggest story of my career, but I'm throwing it away."

They had reached the last, isolated cabin. "Why do you say that?" He shifted Mr. Lorpicar's body. "The keys are in my left hip pocket."

As Jim retrieved them, he said, "Well, what the hell? Who'd believe me anyway?" Then stood aside and let Franciscus carry Mr. Lorpicar into his cabin.

"How'd that fire get started in the first place—that's what I want to know!" Ranger Backus demanded as he and four volunteers from the Lost Saints Lodge guests stood around the smoking ruin of cabin 33.

"I don't know," Mr. Rogers said. "I thought that Mr. Lorpicar had been out of the cabin for two days."

"You mean this is the fellow you had us looking for?" The ranger was tired and angry and the last thing in the world he wanted on his hands was another mystery.

"Yes. Mr. Franciscus and Mr. Sutton saw him briefly earlier

this evening. They suggested that he should avoid the Lodge for a time because of this unpleasant business with the dead Harper girl." He gave a helpless gesture. "The fireplace was inspected last month. The stove was checked out. The . . . remains—" he looked toward the cabin and the mass of charred matter in the center of it—"It appears he was asleep on the couch."

"Yeah," Ranger Backus said disgustedly. "Probably smoking, and fell asleep and the couch caught on fire. It happened in Red Well last year. Damn dumb thing to do!" He rubbed his brow with his forearm. "The county'll probably send Fitzallen out to check the body over. Lucky for you this fellow didn't die like the girl."

"Yes," Mr. Rogers agreed with sincerity.

"You ought to warn your guests about smoking in bed," Ranger Backus persisted.

"Yes." Then Mr. Rogers recalled himself. "Backus, it's almost dawn, and our cook will be up soon. If you'd give the Lodge the chance to thank you for all you've done, I'd be very grateful."

The big man looked somewhat mollified. "Well . . ."

It was Jim Sutton who clinched the matter. "Look, Ranger Backus, I'm a reporter. After what I've seen tonight, I'd like to get your impression of what happened."

Ranger Backus beamed through his fatigue, and admitted, "Breakfast would go good right now, and that's a fact."

Harriet Goodman was pale but otherwise herself when she came to check out the next morning.

"We're sorry you're leaving," Mr. Rogers said as he handed back her credit card.

"So am I, Mr. Rogers," she said in her forthright way, "but since Jim asked me to go to Denver while he covers the trial and there's that conference in Boulder . . ."

"I understand." He paused and asked with great delicacy, "Will you want cabin 21 next year?"

"I . . . I don't think so," she said slowly. "I'm sorry, Mr. Rogers."

"So are we, Ms. Goodman," he replied.

"I'll carry your bags, Harriet," Franciscus said as he stepped out of the library.

"You don't have to," she said bracingly, but with a slight hesitation. "Jim's . . ."

". . . waiting at the car." He came down the stairs toward her. "If nothing else, let me apologize for putting you in danger." He picked up the three pieces of luggage.

"You don't have to," she said, rather remotely. "I never realized that . . ." She stopped, using the opening door as an excuse for her silence.

Franciscus followed her down the steps. "Harriet, you have nothing to fear. This isn't rabies, you know. One touch doesn't . . . condemn you to . . ."

She stopped and turned to him. "And the dreams? What about the dreams?" Her eyes were sad, and though the questions were meant as accusations, they sounded more like pleas.

"Do you know Spanish?" He saw her baffled nod. "*Y los todos están sueños; Y los sueños sueño son.* I think that's right."

"'And everything is dreams; and the dreams are a dream.'" She stared at him.

"The poet was talking about life, Harriet." He began to walk once more. "You have nothing to fear from me."

She nodded. "But I'm not coming back next year."

He was not surprised. "Nor am I."

She turned to him. "Where will you go?"

"Oh, I don't know. Madelaine wants to see Paris. I haven't been there for a while." He nodded toward Jim Sutton, who stood by his three-year-old Porsche.

"How long a while?" Harriet inquired.

He paused and waited until she looked him full in the face. "One hundred eighty-six years," he said.

Her eyes flickered and turned away from him. "Good-bye, Franciscus. If that's your name."

"It's as good as another," he said, and they came to the car. "Where do you want the bags?"

"I'll take care of them," Jim Sutton said. "You'll see that her rental car is returned?"

"Of course." He held out his hand to Harriet. "You have meant a lot to me."

She took it without reluctance but without enthusiasm. "But there's only one Madelaine." There was only disappointment in her words—she was not jealous.

Franciscus shook hands with Jim Sutton, but spoke to Harriet, "That's true. There is only one Madelaine." He held the car door for her as she got in. "But then," he added, "there is only one Harriet."

Then he slammed the door and turned away; and Jim Sutton and Harriet Goodman watched him go, a neat, black-clad figure moving with easy grace through the long slanting bars of sunlight.